Praise for *The White Girl*

'A profound allegory of good and evil, and a deep exploration of human interaction, black and white, alternately beautiful and tender, cruel and unsettling.' ***The Guardian***

'The eerie strength of *The White Girl* is the way Birch writes so convincingly on power and the blinding nature of its corruptive forces ... He writes social realism, his metier is those who are economically and socially marginalised, and his deep emotional honesty when telling their stories resonates throughout.' ***The Sydney Morning Herald***

'*The White Girl* is about our shared history, one that has long been ignored and at times deliberately erased. In a time when our national literature so often seems unequal to the task of reckoning with a world seemingly on the brink of fire, it is a rare thing for a novel to tell a gripping story while also engaging more broadly with the continuing dispossession and violence that are our uneasy inheritance.' ***The Saturday Paper***

'With a uniquely Australian setting, a compelling narrative, malevolent antagonists and determined female protagonists, *The White Girl* will appeal to a wide audience. Readers will find it hard to put down.' ***Books+Publishing***

'Tony Birch contracts the world to one wor
inheritance, and the result is an emotionally el
The Monthly **Awards 2019 (No. 1 Book),** ***Th***

'As a testament to the real calamities that befell generations of indigenous Australians as a direct result of white paternalism and bunk racial ideology – as a record of the pain and hurt suffered, and of the immense bravery and care shown by so many women in communities such as Deane – the novel rings clear as a bell.' ***The Weekend Australian***

'Tony Birch's new novel goes to the heart of black and white relations in Australia, and puts the voices of women front and centre.' ***The Big Issue***

'Tony Birch is one of those writers who's mastered the art of storytelling. There's a natural flow in his stories, so much so that you forget you're reading – instead it's like watching a film unfold before your eyes. His latest novel *The White Girl* is no different, in fact the characters he creates, and the plotlines he weaves so deftly around them are almost hyper-real.'
Daniel Browning, *AWAYE!*, ABC Radio National

'A heart-wrenching story of triumph and hope that's sure to become an Australian classic.' **Mark Rubbo, Readings**

'An outstanding work by a master of the craft, *The White Girl* resonates strongly in the present despite being set in the past. Birch has drawn one of the most memorable and charming characters in Australian literature in the staunch person of Odette, who is compelled by an abiding sense of justice and a steely determination to protect her granddaughter at all costs.'
Judges' comments, NSW Premier's Literary Awards

Tony Birch is the author of three novels: the bestselling *The White Girl*, winner of the NSW Premier's Literary Awards Indigenous Writers' Prize; *Ghost River*, winner of the Victorian Premier's Literary Award for Indigenous Writing; and *Blood*, which was shortlisted for the Miles Franklin Literary Award. He is also the author of *Shadowboxing* and three short story collections: *Father's Day*, *The Promise* and *Common People*. In 2017 he was awarded the Patrick White Literary Award. Tony is a frequent contributor to ABC local and national radio, a regular guest at writers' festivals, and a climate justice campaigner. He lives in Melbourne.

Book club notes are available at www.uqp.com.au

Also by Tony Birch

Shadowboxing
Father's Day
Blood
The Promise
Ghost River
Common People

THE WHITE GIRL

TONY BIRCH

First published 2019 by University of Queensland Press
PO Box 6042, St Lucia, Queensland 4067 Australia
Reprinted 2019 (three times), 2020 (twice)

uqp.com.au
reception@uqp.uq.edu.au

Cover design by Josh Durham (Design by Committee)
Cover photograph by ToscaWhi / Getty Images
Author photograph by Sara Wills
Typeset in 12/17 pt Bembo Std by Post Pre-press Group, Brisbane
Printed in Australia by McPherson's Printing Group

The University of Queensland Press is assisted by the Australian Government through the Australia Council, its arts funding and advisory body.

A catalogue record for this book is available from the National Library of Australia

ISBN 978 0 7022 6038 4 (pbk)
ISBN 978 0 7022 6204 3 (epdf)
ISBN 978 0 7022 6205 0 (epub)
ISBN 978 0 7022 6206 7 (kindle)

University of Queensland Press uses papers that are natural, renewable and recyclable products made from wood grown in well-managed forests and other controlled sources. The logging and manufacturing processes conform to the environmental regulations of the country of origin.

For Archie James
(Born 4 August 2018)

Only women know

CHAPTER ONE

Odette Brown rose with the sun, as she did each morning. She eased out of the single bed she shared with her twelve-year-old granddaughter, Cecily Anne, who went by the name of Sissy. Wrapping herself in a heavy dressing gown to guard against the cold, Odette closed the bedroom door behind her and went into the kitchen. She put a lit match to the wood chips and strips of old newspaper in the stove. She then fetched the iron kettle and made her way out into the yard, filling it with cold water from the tap above the gully-trap. As she leaned forward Odette felt an unfamiliar twinge above her left hip. She placed the kettle on the ground and clutched at her side, breathing in and out until the pain gradually subsided.

Odette closed her eyes and listened. The morning sky was quiet but for a lone bird gliding overhead. It was the black kite Odette knew well, the same bird spoke to her each morning. She opened her eyes and looked across to the town of Deane on the other side of the dry riverbed. To the west she could see a column of smoke wafting lazily over Henry Lamb's junkyard. She watched as the kite hovered above Deane's Line, a narrow red dirt track skirting the western boundary of town. The Line, as the track was commonly known, had been named in honour of the early squatter and land speculator, Eli Deane. Deane carried the blood of so many Aboriginal people on his hands it could never be scrubbed away, not from the man himself or the town that carried his name. The Line had been drawn a century earlier to separate the Aboriginal people incarcerated on the nearby mission from the good white *settlers* of Deane. A government regulation deemed that any Aboriginal person living west of Deane's Line was a resident on an Aboriginal reserve.

Back in the house, Odette cut herself a thick slice of bread from the end of a tin loaf and placed it in a heavy pan with a slab of dripping. She made herself a pot of tea and sat at the table drinking the brew. She cut the bread into small squares and salted it, a tradition she observed with as much ritual as a priest preparing Holy Communion. As a child she'd often had no choice but to eat bread and dripping. Now, at the age of sixty-three, the breakfast was a delicacy she indulged in each Sunday morning. The texture of the warm bread dissolving between her tongue and the roof of her mouth triggered memories of the *big room* on the mission, where she'd sit with the other Aboriginal children, eating in silence at the long bench. Afterwards, they were sent into the classroom for lessons, including religious instruction, reading and writing, followed by long afternoons at work in one of the fields. There would be more prayers of an evening and lonely nights alone in a narrow canvas bunk.

Odette looked into her empty tea cup, aware she'd momentarily been away. In spite of herself, she glanced at the framed photograph hanging on the wall above the stove, a portrait of her only child, Lila. The photograph had been a gift for her daughter on her sixteenth birthday. Lila had been pregnant at the time, a secret she'd managed to keep to herself until she was almost five months gone and could no longer hide her condition. Odette had initially dismissed her daughter's nausea as a symptom of a fever, common across the bitter winters of the district. They had shared a bed and Odette savoured the closeness of her daughter's warmth, until Lila began turning her back and refused her mother's comfort. It was only when Odette caught a glimpse of Lila's swollen stomach though a crack in the bedroom door that her daughter's situation became apparent. When Odette confronted her, Lila didn't bother covering her naked body.

'Who did this to you?' Odette demanded. 'Who put you this way?'

Lila refused to answer.

Odette put the palm of her hand under Lila's chin and forced her daughter to look at her. 'Who did this to you?' she repeated quietly. 'You have to speak to me, Bub.'

Despite Odette's constant grilling, Lila remained silent about the cause of her pregnancy. When the baby arrived, pink as a newborn piglet, delivered by Odette's childhood friend and community midwife, Millie Khan, both women knew the father could only be a white man. After the birth of the baby, any time that Odette probed for details, Lila flew into a rage. The birth of her daughter changed Lila. She'd grown up a quiet girl, thoughtful and calm, but as a young mother she hardened.

No man, young or old, stepped forward to take responsibility for the child. The white community of Deane, thriving on the gossip of a light-skinned Aboriginal baby, exchanged salacious tales about *them wild young gins off the mission* and the so-called respectful men in town who secretly chased after them. Lila became part of that gossip, retreated into herself and rarely left the house.

When Sissy was a year old, Odette woke one morning to the sound of her grizzling in the narrow crib. Odette rested her palm on the bed beside her and felt the hollow where Lila's body should have been. She lifted her granddaughter from the crib and walked into the kitchen. The house was empty and a bitter wind rattled the window panes. Odette noticed a piece of paper on the table. Lila had left her mother a two-line note.

I need to go away for a time. I'm sorry but I have to leave here.
I know you will do better than I can, to care for Sissy. I love you.

Odette held the baby to her chest and re-read the note several times in disbelief. She was convinced that her daughter would not abandon her own child and would soon return home, but Lila stayed away. Following her disappearance, Odette spent many mornings pushing the baby in a rickety pram along the dirt roads circling the town. With no parents to speak for her, Sissy was in danger of being removed from her grandmother's care. From that time on, Odette had no choice but to engage in a dangerous game of cat and mouse with the Welfare authorities.

~

Returning to the bedroom, Odette dressed. As she pulled on her woollen coat she paused and looked down at Sissy, curled in a ball under the blankets. She'd given Sissy a haircut a week earlier, an unappealing bowl cut. For much of her childhood Sissy had been mistaken for a boy, her tomboyish looks and behaviour disguising her beauty. Odette leaned forward and caressed the skin on the back of Sissy's neck and left her granddaughter to sleep.

She closed the front door behind her and put on her gumboots. Gripping the collar of her coat, she went down the veranda steps, crossed to the low wooden gate and walked out past the single row of workers' shacks of Quarrytown. It wasn't a town as such, but a designated zone of the reserve that remained under the jurisdiction of government. The single street took its name from the sandstone mine in the hills north of town, where Aboriginal men from the mission had once been employed. The mine had been closed for decades and most of the workers' huts had been empty for years. The abandoned shacks were slowly being camouflaged by *Morning Glory*, an invasive weed with a deceptively attractive blue flower.

Reaching the narrow footbridge, Odette paused above the trickle of murky water in the riverbed below. Although it had been raining heavily for more than a week, the river, or what was left of it, could no longer quench its own thirst. Over the years its life-force had been stolen by farmers irrigating upstream, their phantom pipelines and open channels criss-crossing the land with little more than a nod and handout to the corrupt politicians who benefited from the theft. After so much neglect, there was little left of the river to give.

Deane's Line was heavy with mud and Odette's boots sunk deeper into it with each step she took. The walk to the Aboriginal graveyard behind the mission was a good mile from home. The smoke bellowing from the chimney above Henry Lamb's junkyard was rich with the scent of eucalypt. Located on the town side of Deane's Line, the junkyard was literally feet away from reserve land. When she reached Henry's rusting fence, Odette saw the front gate was open. Henry was crouched in the dirt, gently patting his dog, Rowdy. The animal had been traded to him a few years earlier. Henry had proudly claimed Rowdy was *pure* Alsatian – *a military dog* – as a way of justifying the dubious exchange of a working tractor for the pup. Rowdy turned out to be no more Alsatian than Henry himself. Regardless, the black and tan mongrel was faithful and strong, and guarded Henry and the treasures of his yard with ferocity when necessary.

Henry got to his feet when he saw Odette. Each day he wore the same sweat-stained Akubra hat with bib and brace overalls over the top of a putrid once-white singlet. He walked with the bandy gait of a man who'd ridden a horse most days of his life, although in his case Henry had never been on the back of a horse. He'd not been near one since he was six years of age, when a wild brumby kicked him in the side of the head and knocked him unconscious. Henry fell into a coma and spent the following two months in the hospital at Gatlin, the nearest town to Deane. When he finally returned home, Henry remembered nothing of the accident and little else about his own life. He eventually returned to school but was constantly bullied in the schoolyard, and no one stepped forward to protect him. When Henry found himself in trouble, which was often, even his father would shrug his shoulders and say, *The boy's an imbecilic, simple as that.*

Henry looked down at Odette's muddied boots. 'Where are you heading to?' he asked.

Odette had a soft spot for Henry. She liked to humour him but would never make fun of him. 'Well, as far as I know Henry, this road goes to one place, which is the mission and the graveyard. Which is also where you've seen me heading every Sunday morning for years now. So, I guess that's where I'm off to this morning.'

Henry kept his eyes on her boots. 'You know that if you were to follow the river track into town and out past the old railway line, your boots would not be so muddy. It's dry over there.'

Odette stuck her hands in her coat pockets. 'Don't you think I know that, Henry? I know every inch of this town and all the country round it.'

Henry patted the dog. 'I know you would know that, Odette. I was just thinking for you, and keeping your boots clean, that's all.'

For years the Aboriginal people living on the mission were barred from entering town, except on Saturday mornings between eight and noon when they were permitted to shop at the company store in the main street. While *crossing the Line* remained an offence, technically at least, the law was generally ignored.

'I prefer to avoid town,' Odette explained. 'Unless I have business there.'

Henry kissed Rowdy's damp nose. 'Me too, Odette. One of your people told me, when I was a youngster, I think it was one of your people at least, that no birds fly over town. Just like you, they go round it.'

Odette knew the story well. She'd heard it from her own father, Ruben. 'Yep. That's the truth, Henry. The birds used to tell the old people, "If you folk aren't allowed in the town, we won't be bothering with it ourselves."'

'The birds, they spoke with them people?' Henry asked, scratching his head.

'They certainly did. And they still do. A morning doesn't pass without one of them talking to me.'

'There you go,' Henry said to Rowdy, sharing the conversation with his dog. 'Just the same way I speak with you, boy.'

Henry was around the same age as Odette. They'd been at school together. Few of the white kids would sit with Henry following his accident. He shifted continuously in his seat and had a habit of wetting his shorts. He found himself thrown in with the Aboriginal children during class breaks. Initially his presence was regarded as peculiar but he gradually felt more comfortable in their company and preferred it to sitting on his own. Henry's schooling, for what it amounted to, came to an end when he turned eleven and his father put him to work in the yard. Old Mr Lamb had been driving his buggy one afternoon when he came across his son walking home from school. Henry was in tears. One of the older boys had painted his face black while others held him to the ground. 'You wanna hang round with the boongs,' one of them screamed, 'you're gonna have to be one.'

Henry never went back to school from that day on. He'd become deeply attached to his new friends and missed their company. On Sunday mornings, he'd sneak over the junkyard fence, head for the mission and wait in the long grass for the boys to gather after church service.

He looked along the length of the Line in both directions. It lay empty and silent. The early morning sun battled the gathering clouds. 'There's not many of us left around here from the old days, is there Odette?'

'No, Henry. Me, you, Millie Khan. Maybe a few others.' She pointed at the dog. 'And there's Rowdy, of course.'

'I heard they have done a count of all the people in the district,' Henry said. 'Around here there is now one hundred and twenty-seven people. In the town and all about.'

'How'd you remember that?' Odette asked. 'The number?'

'I read it in the newspaper and wrote it down. Last week.'

Henry showed Odette the inside of his forearm and pointed to a set of numbers written in fading ink. 'See? It's all here.'

Henry had obviously not washed in the last week or so, but Odette wasn't about to point out such a fact. She had no desire to offend her old friend.

'I wonder where most of them one hundred and twenty-seven people are hiding themselves,' Odette said. 'It's a long time since I've seen that many people round here.' She looked down at the dark earth. 'That wouldn't include my people. They don't count us, Henry.'

'I never heard of that.' Henry appeared genuinely insulted. 'If that was my job, I would count you, Odette.'

'I'm sure you would. And I appreciate that.' She gestured towards the yard. 'Henry, would you have any bicycles in there? I'm after a two-wheeler.'

Henry let out a childish giggle. 'You wouldn't want to ride a bike along here, Odette. It would be a tougher day than walking in them boots. You'd get yourself stuck in the bog, I reckon.'

'The bicycle isn't for me, Henry. I've never been on a bike in my life and I'm not about to start now. Sissy's birthday is coming up and I want to get her something special this year.'

Henry looked over his shoulder. 'I have plenty of bikes back there. Disrepaired though.'

'Could you turn one of them into a rideable machine? One that would hold together?'

Henry rubbed his hands together as he considered the challenge. 'I reckon I could do that. Only one bike?'

'Just one bike, Henry. Riding two bicycles is not easy when you're starting out.'

Rowdy bared his teeth and let out a low growl. 'What are you doing, boy?' Henry asked. In defiance of his name, Rowdy was usually a calm dog. 'You be friendly with Odette. You have known her all your years.'

It wasn't Odette the dog was growling at. A guttural sound could be heard in the distance. It grew louder. Henry, Odette and the dog turned and looked along the Line. A red pick-up truck, belching dark smoke, was sliding from side to side in the congealed ochre-stained mud. Rowdy raced onto the road and raised his chest, defiantly facing the oncoming menace and barking ferociously. Henry desperately patted his thigh and ordered Rowdy to return to his side. The truck careered towards the dog. Rowdy refused to budge. The driver of the truck hit the brakes and the pick-up turned full circle, coming to a halt opposite the junkyard gate. Rowdy started herding the truck, head-butting a hubcap and barking loudly. Henry hobbled over to the dog. 'You stay back here and you behave yourself,' he said, grabbing a handful of fur from Rowdy's shoulders and dragging him back into the yard.

The driver jumped out of the pick-up, followed by a passenger. Odette recognised both boys. The driver, Aaron Kane, was the eldest son of Joseph Kane, a failed farmer whose family had arrived in the district in the previous century. The Kanes had prospered until a decade of drought descended on the land. During the Great Depression of the thirties the soil had turned to dust and the water vanished, leaving behind a haunted and parched landscape. While some farmers walked away from their properties, leaving empty farmhouses and dead livestock behind, the stubborn Joe Kane remained. Over the years he became increasingly embittered by his failure. People wouldn't buy his scrawny, neglected animals for anything more than feed for their dogs.

The passenger in the pick-up was Aaron's younger brother, George. Odette had worked on the Kane farm when the boys were young. She had taken care of the children and tried keeping the chaotic house clean while their mother lay in her bedroom, suffering from an illness never spoken of. Odette felt uncomfortable around the brooding Joe Kane. He looked at her in a way that made her feel uneasy, and had a habit of touching her whenever he walked by.

One hot afternoon, towards the end of summer, Odette was preparing dinner when she heard Mrs Kane moving about in the bedroom. The woman passed by her in the kitchen, without saying a word, and left the house. Odette watched as Mrs Kane walked out across a paddock in a white dress, her straw hair lifting with the breeze. She hadn't returned to the house two hours later when Joe Kane drove home from a trip to Deane. He came out of the empty bedroom and enquired about his wife.

'You seen my missus?' he asked Odette.

'She went walking.'

'Walking?' Kane puzzled. 'What do you mean, walking? There's no place she needs to walk.'

'She headed across the paddock towards town.'

'What did she say to you?'

Odette had never heard Mrs Kane speak a word, not to her own children or anyone else. 'She said nothing. She just went walking.'

Mrs Kane's body was found three days later, face down in a dam that held no more than a foot of water. Odette had been feeding the boys when Joe Kane coldly announced to the children that their mother was dead. George jumped down from his chair, threw himself at Odette and burst into tears. Aaron didn't react at all. He sat motionless in his chair, as if he hadn't understood a word his father said.

The week after Mrs Kane's funeral, Joe Kane asked Odette if she'd consider moving to the farm and looking after the boys on a more permanent basis. Odette declined the offer without hesitation. Kane would not accept her rejection, and a few days later drove to Quarrytown and knocked at Odette's door. Lila answered it.

'What do you want?' she asked.

Joe smiled at the sight of the teenage girl. 'Does Odette Brown live here?'

Lila left him at the door and went searching for Odette in the yard. 'There's a man here for you. A strange white man.'

Odette was surprised to find Joe Kane on her doorstep. It was obvious he'd been drinking. 'Who was that, here just now?' he slurred.

Odette ignored his question. 'What do you want?'

'I want you to come out to the farm and look after my boys. They're running wild.' He rubbed his ample belly. 'You can bring that lovely girl with you.'

'I'm not interested, Mr Kane. I have other work now. You can't be here in Quarrytown,' she said, shutting the door in the man's face.

Over the following months Odette would occasionally see Joe Kane's truck parked along the river track. The sight of him not far from her home caused Odette great unease. One morning she walked past and saw him sitting in the truck, both hands clutching the steering wheel. He appeared to be talking to himself. Returning from town later in the day she was relieved to find the truck had gone. She'd been planning on baking a cake with Lila that afternoon but when she opened the front door and called out to her daughter, to Odette's surprise the house was empty.

Aaron lifted his chin towards the junkyard gate. 'I'm after some parts for the truck. Spare tyres and a new gearbox.'

'I have no gearboxes,' Henry snapped.

Aaron ignored Henry's attempt to brush him off. 'We're racing at the track outside of Gatlin in a month. Course you'd have a gearbox in there, I reckon you'd have dozens of 'em. I'll pay,' he added. 'You can earn yourself some spare change, buy yourself a drink and a feed. Maybe even a bar of soap,' he chuckled, turning to his younger brother for support.

'I have no parts in this yard for you,' Henry said. 'I don't have any parts for any sort of a truck. And I don't need no money for drink. I never take a drink.'

'Henry,' Aaron said, 'I can see from out here all the shit you have piled up back there. You wouldn't know what you have in the yard.'

Aaron walked to the gate and tried forcing it open.

Henry moved between Aaron and the gate.

The boy pushed him away. 'Fuck off, Henry.'

Henry looked anxiously at Odette.

'How have you been, Aaron?' Odette asked. 'Do you remember me?'

The boy looked her up and down. 'I don't know you from any place.'

'Yes, you do,' Odette said. 'You and your brother, I looked after you for a time when you were young. When your Mamma was still with us.'

'I don't know what you're talking about,' Aaron said. 'Nobody has taken care of us but our father.'

'She did,' George interrupted. 'I remember her.' George smiled at Odette in a manner that appeared familiar to her. 'You used to make cakes for us. And at the end of the day you would walk all the way home.'

'That's right,' Odette said. 'I've always enjoyed walking. And they were scones I baked, not cakes. You loved them, George.'

He nodded his head approvingly. 'Scones. Yeah, I remember now. We piled them with butter. You remember Aaron?'

'Shut the fuck up, George,' Aaron sneered. 'Go sit in the

truck. I don't have time to waste here. You going to let us in the yard or not Henry?'

Henry rarely let anyone enter the yard. 'Today is Sunday. I don't open on Sundays.'

'Make an exception,' Aaron said.

Henry again turned to Odette for support.

Aaron looked from her muddied boots up to her dark face. 'I thought there was none of your lot left around here.'

Many years had gone by since Odette had last seen Joe Kane but the man's anger, evident in his older son, was unmistakable. 'Oh, my people are still here, son. A few of us are above the ground, the rest are below it. We've always been here and we're going no place.'

Aaron spat in the dirt, close to Odette's muddied boot. He walked slowly back to the truck and climbed into the driver's seat. 'We'll be back, Henry,' he called. 'I don't care if you're open for business or not. Or what day it is.'

The truck roared away, leaving a spray of mud in its wake.

'Are you alright?' Odette asked Henry, who looked upset.

Henry was just as concerned with Odette's wellbeing as his own. 'You need to be careful with yourself, Odette. Being cheeky with that boy. He's a bad one.'

'Don't you worry about me, Henry, I can take care of myself.'

'Hey, I remember something,' Henry said, changing the subject. 'The bike. I remembered you want one bike.'

'That's right. For Sissy. For her birthday.'

'How much time do I have to make the bike?'

'Three weeks coming. But it doesn't matter if it can't be done before then. Sissy will understand.'

Henry counted to three under his breath. 'I can do that for you, Odette. Three weeks. I'll write myself a note and I'll build the bike for you.'

'Good for you, Henry. And I'll have the money waiting.'

'There won't be any money,' Henry said. 'I will build you the bike for free. For your Sissy.'

'I can't have you doing that, Henry. I don't take charity from anyone. I never have.'

Henry scratched the side of his head, mulling over Odette's comment. 'You don't have to take the charity, Odette. You can take a gift. From me.'

Thanking Henry, Odette said goodbye and walked on. She felt terrible for Henry and the way the Kane boy had spoken to him. Henry had spent his life being bullied and had locked himself away in the junkyard to protect himself.

Odette understood that the young folk around town didn't have much to do and relieved their boredom with occasional acts of mindlessness. But there was something more worrying about the older Kane boy. The summer she'd cared for the children Odette had been struck by the emptiness in his eyes. When she bathed him, Aaron's body often carried bruises and cuts. She was certain the child had been beaten by his father, but being an Aboriginal woman she had no right to interfere in the business of a white family.

She remembered the younger brother, George, also. He was a quiet boy, at odds with his brother. Seeing him again now she realised there was something more about George but she couldn't put her finger on it.

CHAPTER TWO

Odette paused at the iron gates guarding the mission entrance. A stone column stood on either side of an earthen pathway leading to the church. The wooden outbuildings in the yard behind the church lay in ruin, the termite-infested timbers of the old dormitories had rotted and the iron roofing was warped and rusted. Born on the mission, Odette had been separated from family and placed in one of the outbuildings, where she'd spent many nights listening to the sobs of younger girls. Whenever she felt a need to cry, Odette had slipped outside and sat on the back step of the laundry rooms, yearning for her father, Ruben. Although the men's dormitory was no more than fifty yards away Odette was not permitted to speak to her father, except on Sunday mornings after Mass.

Odette had some fond memories of the old church, where families would come together to chorus. After Mass, her relations were allowed to sit together on the ground out front and catch up on their time apart. While Odette had no faith in the Christian God she was told would one day save her, she was prepared to raise her voice and praise Him if it meant she could be reunited with family, however briefly. She would sing from the hymn book, along with her cousins, aunties and uncles, to please the missionaries looking on.

Odette pushed the heavy church door open, announcing her arrival with a heaving creak. Above the altar was an open space where a stained-glass window – the image of Jesus Christ nailed to the cross – had once dominated the far end of the room. When the missionaries abandoned the church they had taken the glass window with them. The oak pews had long since been broken up and used as building material. Odette ran a hand across the back of an imaginary pew. She could see her father sitting alongside a woman, holding her hand in his own. While Odette had no memories of her mother, who'd died on a wooden table after giving birth to her, she had no doubt who the woman was. She'd sensed the presence of her parents in the church many times and was not surprised by, or fearful of, the apparition.

She exited the church, collected a broom and rake from a shed in the graveyard and walked along the narrow paths, each row bordered with blocks of sandstone. The first children of the mission had been buried in nameless unmarked graves, struck down by previously unknown illnesses – whooping cough, measles and fever. The only indicator of the presence of the children beneath the earth were the wildflowers that revealed themselves each year. The seeds had been sown by mothers. In mid-winter the plants lay dormant but by early spring green shoots would appear, followed by yellow and deep red flowers.

Beyond the common burial ground were the marked plots of the children who were born on the mission in later years, some whom Odette had known. Her cousin-sister, Bonita, *Now with the Lord*, had slept in a bed next to Odette. Bonita desperately missed her mother and often sought comfort from Odette. Less than a month after her tenth birthday, Bonita and several other girls contracted measles. They were quickly isolated in a shed away from the main dormitory. Fretting for the children, a group of women approached the head of the mission, Reverend Holman, and asked that they be permitted to take the girls to an important place along the river, *to fix them better.* The Reverend refused, explaining that the girls were too ill to be moved. He ordered the mothers to join a gathering in the church to pray for the girls.

The morning after, desperate to visit Bonita, Odette had placed an empty tea chest below a window at the back of the shed. She stood on it and called Bonita's name. One of the other girls, Ada, her face covered in a mass of red welts, came to the window. She said that Bonita was too ill to leave her bed.

'Can you give her a message from me, please?' Odette asked.

'Yes.' Ada coughed.

'Tell Bonita I love her, and—'

'Go away from here before you get the sickness,' Ada interrupted. 'We're going to be dead soon. All of us. Do you want to die with us?'

'You're not going to die,' Odette said.

'We'll be dying. We know that.' Ada coughed again. 'Will you pray for us and sing to God for our souls when we have gone? I don't want to go to Hell, Odette.'

Odette slipped her hand through the window and took Ada's hand. 'I won't have to say any prayers for you girls, because I know that you won't die.'

'But will you anyway? Say the prayers?'

'I will,' Odette promised. 'I will.'

Odette was wrong in her belief that the girls would not die. Over the following weeks, as each girl passed away she was wrapped in a white bedsheet and quickly buried. Family members were not permitted to attend the graveside, *Lest you become infected*, the Reverend explained to the wailing mothers. When all of the sick children were gone, the mission community was ushered into the church to pray yet again for the souls of the departed. The following day the shed was doused in oil and burned to the ground.

Odette cleared the fallen leaves from the earthen pathways. Her body warmed up as she worked, although she could still feel the pain in her side. When she was finished, she sat near the graves of her parents and her own deceased husband, Daniel, who'd also been born on the mission. Daniel had worked alongside her father at the mine. The inscription below the names of both men recorded: *Perished in a mining accident*. The opening of the sandstone quarry had provided work for Aboriginal men from the mission. Many of them, including Ruben, became highly skilled. With the permission of the Aborigines Welfare Board, the men moved into new quarters in Quarrytown, close to the mine site and within the boundaries of reserve land.

When the stone mine first opened the old people despaired, convinced that cutting into the ground and destroying country with explosives would do great harm, to themselves and the earth. Their *superstitions* were ignored. By the time Ruben moved off the mission, few paid attention to the earlier warnings, including Ruben himself, who had mastered the skill of shifting clean slabs from the quarry wall. On the day of the accident, Ruben had drilled holes at several points along the stone-face, set the charge and ordered his men to safety. At the point of the explosion, the ground beneath Ruben's feet shook violently. He looked across at his son-in-law, Daniel. Three other workers, one of them a young Aboriginal man from the northern plains, and two white workers from town, died along with Ruben and Daniel, buried under tons of stone.

Odette had been standing in the kitchen of the family hut in Quarrytown and felt the vibrations in the earth. She knew immediately that something was wrong. She placed the baby on the bed, lay down alongside Lila and closed her eyes. She felt the same sense of loneliness she'd sometimes experienced in childhood. A mining company foreman knocked at the door later that same day. There was no need for him to explain what he was doing there. The company offered the young widow a *conditional* one-off payment of twenty pounds in recognition of her *pain and suffering.* Although she was in no position to seek anything more, Odette insisted that the slab of stone that had crushed her father and husband be crafted into decorative memorial stones that would stand at the head of their graves.

~

Odette walked back home along Deane's Line. The morning sun had vanished with the stiff breeze. Approaching the footbridge she noticed an eerie and unfamiliar fog hovering over the riverbed. She saw someone standing on the bridge and hesitated. She recognised a cap and silver badge. *Bill Shea.* It was rare for the town's policeman to venture from the main street of Deane, let alone pay a visit to Quarrytown. Odette had known Bill since they were children – they'd played in the dirt together – but she had little respect for him. Shea started his day with a drink to cure himself of the hammering in his head from the night before. He rarely moved from the desk in his office. The only positive to come out of his neglect on the job was that he left the Aboriginal people of Deane to themselves.

'Is that you, Bill?' Odette called. 'If you're looking for any troublemakers, you could start by chasing after that lad Aaron Kane. He was here earlier, tearing along the Line in his truck. The boy was making a nuisance of himself with poor Henry Lamb.'

The figure emerged from the fog. Odette first noticed a pair of black shoes, spit polished and almost gleaming, a task the dishevelled Shea was hardly capable of. She looked up at the policeman's face, at a man years younger than Bill. His skin was opaque. *Like death.* The policeman removed his cap. His hair was cut brutally close to his skull.

'I beg your pardon?' he asked, with a steel voice colder than the morning air.

'I'm sorry,' Odette answered. 'I thought you were Bill Shea. He runs the police station. In Deane,' she added.

'Officer Shea? He doesn't head the station here, not any longer. He is about to retire. I have been sent to replace him.'

The policeman's tone quickly turned interrogatory. 'You obviously know Officer Shea. You are *familiar* with him?'

Odette was careful about how she spoke to white people. She knew that the wider you opened your mouth, the more likely you'd regret what you said.

'No, I don't know him, not too well. He's been in charge of the police station for years.'

'Officer Shea,' the policeman offered, studying his manicured fingernails, 'is one of those fortunate men who was too young for the Great War and too old for the last one.' He pursed his thin lips. 'But with good fortune comes complacency, a debilitating combination. Officer Shea is finished.'

Odette found it unnerving that a policeman, and a stranger at that, would speak so poorly about one of his own to an Aboriginal woman.

'And you are?' he asked, studying Odette.

'Odette Brown,' she answered, avoiding his gaze.

'Of course,' he nodded, as if confirming information he was already privy to. 'You reside in the old mining accommodation.'

'Yes. My home is just across the bridge.'

'Home? Those old huts are in such a state of disrepair, they are worthless.' He looked down at Odette's muddy gumboots. 'You've been out and about early, I see?'

'I like getting out,' Odette said.

'Why so early?' he persisted.

'I like the birds, they get going early as well. Excuse me,' she added. 'I need to get home to my granddaughter.' Odette shuffled past the policeman and felt his cold breath on her cheek.

'Yes, your granddaughter,' he said, his apparent knowledge

of Sissy further discomforting Odette. He reached out and took hold of her arm. 'The child, she is twelve years of age? That is correct?'

Odette had no doubt the policeman knew the answer to his own question. She freed her arm. 'I'm sorry, but I need to be getting home.'

The policeman placed his cap on his head. 'Before you go, let me introduce myself. I am Sergeant Lowe. I'm sure that we will be seeing more of each other.'

Walking towards the cottage, Odette heard the policeman's footsteps on the gravel behind her. When she reached the front gate she turned around. Lowe had stopped in the middle of the narrow street. Odette closed the gate behind her, sat on the veranda steps and slowly removed her muddied boots, watching until Lowe had walked back down the rise and slipped away. She knocked her boots against a veranda post, freeing the mud from the heels, and went inside.

'Sissy, I'm home,' she called, opening the door and taking off her coat. Sissy didn't answer. The bed had been made and the kitchen tidied but there was no sign of the girl. 'I'm home,' Odette called again.

The pain in her side had become worse and she had a headache to go with it. Odette rested her forehead against the back of the closed door. She was conscious of an unfamiliar fear. She'd taken care of her granddaughter for more than ten years and the authorities had mostly left her in peace. In the new policeman, Lowe, she sensed a threat. The man appeared to have been patiently waiting for her in the mist.

~

Lowe walked purposefully along the track beside the riverbed on his way back to the station. Few officers with his experience would have volunteered to be posted to a piece of scrub like Deane, but he had little care for socialising in either his work or private life. He had a few acquaintances from his years in military service, but no real friends or family, and preferred his own company. The offer to head the Deane Police Station, with the responsibility of managing its citizens, had been an attractive one. In his new role he was simultaneously appointed as *Guardian* to the Aboriginal population of the district. He found the title both enticing and apt.

In the years immediately after the war he'd been posted to occupied Europe, serving with the military police. Lowe had dealt with people in situations of great desperation and enjoyed the power he had over those he was responsible for. A person could live or die as an outcome of his actions. He discovered that in times of uncertainty some people made decisions based on moral conviction. For others, a packet of cigarettes, a bottle of spirits, or even a crust of bread was more influential. The contradictions fascinated Lowe and left an impression on him. Children, often hungry, sometimes alone, were the most vulnerable to the decisions of powerful men. More than a decade after returning to civilian life and joining the state police force, Lowe could still recall the faces of those children. He knew similar images haunted other soldiers who had served, having witnessed many horrors. Lowe felt proud that he suffered no such trauma.

He'd been in Deane for only a week, and with little to distract him he'd had time to examine the information on each Aboriginal person under his control, young and old.

The station records revealed that in the decades following the town's foundation, *the blacks* had been kept on a tight rein. The log book for the police cells indicated that a week rarely passed without an inmate from the nearby mission being locked up, from a period of twelve hours to several weeks, and for matters including trespassing, drunkenness, absconding and *co-habitation* with those of a *superior caste.*

Lowe also noted that in recent years the cells had rarely been used, and punishment more generally was almost non-existent. He had little idea of how Officer Shea spent his working day, but he was clearly not concerned with policing. Lowe was determined to bring about change. He would begin with auditing each of the Aboriginal children under his guardianship, with a view to deciding the best outcome for their future welfare.

CHAPTER THREE

Sissy heard her grandmother close the front door on her way to the graveyard and listened to Odette's footsteps recede down the path. Once she was sure her grandmother had left, she pulled the blankets up over her head. She enjoyed having the house to herself. Some mornings she stayed in bed reading a book until hunger pains got the better of her. She would then make herself breakfast, turn the radio on and switch the dial to one of the music stations. Finding a lively song, she'd shimmy across the linoleum floor in her socks. A girl from school, Katie Cole, had taught her the twist and it was her favourite dance, although she never liked to practise in front of anyone else, even Nan.

Sissy also preferred staying home on Sunday mornings as the mission frightened her. She knew some of the older kids at school snuck into the graveyard at night to smoke cigarettes and drink beer. They returned with stories about the ghosts of children who rose from their burial plots crying out they were lost. While Sissy didn't believe the stories, they disturbed her enough to keep her away.

She fell back to sleep and was woken some time later by a bird pecking at the iron roof above her head. She got out of bed and went into the kitchen. As she did each morning, Sissy looked up at the photograph of her mother. She often thought about Lila, but avoided speaking about her, as nothing upset Nan as much as being questioned about her daughter, particularly by Sissy.

The window looking out to the veranda had misted over. Sissy pulled the sleeve of her pyjama-top over her fist and rubbed it in a circular motion to create a port-hole into the front yard. She put her face to the cold sheet of glass, peered through the hole but quickly drew away. A man in dark clothing was standing in the street, watching the house. Sissy crossed to the other side of the room, stood by the stove and waited for the kettle to boil. She made herself a tea, cupped her hands around the mug and went back to the window. When she looked through the port-hole again she was relieved to see that the mysterious figure had vanished.

After breakfast, she decided to surprise her grandmother by preparing their weekly bath. Sissy was worried that Odette had been looking worn down recently and getting the bath ready was heavy work. She didn't want her grandmother getting sick. She would make sure the tub was full and the water was heating by the time Nan returned from the graveyard. As she fetched the wood Sissy thought about how her great-grandfather Ruben first rescued the bath from a muddy ditch along Deane's Line. It was a story Odette had told her many times and she never tired of hearing it. The bath had fallen from old Jed Lamb's buggy, and Jed, being too lazy to retrieve it, left it where it fell. Ruben had only recently moved to Quarrytown and was walking the Line one afternoon after visiting family on the mission when he saw the bathtub. He wasted no time calling in at the junkyard to enquire about taking possession of it.

'You don't want that tub?' he asked Jed Lamb.

'Don't matter if I want it or not,' Lamb grunted, scratching frantically at his crotch like a rat digging for scraps of food. 'It took four men and a donkey to get it onto my horse and cart. Didn't make it as far as the yard, as you can see for yourself, Ruben. I tell you now, the track along this way is worse than our boys had to deal with over there in the trenches. That was a terrible time,' he added, seemingly revisiting the trauma he'd suffered as a foot soldier.

Ruben knew Lamb hadn't left Deane during the Great War, unlike several Aboriginal men from the mission who'd volunteered to fight. He returned Jed to the subject at hand. 'The bathtub here. Can we do a deal on it? I can arrange to have it picked up.'

'You and who?' Lamb smirked. 'You must be a friend of Samson the strongman himself.'

'Maybe I am,' Ruben said. 'But I won't need to call on him. I've got a way of getting that tub. I'm willing to pay you for it.'

Lamb's eyes lit up. He was well aware that Ruben was earning good money, a white man's wage, at the mine. It was a widely known fact that upset some folk in town. 'Oh, you would be paying, son, and a little more than you might be prepared to part with, I'd reckon. I'm not running a charity here.'

Ruben had already given consideration to the amount the tub was worth. He'd calculated a fair price of ten shillings. 'Five shillings,' was his first offer.

'That bathtub is worth more than that,' Lamb scoffed, theatrically slapping a knee. 'I would need to be looking at twelve shillings before I'd give this transaction serious consideration. If I didn't drive a good price, I'd be called a fool across the district, and there would go my reputation as a businessman. Old Jed Lamb would be known as a soft touch for every sly old fox within a hundred miles.'

'It wouldn't be the first time.' Ruben laughed.

The comment grated with Lamb. He tolerated blackfellas who'd come off the mission and made a go of it for themselves. Many walked by his gate, some even doffing their caps as they passed by. It didn't mean he'd tolerate cheek from them. Jed Lamb might have been a junkman, but he was also a *true white man.* 'Don't you be a smart-arse fella with me, Ruben. I could fetch twelve shillings for that bath tomorrow. Jesus Christ himself would tell you, you're out to rob me.'

'Well, I'll give you eight shillings then,' Ruben offered. 'Eight shillings and no more. I can bring some of the boys along here tonight and collect it.'

Lamb showed his tongue. It was grey and cracked. He rubbed his hands together. 'I reckon we're in business. I'll need you to pay upfront, of course. And don't be thinking that it's because I don't trust you. Your health is my main concern right now. Lifting this monster will kill you, I'm certain of it. If your heart doesn't explode in your chest under the strain, you'll most likely snap your back in two.' Lamb offered a gnarled and calloused hand. 'We have a deal.'

Ruben's crew moved the iron bath from the side of the track with more ease than Jed Lamb, or any of the sceptical locals who came to witness the operation, believed possible. Ruben's younger brother, Elias, worked as a rigger at the mine. With the aid of pulleys, ropes and a wooden frame, he rigged an elaborate contraption between the bathtub and a buggy. In less than half an hour the iron bath was secured on the dray with ropes to ensure that it would not fall a second time.

'It's all about physics,' Ruben explained to the bewildered Jed Lamb, watching as the bathtub lowered onto the back of the buggy. 'My brother, Eli, he knows all about physics.'

As they rode off in the direction of Quarrytown, Lamb shouted to Ruben, 'I should have held out for the twelve, you bugger.'

The men set the bath on blocks of stone in the yard behind the cottage. The bath was screened from the hut on the next block by the toilet and laundry. Ruben had promised that one day he'd supply full plumbing to the tub, a task he never completed.

As Sissy carried another large log to rest beside the bath she wished he had. Instead, Ruben had run a length of pipe from the tub to the nearby vegetable garden. Odette still grew potatoes and pumpkins all year round in the same spot, as well as tomatoes in the summer. Each and every Sunday without fail, Ruben would light a fire beside the tub and place the hot coals underneath. Her nan had inherited the task from her dad, and now Sissy, having watched her grandmother prepare the bath for her each Sunday, was returning Odette's generosity.

~

Odette found Sissy busy arranging wood in the fire pit beside the cast-iron bath. She knocked on the window to get her granddaughter's attention. Sissy looked up and smiled. When she was satisfied the fire was ready to be lit she washed her hands under the backyard tap and walked into the kitchen.

'Morning, Nanna.' She hugged her grandmother.

'Morning to you too. Have you had your breakfast?' Odette asked.

'Yeah,' Sissy said. 'I had some bread and jam after I got out of bed. But I'm hungry again. What about you?'

Odette brushed Sissy's fringe away from her eyes and tucked it behind an ear. 'I'm not surprised you're hungry. You've been out there working hard. Take your jumper off and I'll make you a sandwich.'

'You walked all the way to the graveyard and back. That's harder work than I've been doing.'

Odette felt the pain in her side and grimaced.

'What's wrong?' Sissy asked.

Odette dismissed Sissy's question. 'There's nothing wrong with me, Young Miss.' She picked up a box of matches and went into the backyard. Sissy had prepared a good fire. Odette lit the match, stood back and watched as the flames quickly took to the timber. She went back into the kitchen and made lunch. After they'd eaten, Sissy got up from the table and looked out the window at the bath. 'I reckon it's ready, Nan. It's my turn to spread the coals to heat the water.'

'It's hard work,' Odette said, 'but don't let me stop you.'

'You can have first bath today, Nan.'

Odette wouldn't hear of it. 'No, I won't be. You always go first. We'll leave it at that.'

Odette was in the laundry struggling to saw through a rock-hard block of *Velvet* soap when Sissy called out to her, 'I'm ready.'

Until the previous summer Odette had always helped wash and dry Sissy at bath time but now that her granddaughter was developing, Odette left the girl to enjoy some privacy until it was time to wash her hair. She came out of the laundry carrying a tin pail, a hairbrush and a bottle of castor oil. She moved a wooden chair alongside the tub, sat down and dipped the pail into the water. 'Pass me the soap, Sis, and put your head back.'

Sissy closed her eyes and rested her neck against the edge of the bath. Odette gently poured the warm water over Sissy's head, her hair darkening as the water ran onto her shoulders. Odette massaged Sissy's scalp, working the soap into a rich lather. She then rinsed Sissy's hair with several pails of water, poured a few drops of castor oil into one hand and raked the oil through Sissy's hair with her fingers.

Sissy sighed with pleasure. 'I love this, Nanna. It's the best part of the week.'

'I'm happy you do.' Odette smiled. 'I love it too.'

Odette closed her eyes, listening to the call of a bird in a tree branch high above. She had taught Sissy about the importance of birds, telling her that one day they would become the truest friends she could have. Without having to open her eyes Odette knew that the bird was a magpie, the same one that had been visiting the house for two years or more.

'He's a friend,' Odette explained to Sissy when the bird first arrived in the yard. 'As long as that magpie is here, we will be safe.'

‘Safe from what?’ Sissy had asked.

‘From everything,’ Odette had said. She continued to rinse Sissy’s hair while returning the magpie’s call.

‘Hey, Nanna,’ Sissy asked, ‘did you speak with the old people at the graveyard today?’

‘Of course, I always do. To my mamma and your grandpa. And the others.’

‘Are you ever afraid when you go there, maybe that there are ghosts in the graveyard?’

‘Rubbish. Who told you that?’ Odette asked.

‘No one, I was just thinking.’

Odette took a dry cloth from the pocket of her dress and wiped Sissy’s face. ‘Ghosts are what white people put in storybooks and picture shows. They do it to scare people about the dead. The church does the same. It’s about making people afraid. I’m sure they know nothing about the good of a person’s spirit and how it comes forward after death.’

The mission had converted many Aboriginal people into God-fearing Christians. They could sing and pray day and night, and hold to the truth of the Bible as good as any white person. Those on the mission who did not take to prayer were regarded with suspicion by the missionaries, and were sometimes punished. Ruben had taught Odette to sing just loud enough to keep them satisfied.

‘Do you believe in God?’ she had once asked her father.

‘No, I don’t,’ Ruben answered. ‘Not their God. I believe in what the old people teach me, but not the church business.’

‘Why do you want me to sing then?’ she’d asked.

‘Because it’s best to keep them fellas happy, keep their meanness down,’ he’d answered.

'Do you think I'll be able to speak to the old people one day?' Sissy asked, interrupting Odette's thoughts.

'Speak with them any time you like.' Odette chuckled. 'You can start with my cousin, Marcus. He's two rows back from your Pa, Ruben, at the graveyard. Marcus never stops talking. If he doesn't talk back to you none of them old people will.'

Odette fetched a length of clean calico for Sissy to dry herself. She turned her back on the girl until Sissy had stepped out of the tub and wrapped herself in the sheet.

'I saw a man here this morning,' Sissy commented, as Odette was drying her hair.

Odette stopped. 'What man?'

'When I got up and put the kettle on I saw him from the front window.'

'Who?' Odette demanded, raising her voice.

'A man. He was dressed all in black.'

Thinking about her encounter with the new policeman, Lowe, Odette's heart raced. 'And what did he do?'

'Nothing. He was standing out in the street. When I came back to the window after making my tea he was gone.'

Odette wrung her hands together. Sissy could sense Odette's anxiety.

'Is there something wrong, Nan?'

'Nothing,' Odette barked, before checking herself. She patted the small of Sissy's back several times. 'I'm sorry. It's really nothing, Sis. You come inside now and we'll put the brush through your hair before it dries and tangles.'

'What about your bath, Nan? I can shovel more of the coals for you.'

'And get yourself all grubby again? I won't have you doing

that. There'll be no bath for me today. I'm going to be busy with the cards. I have an order to finish.'

'Can I help?'

'Of course. Let's get you out of the cold first.'

Back inside, Sissy sat on the bed in front of a small mirror brushing her hair. Odette stood in the kitchen, looking out of the front window into the empty street.

Later that afternoon Sissy helped Odette with the hand-painted greeting cards she made for the gift shop in Gatlin. The woman who owned the shop had passed through Deane three years earlier, enquiring if there were any *native handy-workers* in the district. She was directed to Odette's cottage by Millie Khan, and had arrived in a small motor car, which she parked on the Deane side of the bridge. When the woman walked up to the house and knocked at the front door Odette was surprised to see a white woman standing on her veranda. She could not recall any white woman visiting Quarrytown, let alone one dressed so elegantly.

Odette had liked drawing since she was a young girl. She kept sketchbooks filled with images of flowers and birds. Once the woman had explained the purpose of her visit and told Odette that her friend, Millie, had described her as an *artist*, Odette showed her some of her sketches. The woman was clearly impressed. She went back to her car and returned with a large case, placing it on the kitchen table. When she opened the case, Sissy, standing on a chair behind her grandmother, looked down at the open box and cried out, 'Wow, Nan. Look at all this.'

Blank white cards were stacked on one side of the case. The other side was filled with coloured pencils, a sharpener, pastel crayons, a tray of watercolours and different sized paintbrushes. The woman took a card from the case, placed it on the table and asked Odette to draw a picture for her.

'What would you like me to draw?' Odette asked.

'Anything that takes your heart, Darling,' the woman smiled, patting Odette on the shoulder as if she was a child.

Within minutes Odette had drawn an image of one of the wildflowers that grew around the children's graves at the mission. The woman was excited and said that she was confident Odette's artwork would sell through her business.

'I have an arrangement with several native women that operates successfully. Each month you would send me your painted cards through the post, and, as long as the work is to standard, I send you a postal order in return for the due amount. We could begin conservatively, with just one package of cards, and see what response we get. There would be no cost to you at all to begin the arrangement.'

'And what would you pay me?' Odette asked, sceptical of such an offer from a total stranger. The woman explained the details of the financial arrangement. Odette did the mental arithmetic and calculated she could potentially earn more from drawing greeting cards over a couple of days than she could scrubbing floors for an entire week.

'What I need from you,' the woman added, 'is your tribal name.'

Odette was puzzled. 'My tribal name?'

'Yes. The tribe of your ancestors, where your people originated from. Whenever I sell native artwork I provide written provenance with the greeting cards, naming the tribe that the artist originates from. It adds to the value of the work, you see?' She looked at the frowning Odette, sympathetically. 'Oh, I'm sorry. Perhaps you have lost all contact with …' The woman blushed with embarrassment.

It never failed to surprise Odette how white people were always going on about *uplifting* Aboriginal people, yet they would demand information about the old ways when it suited them. She looked over to the honey jar sitting on the bread board and read the label to herself. It sounded tribal enough. 'We're the Bilga people,' she explained. 'That's my tribe. The Bilgas.'

The woman lifted her head and looked towards an imaginary and distant landscape. 'The Bilga people. Of course.' She smiled as though she'd had actual contact with the tribe. The woman offered her gloved hand to Odette and the pair shook on the deal. She looked up at the blonde-haired Sissy. 'And who would you be, young lady?'

Sissy proudly lifted her chin but said nothing, having been raised by Odette to remain wary of strangers.

'She's my granddaughter,' Odette offered.

The woman's head snapped, as if she'd been shocked by a bolt of electricity. 'Really? Oh, really,' she repeated, awkwardly. 'Your granddaughter?'

'Yeah. Really,' Odette said. 'The world is full of wonders.'

The woman left the case of art supplies with Odette and over time the arrangement between the women flourished. Each month Odette boxed her completed cards and posted them to the gift shop. In return, she received a postal order and art supplies. Without citizenship, Odette could not open an independent bank account. As a consequence, she cashed the money orders and kept her savings in old jam tins stored at the back of the pantry.

Sissy sat at the kitchen table and watched Odette holding a wattle branch in one hand while sketching with the other.

'You like them ones, don't you?' Sissy said. 'You paint them a lot.'

Odette twirled the branch between two fingers. The yellow flowers performed a pirouette. 'I do like them. So do the birds and insects. I'm painting this one because it comes out early in the season. There's not much else that flowers this time of year.'

'You could paint all these flowers and birds by memory, couldn't you, Nan?' Sissy asked. 'You don't need the branch in front of you.'

'You're right. I don't need them in front of me, Sis. But, as each tree is different, so is each branch and leaf and flower. What I'm painting this afternoon can't be painted again. They're all different. Once this flower dies there won't be another quite the same.'

She handed the branch to Sissy, who closely examined the serrated leaves and fine ball-shaped flowers. 'This comes from the tree in the front yard?'

'It does.'

'They're all the same, the leaves and flowers on that tree.' Sissy sighed.

'No, they're not,' Odette protested. 'You have to look more closely.'

Sissy moved the branch closer to her face, until a leaf tickled her nose and she turned cross-eyed. 'I can't see any difference between them. It's like they're all twins.'

'That's because you're not looking with soft eyes,' Odette said.

'Soft eyes? What's that?'

Odette dropped her paintbrush into an old Vegemite jar filled with water. She picked up a second, finer brush and dipped it in the yellow paint. 'That's something you'll come to know with age and patience. It takes time to learn. You're not ready yet.'

'Will you teach me, Nanna?'

Odette delicately placed the tip of the brush against the greeting card and drew a beautiful flower with the briefest of strokes. If she heard Sissy's question, she didn't answer it.

Odette was thinking of her own childhood and the rare but valued time she spent in the bush surrounding the mission. She often shared these stories with Sissy, yet she also carried other memories of the mission that she kept to herself. These had etched themselves into the telling wrinkles on her face. When Odette looked up she noticed Sissy watching her closely and wondered what the girl was thinking.

Once the cards had dried they wrapped them in greaseproof paper and tied them together with a red ribbon. Odette tidied the kitchen table and swept the floor as rain began to beat on the iron roof. As the rain got heavier, water started dripping onto the floor. Sissy ran around the kitchen with the empty jars they kept for when the roof leaked, placing them on the floor to catch the drops. The half-filled jars soon performed a tattoo, accompanied by the erratic beat of rain on the roof.

'I love this sound,' Sissy said. 'Do you love it, Nanna?'

'Yes, I do.'

In the early evening, they sat across the table from each other, eating bowls of rabbit stew and listening to the radio. Sissy finished her meal, buried her face in the bowl and licked it. She rested the empty bowl on the table. Odette smiled across the table at Sissy, who had no idea that the tip of her nose was covered in rich gravy.

'Will we live here for a long time, Nanna?'

'Of course, we will. Where else would we go?'

'Maybe to the sea.'

'The sea! What gives you that idea? The sea must be hundreds of miles away from here. At least.'

'I'm reading a book that I borrowed from the library. The children in it go on an adventure in a boat, across the ocean. I'd like to see the ocean one day, Nanna. Would you take me?'

It had been a busy day for Odette. Her eyelids were heavy. 'The ocean's a long way from here. That would be a trip we'd need to do a lot of thinking about, and I'm too tired for that now. I'll soon be asleep here if I don't hop up. Let's wash your face and hands, and then put you into your pyjamas.'

'Do you know how long I'm going to live with you?' Sissy asked, wiping her face with a warm flannel.

'You know, Sis, you must have asked me a hundred questions today. You're going to wear me out.'

'Well, this question is a hundred and one. How long will I be living here, with you?'

'I give up, girl. You tell me. How long?'

'Forever.' Sissy smiled.

Forever.

The day her daughter, Lila, was born was the happiest in Odette's life. As a mother she'd battled to ensure Lila would stay with her *forever,* and for many years she'd succeeded in keeping her daughter close. After Lila went away, Odette was forced to confront reality – although her daughter had not been taken from her, for whatever reason, Lila had decided to leave her mother behind. Each night, before Odette fell asleep, she asked the old people for help, that she would not lose Sissy as well.

CHAPTER FOUR

Walking to the mission graveyard a week later Odette saw that a *KEEP OUT* sign had been scrawled in large letters along the junkyard fence and a chain and padlock had been added to the gate. There was no sign of Henry at the yard that morning, or the following week when Odette noticed broken beer bottles and empty shotgun shells strewn across the track. Henry Lamb had gone to ground, as was his habit. Odette suspected there'd be no bicycle for Sissy's birthday, so was surprised on her return home from the graveyard to see Henry in the distance, standing in the open gateway with Rowdy by his side.

'I've been looking out for you,' he called, one arm bent at the elbow to shield his eyes from the precious morning sun.

'Really?' Odette replied. 'I thought you might have left town, Henry Lamb. Gone on a holiday.'

'Not me. I don't go any place.'

She pointed to the shattered glass. 'What's happened here?'

Henry nervously tugged at the bib of his overalls.

'It was them Kane boys. They come round again wanting to have a snoop. I told them the yard is private property and I have nothing for sale. They're not welcome here and I told them so. They smashed the bottles, and I heard someone's boot giving the fence a good kick. There was some shooting too. *Bang! Bang!* Poor Rowdy went off his head with the noise.'

'That's terrible, Henry. When did this happen?'

'Maybe three nights back. Could be more. Could be less.'

Henry appeared to have shrunk into his overalls since Odette had last seen him. He looked more like a child than an old man. Odette briefly considered taking hold of him and giving him a hug, before checking herself.

'Have you reported it at the police station?'

'I've told nobody. But I painted this sign,' Henry said, pointing with some pride in the general direction of his most recent warning to troublemakers. 'And I have the gate bolted double now. I only opened it up because I've been waiting on you, Odette, to talk about your bicycle. For Sissy. I've been worrying that I missed the day. I should have written it down like I was thinking to do. Today is Sunday and I knew to wait here for you to come by. Have I missed her birthday?'

'No, Henry,' Odette smiled. 'That's thoughtful of you, to build the bike for her.' She looked down at the glass shards winking in the sunlight. 'Especially with this trouble you're dealing with. I wish I could do something to help.'

'Don't you worry, Odette. I can look after myself. Some day when they come by I'll have a surprise for them Kane boys.'

'What would that be?' Odette asked. 'Are you going to shoot them or something?'

It was an off-hand comment but the earnest frown on Henry's face suggested he was giving serious consideration to the proposition. 'Haven't thought about that, but maybe I should. Reckon they deserve it,' he said. 'So, when will you and Sissy be coming for her bike?'

'Well, it's her birthday next week. What if I brought her by here on Tuesday after she's finished school, at around four? Would that be a good time for you, Henry?'

Henry lifted his head and closed his eyes, as if mentally checking his diary. 'I reckon I should be here. Yep, the time would be good by me.' He took a pen out of the front pocket of his overalls and wrote a note on his forearm. 'Four o'clock, Tuesday,' he whispered to himself.

'I'll see you then,' Odette said.

'Yep. I'll be right here.'

As Odette walked on she heard the gate shut behind her, followed by the sound of a rattling lock and chain.

The following Tuesday after school Odette had a plan to surprise Sissy. She asked her to help out with a trip to Henry Lamb's yard. Sissy had her nose in a book and didn't want to leave the house. 'Why do you need me to come, Nan? I have homework to do.'

'Homework? You never have homework. I need you to help me.'

'What sort of help?'

'I'm looking for a special part. Henry might have one in the yard. You can help me look for it.'

Sissy wasn't convinced. 'A part? What sort of part, Nan?'

'Just a part,' Odette sighed. 'For a machine.'

'But we don't have any machines at home for a part to go with,' Sissy persisted. 'Maybe it would be best for you to buy a machine from Henry first.' She laughed, testing her grandmother's story. 'And then you can search for a part to go with it.'

Odette had had enough of Sissy's cheekiness. 'That's plenty from you. All you need to know is that you're coming with me, and I'll tell you all about this part I'm after while we're on the walk.'

Deane's Line was drier than it had been in weeks. The sun was out and the walk was enjoyable, despite the pair having to stop a couple of times for Odette to catch her breath.

'It's your birthday tomorrow,' Odette said. 'You're growing up too quick on me, Sweet.' She rested an arm on Sissy's shoulder as they walked and noticed that her granddaughter was almost as tall as she was, with some growing left in her. 'I guess you've been thinking about a birthday present from your nan?'

'Maybe,' Sissy smiled.

'Maybe? And?'

'Well,' Sissy hesitated. 'I'd like a sketchbook of my own and some pencils. I'd like to draw as good as you do, Nan. One day I want to make my own cards and sell them to that lady in Gatlin you work for.'

'That's all you want?' Odette asked. 'Let's say you could have anything you wanted for your birthday. What would it be?'

'Anything?'

Sissy walked ahead of her grandmother as she thought about the question. 'If I could have anything I wanted I would stay in the bath all day, every day for the next year, having my hair washed over and over.'

Odette scoffed. 'And I guess I'd be the one stoking the fire and shovelling the coal all day to keep the water hot. *And* washing your hair. That would be harder than working all day for white people.'

'Nope. You wouldn't be working at all, Nan. We'd have our own worker, doing the jobs for us. All you would have to do would be sit on a couch and drink tea. And there'd be chocolate.'

'You'd need to search a long time to find anyone who'd work that hard for us. Aboriginal people, we do all the work.'

Odette knocked at Henry's gate. He didn't answer immediately. She knocked again, banging against the iron fence with the toe of her shoe. When that didn't get his attention, she shouted his name. 'Henry, it's me, Odette. Me and Sissy.'

She could hear Rowdy barking. He ran at the gate, butted it and sniffed around the bottom of the gate with his wet, black nose. Odette heard the jangling of keys and the sound of several padlocks being opened. Henry pulled on the metal chain attached to the gate and opened it a few inches. He spied Odette through the crack.

'Yep, it's you,' he reassured himself, and threw the gate open. He ignored Odette and offered his grubby hand to Sissy. 'Happy birthday, Miss Sissy.'

'Thank you, Henry,' she said.

'Miss Sissy,' he laughed. 'That sounds like Mississippi.'

'It does,' Sissy said.

'So, you did remember her birthday,' Odette greeted him. 'Thank you.'

Henry frowned, slightly insulted. 'Of course I did. I would not forget this girl's birthday. Come inside.'

Henry stepped to one side and ushered them into the yard. Odette hadn't been inside the Lambs' junkyard before. She'd never seen anything like the collection that Henry and his father had amassed over the decades. One side of the yard was occupied by mountains of wooden chairs, tangled collections of iron bed railings, rolls of rusting agricultural fencing, cattle gates, hessian bags bulging with old clothing, tools, tables, pillars of books ruined by the damp weather and dozens of tea chests filled with pots and saucers, plates and cups, knives, forks and spoons. The rear of the yard was dominated by a long open shed, storing buggies, old tractors, truck parts, three motorbikes and even an old stagecoach.

Odette walked slowly towards the coach, conjuring a distant memory with each step. 'I remember this. I'm sure I do.'

'That one used to go right by here, along Deane's Line,' Henry confirmed. 'I would hear it coming by and run out there on the road to wave at the men inside.'

Yes. Odette remembered it too. The coach brought the managers and a foreman from the mine to the mission each Saturday. They would lunch with the priests, and afterwards stroll through the grounds slapping hard-working backs and handing out boiled sweets for the children and presents wrapped in decorated paper at Christmas. Odette, like the other kids, took the sweets although she felt they tasted a little sour.

She was about to touch one of the large wooden wheels of the coach when a more sinister image flashed before her – a coach full of children being driven away from the mission, crying for their mothers. Odette turned her back on the carriage.

'I don't reckon any person on the planet has gathered so much stuff in one place as you have here, Henry. You've got some collection.'

'I have,' Henry smiled, his chest lifting with pride.

Sissy rummaged through one of the tea chests and picked out a small plate, decorated with hand-painted red roses. The plate was covered in dust. She blew the dust away. 'Is this for sale, Henry?' she asked. 'How much money do you want for it?'

'If I was selling that plate it would be sixpence and not a penny less,' he answered. 'But you can have it for free. There's more of them in the box. You can have a look and take any you want. You could make a set for yourself as good as the Queen of England has.'

Odette was hoping she might spot the bicycle, but all she saw were a couple of rusting frames and a collection of wheels with broken spokes.

Henry shifted excitedly from side to side. 'You can have something more than them cups and saucers,' he said.

Sissy was busy cleaning the dusty plate with the sleeve of her jumper and paid him no attention.

Henry raised an open hand, looking like a dishevelled preacher about to commence a sermon. 'Wait right here, both of you. I will be back with something very special.' He skipped across the yard and disappeared behind a dented old Dodge truck with flattened tyres. He made a terrible racket, the sound of somebody beating a petrol drum with a hammer.

Sissy looked across at Odette, who smiled and lifted her shoulders as if she had no idea what was going on.

'I'm coming,' Henry called. He soon appeared from behind the Dodge, walking a bicycle. The frame was painted red and the wheels, which didn't quite match in size, had been scrubbed and oiled. The handlebar grips, made out of strips of leather from an old car seat, had been crafted by Henry himself. The basket on the handlebars barely resembled the wicker cray pot it had originally been; an item that had somehow travelled far from the sea to the junkyard. Henry brought the bicycle to a halt in front of Sissy.

'Is that your bike?' Sissy asked him.

'No. It's not mine. I don't need a bicycle. I have a motor car that I'm repairing.' He blinked nervously. 'You can tell her, Odette.'

'This is your bike,' Odette said. 'It's a gift for your birthday, Sissy. Henry made it for you.'

Sissy threw her arms around her grandmother and kissed her. 'I love you, Nan,' she said, hugging Odette tightly. 'Thank you, Henry. It's so wonderful of you to make a bike for me.'

'You need to jump on and take a test ride,' Henry said. 'The seat goes up. And it can go down too. The handlebars, they do the same. If it doesn't feel right, I can fix them for you.' Henry held the bicycle and Sissy hopped on the seat. Her foot touched the pedal with just enough bend at the knee.

'I reckon it's a good fit,' Henry said, feeling pleased with himself. He gently pushed Sissy in the centre of her back and the bicycle eased forward, wobbling from side to side. As Sissy slowly found her balance and started to pedal, the bicycle picked up speed.

'You have to steer it,' Henry screamed, running after her. 'Come on. Steer it.'

Odette and Henry watched Sissy circle the yard, a little unsteadily at first. Rowdy, who'd been laying on a bug-infested mattress beneath the wreck of a tractor, bolted out and trotted along behind, barking with excitement.

'I really have to thank you, Henry,' Odette said. She took a ten-shilling note from her pocket. 'And you will be taking some money for your work.'

Henry vigorously shook his head from side to side. 'I cannot do that, Odette. I made you a promise. I don't need to take your money.'

She looked at the volume of unwanted goods in the yard. 'You must need the money, Henry. None of this rubbish looks like it will be moving in a hurry.'

'It's not rubbish,' he corrected her. 'A dealer from Gatlin comes by here every once in a while. What he pays me is enough to get by on. I put some money towards my projects, and I still have plenty left over.'

'Projects? Like building another bike?'

'No. I'm thinking of one of them space rockets, like the Russian people made.'

'Just because you made a bicycle, Henry, it doesn't mean that you could build a rocket,' Odette said, laughing.

'Doesn't mean that I couldn't,' Henry replied, with little doubt that he could.

Sissy quickly mastered the art of bicycle riding. She was soon steering the bike with confidence. Rowdy continued to trot alongside her like a royal escort. 'Has that Kane boy been back here making trouble for you?' Odette asked.

'Maybe,' he said.

Odette was worried for Henry. 'What will you do if he does give you more bother?'

'Rowdy will eat him. He's a brave one. Anyway, like you told me yourself, Odette, I could shoot that boy.'

'I was only joking when I said that, Henry. Shooting him would get you into all sorts of trouble.'

'Don't mean it's not a good idea.'

'Like your rocket's a good idea?'

'Yep. Like my rocket. I've got some gunpowder here to power it up and send it into space.'

'Where'd you get gunpowder?' Odette asked. 'You shouldn't be keeping it here. It's dangerous. You're supposed to have a licence to handle gunpowder.'

'Are you sure?' Henry asked.

'I know because my father had an explosives licence. I still have the piece of paper in a drawer at home. Where'd you get hold of gunpowder?'

'I found it up at the old quarry. I come into the ownership of all sorts of things. Found some detonators too.'

Sissy skidded to a halt in front of Henry. 'I love the bike. Thank you.'

Odette remembered something that had been on her mind since the Sunday morning Henry had first been troubled by Aaron Kane. 'You know, if you ever wanted to give the junkyard business away, Henry, you could sell the lot off. Maybe to that second-hand dealer from Gatlin that you spoke of. There's a couple of decent huts up at Quarrytown that are empty. You could take over one of them. You wouldn't have to be on your own anymore.'

Henry didn't give Odette's idea a second thought. 'I wouldn't be able to do that, Odette,' he explained. 'This is my place. Right here. This is where I was born. I've always lived here. I don't want to be in any other place, Odette. You understand?'

Odette did understand. 'Fair enough. We all have our own place. Or should do. But if you ever change your mind, you let me know.' She nodded to Sissy. 'We'll be having cake and candles tomorrow if you'd like to come over, Henry? You'd be welcome.'

'Thank you, Odette, but I couldn't leave the yard alone. Like I said, I'm busy with my projects.'

'Okay. Well, maybe I'll see you next Sunday.'

Sissy rode ahead and Odette followed behind her across the rough ground, relieved that Sissy didn't notice her clutching at her side.

CHAPTER FIVE

Odette had a canvas bag slung over one shoulder, weighed down with two bundles of greeting cards. 'I'm off to the post office,' she called out to Sissy, who was making the bed in the next room.

'Wait for me, Nan.' Sissy ran into the kitchen. 'I'll bring my bike and you can put that heavy bag in the basket.'

'If you like, Sis. But I don't reckon you'll want to get stuck in town with me. If I run into one of the old girls we could be yarning until the sun goes down.'

'I don't mind. I like listening to your stories. I'm coming with you.'

As they walked over the footbridge Sissy stopped to look down at the riverbed. 'I wish there was water in this river, Nanna,' she said. 'When the weather is warm I could swim the same as you used to do in the old days.'

'Oh, I wish you could too. That water here was once the clearest you would ever see,' Odette lamented. 'The fish and eels would be swimming with us. The old people, they knew the river and its stories from the time it had run free. All along this way the water overflowed into the old billabongs. Now all we have is the muddy bottom and the frogs,' Odette said. 'There's hardly a drop of water left for them.'

'What happened to all the water?' Sissy asked. 'Tell me that story.'

'There's not much to tell. White people got even greedier than we thought possible. That's what happened.' Over the years Odette had witnessed local government officials seizing more and more land and then filling in old billabongs and covering the muddy ground with screening from the mine before selling off the land.

'Between the farmers and the politicians we were left with nothing. Our people have been hurting since,' she said.

'Why's that?' Sissy asked.

'Because the river, all the rivers, we need them. And they need us. This river underneath us, she's not quite dead but if she gets any more sickness she will be gone soon.'

Odette spotted her old friend Millie Khan walking up ahead on the river track, heading towards town. Odette called out and Millie waved back. She'd known Millie all her life and was used to seeing her friend dressed in stockmen's gear, with her hair cut short like a man's. It was a look Millie had perfected as a teenager, disguising herself as a boy so when she worked the stock route with her father she avoided any unwanted attention from the men. Millie also liked to smoke cigars, an expensive habit she supported by braiding the best quality leather bridles, which stock riders and show jumpers travelled hundreds of miles to purchase.

She'd been taught the skill from a young age by her late father, Morgan Carter, the best horseman, *black or white*, in the west of the state.

Morgan had earned his reputation working with the wild brumbies in the mountains. The horses would be driven back to Deane, broken in and sold as valued stock horses. Morgan Carter had a gift. He could command the most stubborn-minded brumby just by looking at it. A local politician and businessman, John Quinn, seconded Morgan from the mission to work in his stockyards. Quinn built his saddlery over the top of a reclaimed billabong and invited Morgan to run the business for him, raising his family in two rooms behind the stables, free from interference. Whenever a Welfare Board official made enquiries about one or more of the Carter children, Morgan directed them to the influential Mr Quinn, who vouched for the character of his most valued worker.

Morgan also worked closely with the Afghan cameleers, who operated between Deane and the stock routes across the desert. The Afghans would herd the brumbies for hundreds of miles and sell them to Morgan. It was how young Millie met her future husband, Yusuf Khan. Morgan Carter had no idea how a romance could have blossomed between Millie and Yusuf, but was pleased enough that the young man wanted to marry his daughter. Yusuf was a hard worker who was prepared to live at the saddlery, which pleased Morgan, as he didn't want to lose his only daughter to the desert. After Morgan's death Millie and Yusuf took over running the operation.

Although the horse trading business was finished, Millie and Yusuf remained in the house she'd been born and raised in. The building had become something of a local curiosity. Over the years the loose ground beneath the saddlery subsided and the old billabong was slowly devouring the house. One corner of the building had sunk completely, while the foundations of the second room had vanished into a cavity below the floor. Millie could rightly claim that she lived in the only house in the district where a person had to struggle uphill to get out of the front door.

'That's some bicycle you have there, Blondie,' Millie commented to Sissy when the pair finally caught up with her. Odette didn't appreciate the nickname and rolled her eyes in protest.

'Sorry,' Millie mouthed.

'It's her birthday gift,' Odette explained. 'Sissy's just turned thirteen.'

'Congratulations, big girl. I wish I was thirteen again,' Millie said.

'What would you do if you were, Auntie Millie?' Sissy asked.

Millie took a long draw on her cigar and thought about the question. 'Well, back then I'd have got hold of the best young colt I could find and headed north. And I wouldn't have stopped riding until I was out of the state.'

'You'd have been in some trouble,' Odette said. 'You'd need to be riding fast to keep them Welfare fellas off your back.'

'Don't worry about that, I'd have been riding fast enough.' Millie shook her head in disgust. 'Fifty years on and we haven't come far. Some of them still treat us like we're children they can do what they like with.'

'What can they do to you?' Sissy asked.

'Never you mind,' Odette said. 'Come on, show Auntie Millie how you ride your bike.'

Sissy pedalled on ahead of the women.

'You going okay?' Millie asked Odette.

'Same as I'm always going. Why you asking?'

'I think you have some weight off you since I last saw you. And you look pale.'

On cue, Odette's pain niggled her. 'Pale? How does a black woman get to look pale?'

'When she's feeling crook, that's how. You need to be seeing a doctor.'

'There won't be any chance of that. The last doctor I saw in this town was more than twenty years back. He was so afraid of touching me he stood on the other side of the room and washed his hands three times without even examining me.'

Sissy rode the length of the track and stopped when she reached the intersection with the main street. She turned and pedalled back to Odette and Millie.

'Well,' Millie said, 'there's this new doctor in town two days a week. A foreigner, he is. Yusuf went to see him not long back when he was having trouble with his eyes. All weepy from the years of dust and sand when he was taking care of the camels. He said this new fella was just fine. *We were like two gentlemen*, Yusuf said when he came home. He has rooms off the main street, behind the bank.'

Sissy circled the track several times, lifted her bum from the saddle and pedalled away. Odette called after her, 'Hey girl, you be careful with my gift cards.'

Millie took hold of Odette's arm. 'We've not only got a new doctor. Have you heard there's a new sheriff in town?'

'I know. He fronted me on the footbridge a few weeks ago. I've never seen a good-looking policeman, but this one had a face like death warmed up. It's taken a long time for Bill Shea's drinking to catch up with him. This new one, he's here to replace him.'

Odette and Millie had known Bill Shea since they were children, after his family moved into a house between Quarrytown and Deane. Initially, Bill and his older sister, Sarah, walked to school a few steps behind the Aboriginal kids, not sure of their place in the pecking order. It wasn't long before the Shea kids fell in with the Aboriginal children. They mixed easily and played together when the school day was over. One afternoon Bill asked Odette if she would like to play in his front yard. When she hesitated, he said, *It's okay, our mum won't be home for ages.*

Odette was wrestling Bill into submission, having pinned his back to the rough buffalo grass, when she heard the rusting hinge on the front gate. Mrs Shea was unable to comprehend the scene in front of her. She looked down at her son lying beneath an Aboriginal girl. Odette never forgot the look of disgust on Mrs Shea's face. Before the woman could get a word of protest out, Odette had bolted across the yard and hurdled the front fence. Sprinting along the track towards home, Odette could hear Mrs Shea yelling at her son. The next time she saw Bill on the way to school she called out his name. He ignored her. Bill's sister turned around and threw stones at Odette. From that day on, Odette had never been inside a white person's home, except to work for them.

~

'It's not Bill Shea's drinking that's getting him replaced,' Millie said. 'Or his shiny arse never leaving that seat in his office.'

'What do you mean?'

'They're bringing in these new police all over the state.'

'Why?'

'Because some of them working for the government don't like our people speaking up, calling for citizens' rights. This isn't the talk they want to hear. I heard they've been hand-picked, and I reckon this new copper is one of them. They want to keep us in our place.'

Odette watched Sissy up ahead as she tried riding the bicycle hands-free. 'Where'd you hear this from?' she asked.

'I heard it. That's all you need to know for now. I was also told that some coppers have been doing the old count again. Names. Age. Colour. Blood. The lot.'

'Blood? There mustn't be more than two dozen blackfellas between here and the ranges. Why would they bother with us? We don't make a nuisance of ourselves and we ask for nothing. And there's been no meetings about the citizenship round here. You can stop acting mysteriously towards me, Millie. If there's trouble ahead for me and Sissy I need to know what it is, and I need to know where this story's coming from. This might be nothing but drunk yabber or crazy talk, for all I know.'

'There's nothing crazy about it. Yusuf's cousin, Miriam, over at Thunder Ridge, she told me herself. The policeman out there, he's a new fella as well. He came round not long ago and was quizzing her. Asking all types of questions. He even took photographs of her grandkiddies. I heard one of the women, a young girl, she recognised his face from when she was in the Homes, said that he'd worked there before he joined the coppers. She took one look at him and ran off into the desert.'

'What did the woman say about him?'

'Nothing. She went away for two nights and when she came back she wouldn't speak about him. Not a word.'

'You say he took photographs?'

'He did. A couple of them kids are real light-skinned. Same as your Sissy. Their daddy is a Swedish man, a rigger. Miriam put this copper off by showing him her papa's immigration papers. He was born in the Punjab over there. Same as Yusuf's people. She told the copper they are *pure* Afghans.'

'But Miriam's mother, isn't she from country round here?'

'Sure is. But she wouldn't be telling a copper her true identity. Miriam's worried sick over the grandkids. The whole mob is thinking of getting on the move, heading further out on the stock run, to the desert.'

The women reached the main street of Deane. Sissy was waiting for them, resting on her bicycle, looking pleased with herself. The morning sun captured the light in her hair and the pale skin of her face. A knot of fear gathered in Odette's stomach.

Millie tapped Odette on the arm. 'I have to get to the hardware store. You do me a favour and go see that doctor.'

Sissy rested her bike against the horse trough outside the town's only surviving hotel, *The Squatter*, and walked along the street with Odette. They first went into the post office and had the greeting cards weighed, stamped and posted. Odette converted her most recent money order to cash. The cashier,

Estelle Slocomb, the current mayor's daughter, had a habit of never looking directly at Odette as she counted out the one-pound notes. It was clear to Odette that Estelle felt the task of handling money for an Aboriginal woman demeaned her. She once heard the cashier say to the postmaster, 'I don't know what she does with all that money.'

Next, they went to the general store to buy groceries. Owen Healy, the owner of the store, was close to ninety years of age. He had outlived his wife and eldest son, and continued to run the business with his youngest son, who was close to sixty years old himself. Owen always spoke politely to his customers and was well liked.

'How are you, today, Odette?' he asked.

'Very well, Owen, but not as fit as you.'

Sissy helped Odette load the shopping into the basket on the front of the bike. 'This is too heavy for you,' Odette protested. 'Let me share the load.'

'Maybe you could ride the bike home,' Sissy teased her nan.

'I hardly think so. I'm too old.'

'You're not old, Nan. Not like Mr Healy is old.'

Odette had felt old in recent weeks. 'Not too many people get to be as old as Mr Healy,' she said.

They walked back, past the bank, the bicycle between them. Odette glanced down the side street and noticed the *Surgery* sign hanging from a hook above an open door. She stopped outside the local picture theatre, *The Palace*, which had closed down two years earlier.

'Sissy,' Odette said, 'I need you to wait for me.'

'Where are you going, Nan? I could come with you.'

'No, I need you to wait. There's a doctor along the street

here. I'm going to call in and see him and get some powders for this pain I've been having. I won't be long. You don't move, and I'll be back soon.'

As soon as Odette was out of sight Sissy thought about jumping on her bike and tearing along the main street. The first time she'd ridden her birthday bike in Henry Lamb's junkyard, Sissy felt an exhilaration she'd not experienced before. She knew it wasn't anything to match the magic a bird must feel, gliding across the sky, but just the same she liked to imagine she was flying. Her grandmother had told her she was allowed to ride along the river track on her own, but only as far as the turn-off to town, unless she was riding to school. Each day Sissy secretly defied her grandmother, venturing further along the snaking river trail, setting herself a new marker to reach before turning around and heading for home.

Instead, Sissy took an apple from the shopping basket and sat on the bench outside the picture theatre eating it. She looked up at the faded movie posters in the front window of the theatre. The final movie to be shown there had been *Imitation of Life*. She and Odette had not been to see the movie, but Sissy had heard a group of white girls from school talking about it.

Angeline Adams, the publican's daughter, believed it was the saddest movie ever made.

'What's it about?' one of the other girls asked.

'It's about a part-black girl who doesn't want to be black and she treats her own mother like she's dirt,' Angeline explained to the girls gathered around her. 'She even pretends that she doesn't know her mother,' she added. 'They do that around here too, some of them.' She looked directly at the Aboriginal girls, including Sissy.

The stars of the movie, Lana Turner and Juanita Moore, had been trapped in the cobwebbed theatre window since the night of the final screening. In another poster, a white girl and a brown-skinned girl, around the same age as each other, were sitting on a beach, smiling. Sissy stood up and walked across to the window. She rested her back against the glass, rolled up the sleeves of her jumper and placed one arm alongside the bare skin of the brown girl. She did the same with the other arm against the skin of the young white girl. She then stood between the two girls, looking up at them watching her.

The surgery waiting room consisted of two wooden chairs, a bench seat and a framed photograph of Queen Elizabeth on the wall. A sign on a closed door read *Dr Nathan Singer M.D.* Odette could hear someone moving around in the next room. The door opened suddenly, startling her. A man around ten years younger than Odette appeared. He was wearing a dark three-piece woollen suit, an older-style rounded shirt collar and a polka dot bow tie. His thick, dark hair was flecked with streaks of silver around the temples.

'I am so sorry,' he said. 'I did not realise that there was someone waiting. Please come in and take a seat.'

Odette hesitated before walking into the room. The doctor followed. She immediately began to feel nervous and remained on her feet.

The doctor gestured towards the chair. 'Your name is, please?'

'My name is Mrs Odette Brown,' she said. 'I live in Quarrytown.' She took her purse out of her coat pocket. 'I have my own money,' she said. She took out a two-pound note, which she offered to the doctor.

The doctor was clearly puzzled. 'Money?'

'I am able to pay you myself. There's no need for you to bill the Welfare people. I can take care of this.'

The doctor frowned. 'There is no need to discuss payment now. Please, Mrs Brown, do take a seat and tell me why you are here this morning.'

Odette sat and nervously looked around the room, which was sparse but clean. Several leather-bound books sat on the mantle above a fireplace behind a large desk. On one side of the room was an examination table and screen, and on the other, a trolley containing medical instruments, medicines and a sterilisation oven. The doctor waited for Odette to say something. When she didn't speak, he prompted her.

'How can I help you today, Mrs Brown?'

'Some time back I started to get these pains in my side. I get it mostly when I'm walking, and other times when I need to lift something heavy. I've been expecting the pain to go away. But it hasn't.'

'Which side of your body is the pain on?' the doctor asked.

'Underneath my ribs.' Odette rested her hand above her left hip. 'In here.'

'Okay.' He smiled. 'Do you have any other symptoms?'

She thought for a moment. 'I haven't been eating much as I haven't felt hungry lately. And my sleep has been poor. I get tired early but wake up in the night.'

'Is it the pain that wakes you?'

'Yes, it's the pain.'

The doctor nodded towards the examination table. 'It will be necessary to take your blood pressure and your temperature. I need to know if you're running a fever or have an infection. I do think it best if I can also examine you, Mrs Brown.'

Doctor Singer detected Odette's look of concern. Her experience with medical people, as limited as it was, had always caused her anxiety. The doctor manoeuvred the screen into position beside the examination table. He opened a cupboard door, brought out a dressing gown and handed it to Odette.

'I'm sorry. This is a gentleman's robe. It's all I have for now but it is clean. Please remove your clothes, place this over your underwear and lay down on the table. Call me when you are comfortable.'

Odette undressed and lay down. She concentrated on the web of cracks in the plaster ceiling as Doctor Singer examined her. She answered each of his questions, delivered in a quiet voice, as thoughtfully as possible. He'd removed his coat and rolled up his shirtsleeves. Odette noticed a set of numbers tattooed onto his forearm. Their eyes met. Odette looked away.

'You'll need to have an X-ray at the hospital in Gatlin,' the doctor explained. 'I work there three days a week, where we have the equipment to complete some tests for you.'

'Tests for what?' Odette asked.

'Well,' he said, 'I can't be sure at this stage. You certainly have some swelling on the left side of your abdomen. But without an X-ray and perhaps some pathology tests to follow up I can't be certain. Do you know the Gatlin hospital?'

The only time Odette had visited Gatlin was twelve years earlier when she'd walked the streets searching for her daughter, Lila. 'I can find the hospital,' she answered.

'Good. I will arrange an appointment date and time for you to attend. I will have a detailed letter ready for you to collect by Monday morning.'

The doctor rolled his shirtsleeves down and buttoned the cuffs. As he did so, Odette again noticed the tattooed numbers on his bare arm. She knew a little about the war in Europe and what had happened to the Jewish people. Some years earlier she'd seen a magazine with photographs of thin and starving people waiting in line for food at a Red Cross station. In one photograph three men displayed tattooed numbers on their arms, similar to Doctor Singer's.

'Have you always lived here, in this town?' the doctor asked Odette after she had dressed.

'Yes. I've never lived any place else.' She was curious about the doctor's own story. 'Where are you from?' she asked, surprising herself with her forwardness.

'I'm from the other side of the world. Poland,' he smiled.

Odette was curious about why a person would travel many thousands of miles from Europe to a lonely town in Australia, stuck between the mountains and the desert. The doctor opened the door. He followed Odette into the waiting room.

'We should have an appointment for you at the hospital within two weeks. My letter will contain all the necessary details. In the meantime, it would be best if you are able to get some rest.'

'Thank you,' she said. 'I'm grateful for your help.'

'It's what we do,' he said. 'Help people.'

~

Walking back to the main street Odette saw Bill Shea outside The Palace looking down at the ground, his hands resting in the small of his back. She could also see Sissy, who was using her bicycle as a barrier between herself and Sergeant Lowe.

'What do you want with her?' Odette asked more abruptly than the policemen may have expected.

'Whatever I think is necessary,' Lowe answered.

'I need to know what your business is with my granddaughter.'

'Do not be alarmed,' he said. 'I have been talking with young Cecily. She has been telling me that she had a birthday recently and was presented with this bicycle. I have been asking Cecily what plans you have for her future, Mrs Brown.'

Odette felt a single bead of perspiration run from the base of her neck down the centre of her back. 'Oh, we don't have any plans,' she answered, doing all she could to remain calm. 'We're on our way home. Come on, Sissy, we need to be going.'

'Not just yet,' Lowe interrupted, gripping the handlebars of the bike. 'The welfare of the child is my concern.'

Odette looked nervously towards Bill Shea, hoping he might have the courage to intervene. Shea dropped his head, finding a sudden need to study the frayed cuffs of his trousers.

'Come on, Sis,' Odette ordered a second time. 'Let's get home.'

'Not yet, Mrs Brown,' Lowe said. 'Not until you hear what I have to say. Change is coming to the town of Deane and it's best that people prepare for it, yourself included.' He patted Sissy's hand. 'She is a smart young lady, your granddaughter. I would not want to see a girl with such potential slip back. It is my duty to uplift children such as Cecily and I will not fail her. Good day.'

He strode purposely across the street in the direction of the police station. Shea followed him like a clumsy but loyal pup.

'What does he mean by that, Nan? *Uplift?* What does that mean?' Sissy demanded.

'It means nothing,' Odette said. 'Don't be worrying yourself over this. It's just police talking the way police have always talked.'

Sissy looked at the movie poster of the two girls comparing their skin colour. 'I bet it does mean something, what he just said to you.'

'Whatever it means, you're not to get upset about it. It's my job to care for you, and nobody else. We need to get these groceries home. I've got butter in this bag for making a cake. I don't want it to melt.'

'I'm not leaving until you tell me what the policeman was speaking about,' Sissy insisted. 'I don't like him.'

'Aren't you just? There's nothing to tell you. And by the way, I don't like him either.' Odette slapped her hands together. 'We're going home, Sissy.'

'But Nan.'

'No more!'

Sissy rode her bike slowly, sulking the whole way home. She went straight to the bedroom and lay down and read. A little while later Odette went to check on her. Sissy wouldn't look up. Odette sat on the bed next to her granddaughter. After Lila left she'd sworn that no harm would come to the girl while she was alive. It was an oath she'd reinforced to herself many times over the years.

'Are you going to keep this up, ignoring me?' Odette asked.

Sissy could never stay angry with Odette for long. 'I'm just reading, Nan.'

'Are you going to eat, then?'

'If you are, Nan.'

'I don't want you worrying over what that policeman was talking about,' Odette said to Sissy as they ate.

'I'm not thinking about him, Nan.'

Odette doubted her granddaughter's response but let the matter be.

CHAPTER SIX

When Sissy arrived home from school one afternoon the following week she found Odette in the backyard stoking hot coals under the bathtub and running buckets of water from the laundry.

'Nanna, do you know what day it is?' Sissy asked. 'You know that it's not Sunday, don't you?'

'Of course, I know what day it is,' Odette answered, annoyed at the suggestion that she may not. 'Today is Wednesday, and tomorrow will be Thursday. How's that for you, Missy?' she grumbled. Odette marched breathlessly back and forth across the yard, spilling more water on the ground than she managed to tip into the tub.

'But you're heating the bath water. You've never done that on a Wednesday. Why are you putting water in the bath?'

'Because I'm about to get in it and wash myself,' Odette snapped. 'I can take a bath any day I feel like it,' she added, 'after all, I'm a grown woman.' She stopped suddenly, dropping the bucket at her feet. Water splashed over her legs. She fell back into the dirt, muddying the back of her dress.

'Oh, Nan. What's wrong with you?' Odette could see Sissy was trying not to laugh. Sissy ran over and took hold of her hand. 'Let me help you.'

Odette struggled to her feet and felt the back of her dress. 'Oh bugger. Look at it. The dress is filthy.'

'Let me look after it for you, Nan.' Sissy walked over to the bathtub and ran a hand through the water. 'It's just right, the water. You hop in and I'll rinse the dress in the trough.'

Odette struggled out of her dress and hopped into the bath. She lay back and closed her eyes. Sissy scrubbed the dress with soap and a brush and hung it on the washing line, stretched between the laundry and a gum tree. Odette was almost asleep when she felt Sissy's fingertips caressing her forehead.

'Will you let me wash your hair for a change, Nan?'

'I wouldn't say no to that,' Odette smiled, feeling calmer. Her silver mane glowed in the sweet light of dusk.

'You should do this every day,' Sissy said, rinsing Odette's hair a second time. 'Give yourself a rest and a bath.'

'I don't think so. We'd run out of fuel in a week if I did that. There'd be no wood for cooking.' She asked Sissy to pass her the calico sheet folded over a wooden chair. 'I need to tell you something, Sweet. The reason I'm having the bath tonight is that I have to go to the hospital in Gatlin tomorrow. I'll need to catch the early bus and will have no time to wash in the morning.'

Sissy frowned. 'Why are you going to the hospital?'

'Remember I saw that doctor in town?'

'Yeah.'

'Well, he told me I need to have an X-ray.'

'What will they be X-raying?'

'Just my leg,' Odette lied. 'I have a sore leg.'

'When did you hurt your leg?'

'I never really hurt it. It's just worn out over the years. The bones, the doctor thinks.'

'Will it hurt you? The X-ray?'

Odette rested a hand on Sissy's shoulder. 'Stay still, Love, I need some help getting out of this tub. And no, the X-ray won't hurt. The machine takes a picture of the inside of your body. That's all it does.'

'And did he say what they will do at the hospital to fix your leg?'

Odette tousled Sissy's hair. 'It's always questions with you. Don't worry yourself over me. Hey, it's getting cold out. We'll have an early tea tonight and listen to the radio.'

Later that night, lying in bed, Sissy listened as Odette explained what her granddaughter was to do while she was away in Gatlin. 'I don't expect I'll be back until late at night. You be sure to come straight back here after school, won't you?'

'I always do, Nan.'

'And the spare key to the door. I'll tie it with some string and leave it on the kitchen table for you. Before you leave for school you hang the key around your neck and leave it there for the day. You'll be sure not to lose it.'

Sissy couldn't understand why her grandmother was fussing so much. 'We never use the key for the door, Nan.'

'Well, I want you to use it tomorrow. You lock the door

when you leave the house for school and again when you come home.'

'Why would I lock the door when I'm in the house?' Sissy asked, suddenly a little anxious herself. She thought back to the Sunday morning she'd seen the shadowy figure out on the street, through the front window, and realised it could only have been the new policeman in town.

'Because I'm telling you to,' Odette said. 'That's why. Like I've just explained to you, I don't expect to be back here until after dark.' She took hold of Sissy's hand. 'There's bread and cheese. Biscuits, too. If you want to make yourself something warm, there are tins of beans in the pantry.'

Sissy squeezed her grandmother's hand, attempting to reassure her that she would be fine. 'I'll wait for you for my teatime, Nan. I don't want to eat until you get home.'

'Please yourself then.'

Sissy rested her head on the pillow and listened to her grandmother's deep, slow breaths as she drifted off to sleep.

Sissy woke in darkness. The feeling of being alone in the house that morning was different from how she felt when Odette went to the mission or into town. Although Gatlin was only forty miles away, it could just as well be another country. She pulled the blanket over her shoulders and tried to go back to sleep but soon gave up. She lit the fire in the woodstove and made her own breakfast, then washed and dressed. When she left the house, she locked the front door and hung the key around her neck, just as Odette had instructed her to do.

Riding home from school that afternoon, Sissy followed her usual route. When she reached the riverbed track she stopped. She looked along the trail leading away from town. The afternoon sun was at her shoulder and the sky was big and blue. She put her foot to the pedal and rode on, enjoying the freedom as she pedalled past dilapidated farm sheds, empty silos and the occasional herd of scrawny cattle. The track narrowed, widened again and skirted the bends of the riverbed. Sissy steered the bike around a corner and saw a horse up ahead, leaning its head over a wire fence. She was fond of horses and had read many books about them. She lay the bike down on the track, pulled up a clump of dry grass and slowly approached the animal.

'Hello, boy. I bet you're hungry.' She offered the horse the grass. He lifted his head in the air, showing no interest in either Sissy or the offering. 'You want it? I know you want some grass.' The horse slowly lowered his head. His neck brushed against the wire fence. He sniffed the grass and bit into the clump, displaying a set of yellowed teeth. 'There you are. Good boy,' Sissy whispered, gently petting the horse on the neck. She fed him another handful of grass and looked across to the field beyond, infested with thistle and blackberry weed and strewn with machinery. There was an old farmhouse in the distance. She looked over her shoulder. If Nan discovered that she'd trespassed on someone's property, *white* property, she would be in trouble. But there was nobody around and Sissy could not resist the temptation to explore.

She crossed the paddock and made her way along a pathway to the front veranda. The windows of the house were boarded up with sheets of corrugated iron and the front door hung limply from its hinges. Sissy hesitated before going inside. The ceiling in the hallway had collapsed and the floral wallpaper was peeling away from the walls. In one of the front rooms a sheet of plaster had fallen from the ceiling onto a bed. Dust covered every surface. The tracks of either a rat or possum were visible on a sideboard under the front window.

Sissy opened the door of an ornately carved wardrobe. It was full of women's dresses, scarves and coats. She reached out and touched the sleeve of a red velvet dress pitted with moth holes. The material fell apart in her hands. In the mirror in the centre of the wardrobe, Sissy could see the fireplace and mantle behind her. A large gilded portrait sat above the mantle. She walked across the room and stood in front of the frame. It was a photograph of a white family, standing in front of the house. The men in the photograph wore suits, the women dresses and straw hats. Children sat in front of the adults. The girls had beautiful long hair and wore white dresses. Sissy put a finger to the glass and imagined herself wearing such a fine dress. On the edge of the group, at a slight distance from the family, stood two Aboriginal women. The older woman had her arms crossed over her breasts and looked sternly into the camera. The younger woman refused the lens completely, looking off to one side.

Sissy left the room and continued to explore, walking lightly and breathing quietly. In the kitchen at the rear of the house a long wooden table was set for dinner, the crockery and cutlery neatly arranged. She counted eight places. Each of the dinner plates was covered in a layer of dust and the tarnished cutlery had blackened. She heard the scurrying of feet, turned and saw the head of a large ginger bush cat pop up from a hole between the rotting floorboards. Sissy had seen wild cats before and wasn't afraid of them, although she knew they could be dangerous.

'Hey, puss,' she whispered. 'Is this your house?'

The cat hissed violently and disappeared into the hole. Sissy felt a chill at her back and quickly left the house.

Walking back to the track to collect her bike, Sissy puzzled over the family in the portrait. What would cause them to abandon their own home and leave all their clothes and furniture behind? She had no idea. She wondered about the two Aboriginal women. They would have been away from their own families, working for the white people. Although her grandmother never spoke to her about girls in the district who'd been taken away from their families, Sissy had heard stories at school about missing sisters, cousins and friends. In the schoolyard at lunchtime they would sometimes argue over who the Welfare Board went after, the dark or fair children. They would line up from the darkest to the lightest skinned. Sissy always found herself at the end of the line, not sure if she was the safest or if she might be the next child to be taken.

It wasn't long before the track veered and ended at a wooden bridge. On the other side of the bridge the track widened into a gravel road. Sissy absentmindedly pedalled on, listening as the gravel crackled beneath her. The sun was almost down before she realised how far she'd ridden. She was hungry and tired. The front wheel of her bike started wobbling from side to side. She hopped off the bike and felt the front tyre. It had a puncture in it. A dog howled in the distance. A little further on she saw a dull pair of eyes heading towards her. It was a truck, its engine grunting like an angry old man.

The engine coughed and murmured as the truck pulled up alongside her. A teenage boy stuck his head out of the window, a cigarette resting lazily on his bottom lip. He didn't speak. He looked down at Sissy, drew on his cigarette and flicked the butt onto the road.

Sissy attempted to straddle the seat but knocked her leg against the back wheel of the bike and fell to the ground. The truck inched past and pulled up ahead of her.

The driver jumped out of the cabin, springing to the ground like a cat. He stood in the middle of the road, resting his hands on his hips. 'What are you doing all the way out here at night?'

Sissy sat up, aware she may be in danger. She heard Odette's voice in her ear, *Stay strong.* 'I've been riding my bike,' she said. 'And I got a puncture.'

'You're a long way from home. Ours is the only place this far out of town. Where'd you come from?'

She was unsure how she should answer. 'I live at Quarrytown,' she said.

The driver stuck his head in the truck. 'You hear that, George? The girl's from Quarrytown.' He leaned his back against the truck. 'Shit. You're some distance from Quarrytown,' he said to Sissy. 'How'd you end up out here?'

While the boy appeared friendly, Sissy didn't trust him. She got to her feet and picked up the bike. 'Like I said, I rode the bike.'

'You hear that, George?' he called to the passenger. 'This girl's been doing some riding. Give me a look at that bike,' he said, turning his attention back to Sissy. 'It's a strange looking machine. Where'd you get it?'

'It was homemade for me. For my birthday.'

'It looks homemade. By who?'

'By Henry Lamb. He's a friend of my nan's.'

The boy laughed. 'Well, Henry Lamb, the retard from the junkyard.' He walked over to Sissy and picked up the bicycle. 'Looks like it was made by a retard.'

'It's my bike and I need it,' Sissy said.

'You'll get it back.' He inspected the bike. 'Henry Lamb made this thing all by himself? Fuck me. George, take a look at this bike. It's a miracle.'

'Can I have it back, please?' Sissy pleaded.

George hopped out of the truck. 'Give her the bike, Aaron.'

Aaron was too interested in Sissy to bother with his young brother. 'You say you're from Quarrytown? We've always called it Abo-town because it used to be overrun with Abos. But you don't look like an Abo to me. Does she look like an Abo to you, George?'

'Leave her be,' George said. 'She's just a kid.'

'You're right, George. She's a kid. That's why we can't leave her out here all alone.'

Sissy reached for the bike. 'I don't need your help. I can get home on my own.'

Aaron lifted the bike in the air and hurled it into the scrub. 'You won't be riding that bike home tonight. You're coming with us. Get in the truck.'

Sissy didn't know what to do. She listened for Odette's voice but heard nothing.

George stood between his brother and Sissy. 'Don't do this, Aaron.'

'Let me apologise for my brother,' Aaron said 'He'd just as soon leave you in the dark by yourself. But not me. Get in the truck.'

'No, Aaron,' George repeated. 'Leave her.'

'Leave her? Fuck off, George. We can't leave this girl out here. She could get herself in trouble. We can't let that happen. We found her and we're responsible for her.' He winked at Sissy. 'I apologise for my brother. He should have done a couple of years in the Boy Scouts and learned something about responsibility.'

George walked into the scrub, retrieved the bicycle and handed it to Sissy. 'The moon is out,' he said, 'if you stick to this road it will take you back to town. You can ride on a puncture, just as long as you keep the pedals moving.'

Aaron pushed his brother in the chest. 'What the fuck do you think you're doing, George? I said the bike stays here.'

'No!' George said. 'Let her have her bike and let's get out of here.'

Aaron put his arm around his brother's neck and whispered to him. 'Take a good look at her, George. I want to have some fun, that's all.' He pushed his brother in the shoulder.

George pushed his brother back, forcefully.

Aaron punched George in the mouth. George fell to the ground. Aaron jumped on the front wheel of the bike, breaking the spokes and bending the rim out of shape.

'Hey, look at this,' Aaron laughed. 'This bike's no good to anyone now.'

Sissy realised her only chance of escaping Aaron was to run.

She willed herself to move but was too slow. Aaron grabbed her by the arm. 'Get in the truck. You Abo girls don't get to make choices. Our old man taught us that.'

A second set of headlights loomed into view. The lights grew brighter, blinding Sissy. It was the Deane ambulance, which sometimes doubled as the police van.

Bill Shea got out of the van and pulled on his policeman's cap. He looked down at the broken bike and over at Aaron Kane. Shea had dealt with Aaron's father, Joe, many times. They'd crossed paths well before Mrs Kane's body had been found in the bottom of the dam on their farm. While the once prosperous Kanes were not the only family in the district to have lost their wealth, few had fallen as far. What he couldn't make up legitimately Joe Kane chased illegally. It was rumoured that most of the cattle that went missing across the district were rustled by him, although Shea had only ever arrested him for public drunkenness and minor theft.

Shea knew Joe Kane had treated his sons badly after their mother's death. The headmaster at the school, Tony Wills, had turned up at the police station once when the boys were kids and reported that the older boy, Aaron, had been badly beaten by his father.

'I'm sure that it's happened more than once,' Wills reported. 'I've seen the boy in the schoolyard with belt marks over the back of his legs, a black eye another time, and this morning a bruised lip and even a clump of hair missing.'

'Can you prove it?' Shea asked, to the surprise and anger of the headmaster.

'Isn't that your job, Bill? To investigate these matters?'

Maybe it was. But few police were willing to interfere with a family's privacy, not a white family at least. The next time Bill saw Joe in town he'd asked after the boys, prodding Kane a little. Kane said the boys were in good health and the issue was left at that.

'What's happened here?' Shea asked the boys.

'Well,' Aaron smirked, 'there's been an accident. We came across this girl and her broken bike. We're just helping her out, Bill.' Aaron Kane had inherited his father's disregard for the law.

'It's Officer Shea to you, son. Keep your cheek in your mouth.' Shea was surprised to see Sissy Brown on a lonely road in the dark. 'Where's your grandmother tonight?'

'Nan is at the hospital in Gatlin. I just went for a ride after school, and I was coming along here and couldn't see where I was going,' she said. 'I think I must have hit something.'

It sounded like a far-fetched story to Shea. 'I can't see anything you might have run into.'

'Me either,' Sissy shrugged. 'It was getting dark and I couldn't see.'

'Like I told you,' Aaron interrupted, 'it was an accident. *Bill*,' he added purposefully.

'Don't talk rubbish to me!' Shea shouted. 'Get going or I'll ticket this bomb and put it off the road. On your way.'

'A ticket, Bill? I don't reckon you could write one.'

Shea drew his cosh out of his trouser belt and smacked Aaron across the face with it. He belted the boy a second time across the shoulder. Aaron screamed out in pain and fell to his knees. Shea kicked the boy in the chest with the heel of his boot and waved the cosh in George's face, who was visibly shaken. 'Get him in the truck and fuck off home,' Shea growled. 'Unless you want a taste of this yourself?'

George dragged his moaning brother to his feet and into the passenger seat of the truck, then drove away.

The policeman collected the bicycle and checked the front wheel. 'You won't be riding this in a hurry. I'll throw the bike in the back of the van and drive you home.'

Sissy was afraid to move. Although the policeman seemed to have calmed down as quickly as he'd exploded, his sudden turn of violence had frightened her.

'You don't have to come with me,' Shea said, sensing her apprehension. 'But if you decide to make your way home in the dark, you're likely to run into more trouble. It will take a lot more than a whack on the skull to cure that Kane boy of his madness. I've known your grandmother for most of our lives,' he added, attempting to reassure Sissy. 'She's a good woman, Odette Brown.'

Sissy was not about to tell the policeman that Odette's opinion of him was not nearly as generous. She heard the growl of Aaron Kane's pick-up in the distance, walked over to the van and waited by the passenger door. The policeman opened the door for her and Sissy got in. On the drive back to Quarrytown, he lectured Sissy about being on the backroads outside Deane, which he said was no place for a teenage girl. 'It's not safe out here,' was his final comment before dropping off Sissy and her bike at the footbridge.

Sissy crossed the bridge, pulling her bike along the street

in darkness. She was relieved to finally be home. At the house she rested the battered bike against the gate and reached for the door key hanging around her neck. It was gone.

CHAPTER SEVEN

Odette left for Gatlin well before first light. The sky was clear and a blanket of stars, stretching across the sky from east to west, greeted her as she set off to catch the bus. When she was a child, her father would sit her on his lap and tell stories about the connection between the stars and the surrounding country. Odette never forgot her father's words: *Them whitefellas, they can never touch the stars, no matter how clever they think they are.*

Odette boarded the bus outside the Deane Town Hall and took a seat towards the back. The only other time she'd visited Gatlin was when she'd gone searching for her daughter. In the days after Lila vanished, Odette was hopeful the girl would soon come home for the sake of her baby. On the third day, after Lila still had not returned, Odette arrived on Millie Khan's doorstep with Sissy under one arm.

'Lila, she's run off somewhere,' Odette explained to her old friend. 'She'd have no money, so I can't see her getting further than Gatlin. I need to go and fetch her back.'

'Run off?' Millie shook her head. 'She can't go running off. If the Welfare track her down before you do, they'll have her trained up for some country mansion.' Millie took Sissy from Odette, held her in her arms and kissed her on the forehead. 'And they'll be after this little one as well, the buggers. Have you had a word to Bill Shea?'

'Why would I? If he bothered to shift himself at all, he'd only move as far as the telephone to call the Welfare Board himself.'

Millie considered Odette's words. It wouldn't be the first time Bill Shea had stood idly by and allowed the kids of his childhood friends to be taken away by Welfare officers.

'You're most likely right. The best we can hope from here, I suppose, is that Bill does nothing.'

Searching for Lila in Gatlin, Odette had walked every street surrounding the town centre, enquiring after her daughter in shops and cafés where she may have sought work. By the end of the day, exhausted and at a loss, Odette found herself standing outside a stone church. The building was similar to the one on the mission, except for the addition of a large metal crucifix adorning the steeple. Her search for Lila had drained her of both energy and hope. She had nowhere to go but home, yet was reluctant to return without her daughter. When it began to rain, Odette had no choice but to seek shelter. Inside the church, she wearily took a seat, rested her hand on her chin and closed her eyes.

A little while later someone was gently shaking her shoulder. 'You look beat, love,' she heard someone say, and sat up. An Aboriginal woman around her own age, but with lighter skin, was smiling down at her. Before Odette could respond, the woman took her by the hand and guided her along the aisle to a small room behind the church. She introduced herself as Delores Reed, and said she was from the south coast. The woman seemed desperate to talk, as if she'd been waiting for Odette to come along. She spoke in a rush of words and Odette had difficulty following her story.

Delores had moved to Gatlin three years earlier to be closer to her two daughters, who'd been placed in a Home attached to the Convent.

'I'm a lucky one,' Delores said.

'You're lucky?' Odette replied, puzzled. 'How's that?'

'Well, when I found out where my girls were, I made my way up here. It was good news, to hear that they'd been kept together. Best for them that way, to comfort each other. One of the nuns from the Convent, she looked out for me when I got here. She had words with the priest, Father O'Brien, on my behalf. The Father is dead now. Only six months ago. His heart,' Delores explained. She made the sign of the cross and uttered *Amen* before going on. 'That same nun organised for me to take this job here.'

'What sort of work do you do?' Odette asked.

'Well, I clean the church and help in the kitchen. In return, I get all my food and board.' Delores pointed to the narrow doorway off the room. 'I have my own little crib in there.'

'And wages?' Odette asked. 'What do they pay you?'

'It's not about money,' Delores snapped, as if the suggestion was an insult. 'I'm taken care of and I get to see my girls once every month.'

'Once a month?' Odette could barely hide her disgust.

'Yes. Father O'Brien, he didn't think it would be good for any of us, the girls or me, to see each other, not at the beginning. He said the visits might be too much, get us all emotional. But it has worked out for the good.'

'You must miss them between visits,' Odette said. 'A month is a long time not to see your own kiddies.'

'Oh, it is,' Delores said. 'But I keep myself busy with the cleaning. Takes my mind off the worry.' She leaned into Odette and whispered, 'Sometimes I sneak over to the school and look at them through the fence. They look so happy, skipping about with the other kids. They're all so happy here. And I pray, of course.'

'The other children here, do their mums come and visit?'

Delores vigorously shook her head from side to side. 'Oh no. It's not allowed. I'm the only one. Father O'Brien always believed that the children were as good as orphans. It's the best outcome for half-castes, he said.'

'Half-castes?'

'All of them here are half-caste or quarter-caste. Sometimes a bit less. But they're all treated the same. The church finds homes for them. With white families.'

Odette supposed the same fate must be awaiting Delores's children. As they sat together at the scarred wooden table drinking tea she told Delores about Lila's sudden and mysterious decision to leave home. 'She has her own baby girl. I can't understand what would have caused her to leave.'

'Is she light-skinned, your granddaughter?'

'Yeah, she's light. Why are you asking?'

'The Welfare, they're in love with the fairer ones these days. My ex, he was an Irish fella, red hair, freckles. Skin the colour of a fresh bedsheet. My girls look more like him than me. After they were born a nurse at the hospital told me it's because our Aboriginal blood is weak. Both of them babies, I sat them in the sun from the day I took them home, wanting to darken them up. It didn't work that way. They turned bright red and ended up with freckles all over them. I guess that nurse at the hospital was right. Our colour is weak.'

Odette observed Delores gripping the edge of the table with both hands, her eyes sharp and her cheeks reddening.

'The first time the Welfare lady set eyes on my babies,' Delores said, 'I knew I had no hope of keeping them.' She took one hand away from the edge of the table and slammed it against her chest, alarming Odette. 'From that day on, that bitch followed us around like a bloodhound. My eldest girl, Colleen, she was the first to go. We'd put her in the local school, a Catholic school. My hubby thought it might work in our favour, putting on the God act. He was in the merchant navy. He'd been away at sea six weeks and then his pay stopped coming to me from the company. I never knew it at the time, but he'd jumped ship and took off on me and the girls. I haven't laid eyes on him since.' Delores took a worn handkerchief out of the sleeve of her cardigan and wiped her nose. 'I ran out of money in no time. No sooner was I spotted in the line outside the House of Charity than Colleen was taken. They picked her up at school.'

'Did you fight it?' Odette asked.

'Fight? There was nothing I could do.' Delores put a fist into her mouth and bit down on a knuckle to stop herself from sobbing. 'You know what the nun at the school said when I fronted her? Do you know?'

Odette shook her head.

'She said, "This is best for you. We're doing this to help you as much as your daughter." I wanted to spit in that woman's face. I went straight home and pulled a case out of the cupboard. I poked some air holes in it with a screwdriver and put my baby girl, Iris, in that case with our clothes.' Delores took a deep breath. 'And then we took off.'

Odette wasn't certain what she'd just been told. 'You put your daughter in a suitcase?'

Delores wiped her nose and laughed hysterically. 'Sure did. That was my plan.' She laughed again. 'Didn't work out for us, though. We only got as far as the bus station. I was ready to jump on any bus that would get us out of the city. I didn't care where it was heading. And then, *bang*, the case sprung open and poor little Iris, she fell out.'

Delores looked down, as if the child was on the floor at her feet. She stood up and began circling the table. Odette wanted her to stop, both her manic pacing and the story, which she didn't want to hear. But Delores couldn't stop.

'I mean, it was funny. Really funny,' she cried. 'We both laughed. My beautiful baby girl, she was giggling and I thought I was going to wet my pants.' Delores walked over to the back door and looked outside, concerned she was being overheard. 'I hadn't noticed that there was a copper right there. He'd been a couple of footsteps behind us the whole time, writing a ticket for some fella who'd parked his car illegally. The copper saw what happened and I knew we were in trouble. I knew it, but I couldn't stop laughing. Everyone waiting for the buses, they all thought I'd gone mad. After Iris was taken away I was put into one of those hospitals. You know? For *sick* people? And by then I was mad.'

Delores had exhausted herself. She could hardly look at Odette. She quickly changed the subject and offered to contact Odette if she heard any news about Lila.

Odette thanked her, and left the church and the town that night on an empty bus. The story of Delores losing her young daughters shook Odette. Although she never searched for Lila again, she lived in hope that her daughter would return home. About a month after her meeting with Delores Reed, Odette received a letter. The postmark was illegible and there was no return address on the back. The few lines from Lila, accompanied by a one-pound note, asked that Odette care for Sissy, *until I make it back there.* The letter gave no indication where Lila might be. It was obvious she wouldn't be coming home. Odette got a job cleaning at a hotel in town and Millie Khan took care of Sissy during the day. Over the following years additional letters from Lila occasionally arrived, with little comment and giving nothing away.

At the Gatlin hospital, Odette once again found herself laying on a padded table behind a screen. Doctor Singer was as polite and considerate as she remembered him.

'I'll be wearing a heavy apron during the procedure, which alarms some people,' he said. 'I'll look a bit like a mad scientist, but don't worry, I'm not out to frighten you.'

Each time he asked Odette to shift her position on the table he said, 'Please' and 'Thank you'. When he had finished with the X-ray and Odette had dressed he sat beside her in the waiting room. He looked at his watch. 'It's just before eleven now. I'd like you to come back here at two o'clock for the results.'

'Today?'

'Yes. I can see that you are in constant pain, Mrs Brown. We need to find out what is causing it, and we need to deal with it as quickly as possible. Do you know anyone here in Gatlin?'

'No, I don't.'

'Well, perhaps you can get some lunch? Also, they have a decent public library in Gatlin. I use it myself.'

Odette walked aimlessly along the main street to pass the time. She looked in the shop windows, at bright dresses, cookware, and dominating the window of an electrical store, a television set. She stood in front of a display TV and watched a woman cleaning her teeth. Odette didn't own a television and thought nothing could be more absurd than a person cleaning their teeth in public. The woman on the screen opened her mouth widely. Odette had never seen teeth as white or straight.

Another window shopper, standing next to Odette, chuckled to herself and pointed at the screen. 'I don't see why she'd need to bother with the toothbrush. You couldn't get them teeth any cleaner if you scrubbed them with bleach.' The woman removed a full set of nicotine-stained dentures from her mouth and proudly showed them to Odette. 'These fangs would test that stuff. If they could get these white I'd buy a truckload of that paste myself.'

In the next window, a gift shop, Odette admired a set of greeting cards arranged in a wire-framed stand. It took a moment for it to register that the cards were her own artwork.

A notice above the stand announced that the cards were *painted by a native woman of the Bilga tribe.* Odette lingered, watching the proprietor select several cards from the display to show to a customer. She remembered the woman as the one who'd sat at her kitchen table a few years earlier. The woman looked out the window at Odette and smiled; it was not an expression of recognition but one of general politeness.

Odette walked to the end of the street and looked up when she reached the clock tower of the Gatlin Post Office. She was not due back at the hospital for another hour. She began walking with a sense of purpose. After some initial confusion, she found the old church she'd visited years earlier. In the yard Odette could see a man kneeling in a garden. He was crouched on all fours, turning the soil over with a spade. He heard Odette's footsteps and turned towards her.

'Excuse me. Are you the priest here?' Odette asked.

'Oh no. I'm the gardener, Robert. Not one so worthy as a priest.'

Odette looked down at the clumps of soil stuck to the front of his woollen jumper. He also noticed the dirt and brushed it away. 'Can I be of any help to you?'

'I'm in town for the day,' Odette explained. 'I'm looking for someone who used to live here. Her name is Delores Reed. She worked here some time ago. At the church.'

The man frowned as he stood up. He had a soft and gentle face, reminding Odette of Henry Lamb.

'Are you related to Mrs Reed?' he asked. 'Or a friend?'

'I'm neither. Not really,' Odette said. 'She was a help to me many years ago. I was thinking about her this morning. I hoped I might find her here.'

'Oh, she was a very kind woman,' Robert said.

'You know her?' Odette asked.

'Yes, I did. We sometimes worked together. She helped in the garden occasionally. Delores was a wonderful woman.'

'You say *did*. She doesn't work here any longer?'

'No, she's gone.'

Robert picked up a metal rake and methodically worked the ground. He spoke slowly but deliberately, concentrating on his task. 'You knew about her children?' he asked.

'Yes. She talked about visiting them here. They would be young women now.'

The gardener let out a long, anguished sigh. He leaned on his rake and looked away. 'I don't know why they did it. It was wrong.'

'Wrong?'

'The church authorities, about eight years ago, they decided to move a group of the girls away, including Mrs Reed's daughters.' Robert briefly concentrated on the pattern he'd created in the soil below his boots. 'She wasn't told what had happened to them until after they'd gone. It was more than a week after when the priest came to her. It was too late by then. There was nothing she could do.'

'Taken? Where to?' Odette asked.

'To the city. A long way to travel for a woman without means.'

The gardener placed the rake against the trunk of a gracious elm tree. 'She lay in the room there for days on end, unable to move. It broke her, what they did to her.'

Odette dreaded her next question, but had to ask. 'What happened to Delores?'

Robert looked up to the sturdy limb above his head. 'Delores took her own life.'

Odette gasped. 'Her life?'

'Yes. It was terrible.' Robert took a set of keys out of his pocket. 'Come with me. I want to show you something.'

Odette was still trying to comprehend what Robert had said. Her body shook involuntarily. He opened the door to Delores Reed's old room. 'Nobody has used it since she …'

Odette stood in the doorway. The gardener went inside and returned with a faded envelope. He opened it and took out two coloured photographs of young children, both with red curly hair. They were pale-skinned, except for a sprinkling of dark freckles on their cheeks. The names of the children, *Colleen* and *Iris*, were written in lead pencil on the back of the photographs.

'This is all she left behind,' he said. 'I was asked to clean her room out and found these in a drawer. We couldn't find any other family. This envelope has been sitting here ever since.'

Odette looked closely at the photographs. The girls looked so happy, just as Delores had said. 'Were the girls told about their mother's death?'

'I wouldn't think so. I don't believe any children in the care of the church are informed about the death of a parent. It would be traumatic, I suppose.'

'Care? Is that what you call it?' Odette replied, her voice rising.

'I'm sorry,' he shrugged, looking beaten. 'I don't know what to call it.' He coughed nervously, realising there was nothing he could say that would appease Odette. 'The photographs … it would be best if you could take them. They may be misplaced, or thrown out once I—'

'But they're not mine.' Odette was distraught at the very idea. 'These babies, they're not my children. I can't take them. It would be too much.'

'No. Of course not. I'm so sorry. I was only thinking …' He paused. 'They belong with *your* people. If not, they may eventually become lost.'

'Lost? Photographs are not enough. It's the children in the photographs who are lost.'

'You're right,' Robert conceded. 'But perhaps, one day …'

Odette noticed the look of sadness on the gardener's face.

'You say you're not a priest?' she asked.

'No. I'm an orphan.'

'I see,' Odette said. And she did *see*.

'I was a foundling, as they used to call us back then. I was left on the doorstep of this very church as a newborn, and fortunately I was taken in.'

'Your whole life has been spent here?'

'Most of it. I was let go at sixteen so I could find a means of taking care of myself. The church assisted me in finding work and accommodation. I found my way back here. Three times. Eventually they allowed me to stay on and put me to work.'

'Why did you do that, come back, if you could go anywhere you wanted to?'

The gardener considered the question, but did not have a satisfactory answer. 'I cannot say, except that being outside, on my own, I did not know what to do with myself.'

Odette looked up at the heavy limbs of the elm tree. She felt an urgent need to leave and apologised to Robert. She collected the photographs of the girls without thinking of the consequences and quickly headed back to the hospital.

In the waiting room Odette couldn't stop thinking about Delores's children. She took the photograph of the older girl, Colleen, out of her bag and looked into the girl's eyes. The beauty of the child's face was upsetting. When her name was called, Odette was once again ushered into Doctor Singer's office. He guided her to a chair and pointed to a set of X-rays, clipped to a light-box. Looking at her own skeleton, Odette eerily felt she was witness to her impending death. The doctor held a tongue depressor in his hand and used it to point to a mass above Odette's pelvis.

'This dark shape here, this is where your pain is most acute, between your left hip and your ribs. And this,' he tapped the X-ray with the end of the depressor, 'is the cause of that pain.'

'And what is it?' Odette asked.

'It's a tumour.' He raised an open hand. 'Although I cannot be certain, I am confident it is likely to be benign. Due to the size.'

The word meant little to Odette. 'What does that mean?'

'Essentially, and again, I'm not certain, but it means the tumour is non-cancerous.' He tapped at the X-ray a second time. 'When I examined you in Deane, and again this morning, the swelling was soft to the touch. A good sign in a difficult situation,' he said, raising his eyebrows.

'Difficult?'

'I can't be sure how long the tumour has been growing, but it would be some time. And it will keep on growing if we do nothing. What we do not want to happen is for the tumour to attach itself to your spine. Whether it is benign or not, it would make an operation difficult to perform.'

Odette looked up at the X-ray and pressed the fingers of her right hand to her left side, imagining the tumour growing inside her body. 'You're saying I need to have an operation?'

'Yes. And sooner rather than later. You may be able to cope for now, but any further growth of the tumour could debilitate you completely, as it is also pushing against your left lung, hence the breathing difficulties you are experiencing.'

'Would you be doing the operation?' Odette asked, seeking assurance from a man she felt she could trust.

'No, no. I'm not a surgeon. The operation would be performed here at the hospital by another doctor. We would also need to provide you with after-care. For some weeks in fact, much of it spent in bed, unfortunately.'

The thought overwhelmed Odette. 'But I can't do that. This can't happen.'

The doctor frowned. 'Mrs Brown, are you anxious about the thought of surgery? Please don't be.'

Odette's fears were not for herself. 'I have a granddaughter to look after. She can't be left alone.'

'Left? Why would she be left alone?'

'Well, because I'm her only relative. I want to thank you, doctor, but I don't need this operation. My granddaughter, she's only young and she's—'

Doctor Singer took Odette by the hand and spoke quietly. 'Please, don't be alarmed. As I stated, I am confident that this tumour is benign, Mrs Brown. We can wait a little longer if you like, giving you the time to make arrangements for your granddaughter's care. We will schedule an operation once that's done.'

'I don't know that I can make any arrangements. We don't like to be apart, my granddaughter and me. There's only the two of us. Most of our family are gone and we're alone. Do you understand?'

The doctor understood only too well what it felt like to be alone. 'I promise we won't do anything until your granddaughter's care is assured.'

On the bus back to Deane Odette rested her head against the window and closed her eyes. She had left the hospital agreeing to contact Doctor Singer as soon as she'd made the appropriate arrangements for Sissy's care. When she got off the bus outside the Deane Town Hall it was late. Sergeant Lowe was standing across the road outside the police station. Odette could feel him watching her as she walked along the street towards home. By the time she'd reached the river track, Odette was clear about her decision. There would be no operation.

CHAPTER EIGHT

Odette found Sissy sitting alone on the dark veranda. The damaged bicycle rested up against the veranda post. When she saw her grandmother Sissy burst into tears. Odette put her arms around her and tried to make sense of what had happened. 'Why aren't you inside? It's bitter out here. I'll put the fire on and then we can talk.'

Sissy began by apologising to Odette for disobeying her and taking off on her bicycle. She explained that she had ridden further than she'd meant to, became lost and then punctured the front wheel.

Odette initially tried to make light of Sissy's act of disobedience. 'It doesn't matter, Sweet. We've all done something a little too bold. This is your first time. When I was your age I used to sneak off with the other tearaway kids. When my father found out, he would threaten me with a broom handle on the bum. Not that he ever used it. He was too soft on me. It doesn't matter that you got up to mischief, as long as you're okay. What did you do to that front wheel, hit a rock?'

Sissy went quiet. 'No, I never hit a tree. The bike was jumped on.'

'How could it have been jumped on?'

'It was a boy. His name is Aaron. He found me on the road. The policeman, Mr Shea, came along afterwards.'

Odette listened closely as Sissy told her about being confronted by Aaron Kane and the fight between the brothers.

'Mr Shea whacked Aaron around the head and brought me home.'

Odette was surprised. 'Bill beat him?'

'He did. The boy, Aaron, he was bleeding.' Sissy wiped her runny nose on the sleeve of her jumper. 'I did what you always told me to, Nan, I wouldn't go in the truck with him, even when he yelled and pushed me. I shouldn't have been there, I know that. That's what the policeman told me. He said I shouldn't be out at night, and I wasn't to do it again. Or I'd be in trouble.'

Odette slammed her open hand on her knee, startling Sissy. 'You'll be in trouble? And what about that lunatic of a boy? He'll be in trouble when I get hold of him. What else did Bill Shea say to you?'

'He said that I wasn't to tell anyone but you about what happened. I'm afraid, Nan.'

'Of who?'

'Aaron Kane.'

'Well, don't be afraid of him,' Odette said, looking down at her dark, wrinkled hands. 'Your grandmother will take care of this.'

Odette wouldn't admit to Sissy that the girl was right. That Aaron Kane, while only a teenage boy, was his father's son and could be very dangerous. Something had to be done, but she had no idea what or who to turn to. Even though Bill Shea had come to Sissy's aid, he was useless when it came to doing his job, and the new policeman in town, Lowe, could not be trusted at all.

The following Sunday Odette organised their regular bath. She washed Sissy's hair, but hardly spoke a word.

'Is everything alright, Nan?' Sissy asked, as Odette rinsed her hair.

Odette answered, *fine*, but said nothing more. She wasn't fine at all, and didn't want Sissy questioning her. She could see Sissy was tired of being stuck at home all weekend, and would have enjoyed nothing better than taking her bike out but it was still broken. It would have remained so had Henry Lamb not called by the house later that day asking Odette if she'd seen Rowdy playing along Deane's Line or down at the river.

Odette had been surprised to see Henry standing on her veranda after hearing a tap at the door. She invited him inside for a cup of tea but he declined the offer.

'I don't think I will do that. I'm worried about my boy, Rowdy, that's all I'm here for today,' he said. 'He goes out through the back fence for a wander some days but is always home for his tea. I don't know where he is.'

Odette tried reassuring Henry. 'It's best not to fret,' she said. 'He loves you, Henry. He'll be home soon for his tucker.'

'Maybe he will, Odette. But I reckon he'd be plenty

hungry by now. I don't feel good about what's happened to him.' He was about to leave when he saw Sissy's bike resting against the side fence. He walked across the yard, picked it up and tried to wheel it. 'What's happened here? The bike has gone bung.'

Odette knew Henry was having enough trouble with Aaron Kane himself without hearing about how he'd jumped all over Sissy's birthday gift. 'Oh, we had an accident there. I was going to let you know the next time I was by your place.'

Henry lifted the front wheel and turned it. The wheel wobbled and caught in the front forks. 'This is no good, Odette. We need a new wheel on this bike. I'll get home and come back with another wheel.'

'No, Henry. That's generous of you, but it can wait. Truly.'

Henry wouldn't hear of it. 'No, I'm sorry, Odette, but this job has to be done quick smart. Or Sissy won't be riding to school. This was for her birthday.' He rushed from the yard and was back at the house within half an hour, a toolbox in one hand and a spare wheel in the other.

'That was quick of you,' Odette said. 'You must have run the whole way.'

'I've run no place, Odette. I could have a heart attack doing that. Across the bridge there you'll see I have my own motor car. A utility, it's called,' he said, proudly.

'You bought yourself a car, Henry?'

'I didn't need to buy anything at all. I fixed it up myself. And I put petrol in it.'

'Well, cars do need petrol,' Odette said. 'I didn't know you had a driving licence.'

'Oh, I don't need one. My Pa taught me to drive as soon as I left school. I used to drive the truck back home for him when he had too many bottles of beer. He told me the licence wasn't needed if I didn't drive into town. And I never do that, drive into town.'

'Well, that's an interesting way to think about the law, Henry. I don't know how you'd fare in court with that defence.'

Henry changed the bike wheel and refitted the tyre and tube. He knocked at the door again when he'd finished. 'It's done, Odette.'

'Give me your hand,' Odette ordered. 'Don't think you're not taking the money this time, Henry,' she said, placing a ten-shilling note in it. 'You've done more than enough for us.'

Henry studied the note, folded it and stuck it in the side pocket of his overalls. 'I could offer this as a reward for the return of Rowdy,' he said.

'I'm sure he'll come home soon, and you'll get to keep your ten shillings,' Odette said.

'Do you really believe that, Odette?'

'I do, Henry, I do.'

Henry picked up his toolbox and the buckled bicycle wheel. 'I miss that boy,' he said. 'When he gets home, Odette, I'll put him in front of the fire. A big feed and some bones and he'll know he's home.'

About a week after Henry Lamb repaired the bicycle, Odette sat at the kitchen table waiting for Sissy to finish her breakfast so they could go shopping. She was taking far too long.

'What's up with you, Sis? You're not yourself lately. We need to get into town before the shops shut.'

Sissy licked her spoon clean of porridge. 'I think I have a flu, Nanna. There's something up with you, too. I can tell.'

Odette knocked on the wooden table with the knuckles of her hand. 'Don't you be funny with me, and don't be dodging the question. You tell me what's up. *Now.*'

'It's that boy,' Sissy said.

'The Kane boy? Don't you worry yourself over him, I won't let that boy near you.'

Sissy looked unconvinced. Odette sensed there was more to it. 'You've seen him again, haven't you?'

'Twice,' Sissy said, her voice breaking slightly. 'After school.'

Odette reached across the table and tugged at Sissy's arm. 'You should have said something before now.'

'I didn't want to make trouble. I know that you've been sick.'

'Don't be worrying over your grandmother. I'm as strong as a bull. What did he say to you?'

'He didn't say anything. He just drove the truck alongside me until I got to the footbridge and then he drove away.'

'That boy!' Odette screamed. 'From now on I'll be walking you to school, and waiting at the gate when last bell goes. I won't have him troubling you.' She kissed Sissy on the cheek. 'Come on, now. We have a busy morning.'

They were crossing the footbridge when Odette realised she'd left her shopping money at home. 'Hey, Sis,' Odette called. 'I've forgotten my purse. Wait for me here.'

When Odette returned with her purse a few minutes later there was no sign of Sissy. She searched the road. Aaron Kane's red pick-up was weaving erratically from side to side and Sissy was running ahead of the truck. Odette watched as the truck swerved in Sissy's direction. She saw her granddaughter stumble and fall to the ground. The truck sped off.

Odette hobbled to where the girl lay. Sissy had a cut on the side of her face and grazes on her knees and hands.

'That bastard,' she said. 'He's hurt you this time.' She held Sissy to her chest and looked into the distance, at the trail of dust left in his wake. 'I've had enough. That boy needs to be dealt with.'

Sissy didn't want her grandmother causing trouble for either of them. 'I'll be okay, Nan.'

'No, you won't. Not until that boy is stopped.' Odette helped Sissy to her feet. 'I want you to get yourself down to Auntie Millie's. You're to stay there until I come back for you.'

Standing at the Kane's farm gate an hour later, after struggling all the way from Deane, Odette looked along the driveway. There was no sign of the red pick-up. It had been many years since she'd been at the property. The last she'd heard of old Joe Kane, he'd been in a car accident that had left him with a crippled leg. She walked around the side of the house to the squat stone building opposite the back porch, and peered through the open door. A frenzy of blowflies hovered above a concrete trough. She could see the bloodied carcass of a kangaroo. On the bench beside it was a slab of meat and a shallow bucket of broken glass. She knew that some farmers laced kangaroo meat with glass and left it out for foxes. She turned away, gagging on the terrible smell.

The kitchen door was ajar. Odette could see the room was empty. She barely hesitated before walking inside. A large table was littered with food scraps and dirty dishes. She walked through the kitchen into the hallway and stopped at the doorway of the room she remembered as Mr and Mrs Kane's bedroom. The room was empty except for a couple of pieces of furniture and a double-bed mattress sitting on a wire-sprung base. The mattress was stained and a single blanket lay on the floor beside it. Odette was about to turn away when something caught her eye. A set of Rosary beads hung from a brass hook on a rounded mirror above a bedside table. There was a necklace hanging from the same hook. It was a deep red colour. Odette walked into the room, lifted the necklace from the hook and held it in her hand. It was unmistakable. Millie Khan had made the necklace for Lila out of eucalypt seed pods for her sixteenth birthday. Lila had told Odette that she lost it, and now here it was.

Odette clenched her fist, crushing several of the pods in her hand. Her mind flashed back to the day she'd seen Joe Kane's truck parked at the footbridge all those years ago when she'd been heading into town. She'd arrived home to an empty house. Lila had returned some time later, clearly distressed. She told Odette she'd gotten lost.

'Lost? You can't get lost around here, Lil. You know this country as good as I do.'

'It was a track I've never walked before,' Lila explained.

'Well, you'd only need to follow it back,' Odette scoffed. 'You're no bush girl, that's for sure.'

It was then Odette had pointed to Lila's neck. 'Where's your necklace from Millie got to?'

Lila had clutched at her throat, unaware that the necklace was missing.

Odette opened her hand. A seed pod was embedded in her skin. The cut was bleeding. She heard someone coughing furiously and walked further along the hallway. Joe Kane was sitting in an old armchair wearing nothing but a frayed dressing gown. His bare feet were covered in scabs. On the wooden tray next to him was an apple that had been cut into pieces and turned brown, along with a skinning knife.

Joe Kane squinted up at Odette. She wondered if the old man remembered her. She dangled the necklace in front of him. Kane seemed to recognise it. Odette could no longer contain a rage that had been building for years.

'Hey, Joe,' she said. 'This belongs to my girl, my Lila. You took it from her.'

Kane snarled. One side of his face had dropped and his top lip curled upwards. He couldn't speak.

'It was you, you bastard,' Odette said. 'You hurt my daughter.' She snatched the knife from the tray. The old man responded with a wheeze of yellowish phlegm that dribbled down his chin. 'You're an evil man, Joe Kane. And so is your boy.'

'Don't do that! Please stop.' George Kane was standing in the doorway, an open hand raised towards Odette. 'Please, leave him be.'

'The man is a monster,' Odette screamed. 'He hurt my daughter,' she said. 'And your brother, he's out to do the same to my grandchild.'

'I'm sorry,' George said. 'He's hurt a lot of people, I know that. But you have to leave. Aaron will be back here soon. He's angry over the policeman hitting him. He says it's the girl's fault. Please, you have to leave,' George begged.

Odette was struck by the look of fear on George's face. What she'd puzzled over on the morning she'd seen him outside Henry's yard, was now suddenly clear to her. His dark eyes, long lashes and wide face were as much Sissy's features as his own. The sudden knowledge that Sissy was connected to the boy's father by *blood* was too much for her to comprehend. She dropped the knife on the floor.

'Please, I want you to go,' George repeated.

The boy's gentleness could not be more of a contrast to the violence of his father and older brother. He looked so fragile, Odette was certain he was in danger. 'What about you?' she asked. 'What are you going to do?'

'I don't have any place to go,' he said.

'You can't stay here with him,' she said, gesturing to the old man.

'But I have to. He's always been mean, even before my mother died. After she went he was worse. I know Aaron is a lot of trouble, but you don't understand what happened to him.'

'What do you mean?'

Joe Kane spluttered and shook his chair from side to side in protest. 'He was cruel to Aaron,' George said. 'He did terrible things to him. Now go. *Please*.'

Odette stumbled back along the dry riverbed, holding the necklace in one hand, thinking about Lila and the crime Joe

Kane had committed against her. She now understood the fear and shame that had driven Lila away.

She thought about Sissy's bloodline to the Kane family, consumed with anguish and a rising fear that the revelation would damage her love for her granddaughter. Putting the thought out of her mind would be difficult.

As she walked on Odette started to feel stronger, as if she was being carried along by a current of water. She could hear water flowing beneath her and remembered the story her father had once told her, that water is never lost from rivers, not even when they appeared dead. Water could always return. *The water is always with you*, he'd said. It had made little sense to her at the time, but Odette could now hear the old people, guiding her home. They were listening to her as she anguished over what to do.

When she arrived at Millie Khan's door, Odette took her aside and showed her the necklace. Although Millie had made many necklaces over the years, she had no doubt that the one in Odette's hand was the same one she'd given to Lila years earlier.

'Where'd you find it?' she asked.

'Out at Joe Kane's farm. I just come from there.'

Millie took the necklace from Odette and massaged the seed pods between her fingers, contemplating the meaning of the find. She turned and looked over at Sissy, quietly sitting next to Yusuf, who was reading from a decoratively bound book.

The women sat together out the front of the house. Odette talked about Lila, Sissy and her trouble with the oldest Kane boy. She didn't mention her visit to Doctor Singer, or her need for an operation. 'I've had enough,' she sighed. 'Something has to be done.'

'And what's that?' Millie asked, knowing that the choices available to an Aboriginal woman were limited.

'Let me worry about that, not you. I'll think of something.'

Yusuf walked out of the house carrying his prayer mat. He laid it on the ground, knelt and prayed. The women sat quietly. When he'd finished, Yusuf collected the mat and walked back into the house.

'Yusuf dealt with Joe Kane one time,' Millie said. 'The man came by here wanting to buy a horse from us.'

'Did you sell it to him?'

'I would have. Joe was cashed up at the time. Must have stolen some cattle and sold them on, I reckon. Yusuf stepped in and said no. Joe cursed him and left here in a rage. I asked Yusie why he wouldn't do business with Joe, and he said it would be a sin to sell a horse to such a man. He said he was sure that the animal would be badly treated and he couldn't let that happen. We found the same horse dead a week later in the corral, here behind the house.'

CHAPTER NINE

Odette prepared Sissy's favourite meal, lamb chops and mashed potato. She ate quietly, thoughtfully, as though she was rehearsing a conversation. Odette instructed Sissy as they washed and cleaned the dishes together. 'I have to go out shortly, just for a bit. I need you to lock the door after me.'

Sissy slung the tea-towel over her shoulder, surprised. 'Going out? It's late, Nan. Where are you going?'

'There's something more I need to talk to Millie about.'

Sissy listened as a strong wind rattled the iron roof above them. 'Maybe you could talk to Auntie Millie tomorrow? I think it's going to rain soon.'

'I have to do this tonight.'

Odette put her coat on, kissed Sissy on the cheek and left the house. Sissy stood at the window and watched Odette walk down the path. She was sure that her grandmother was up to something secretive but couldn't work out what it might be, except that it had something to do with Aaron Kane. She opened the door, stepped out onto the veranda and watched Odette cross the footbridge. Auntie Millie's house was to the right of the footbridge. Her grandmother turned left.

Odette paced the footpath in front of the police station, took a deep breath and walked through the heavy wooden doors into a room of polished floors and wood-panelled walls. The national flag hung from the ceiling between a pair of photographic portraits. One of the Queen, resplendent in a velvet gown and tiara, the other of the Australian prime minister, Robert Menzies, looking adoringly towards the young Elizabeth. Standing at the counter, Odette could see her own reflection in a mirror above the door. Sergeant Lowe had ordered its installation on his first day at the station. The positioning of the mirror allowed him to view anyone who came into the office, without them knowing that they were being watched.

Odette rang the bell. Bill Shea came to the counter. He ran a nervous hand through his thinning hair.

'How can I help you, Odette?'

'I'm here to see your boss, Sergeant Lowe.'

Shea rested both hands on the counter. 'What is it? The matter you need to see him about? I'll need to explain to him why you're here.'

Odette pursed her lips. 'The *matter* is private, Bill. It will take some telling and I need to talk with him directly.'

'You might want to take a seat then,' Shea said, and pointed to a padded bench seat on the other side of the room. 'He's busy, and doesn't like to be disturbed unannounced.'

Odette sat listening to the ticking clock on the wall. She'd never been inside the police station before. The local police had total control over the lives of Aboriginal people, and very few of them walked through the station door of their own accord. She'd heard plenty of stories over the years about what went on in the cells out the back; a stone building with narrow steel doors and a small iron-barred window. During mission times, any Aboriginal person found within the town boundary without permission was given a warning. A second offence resulted in a night or two in the cells. Any *habitual absconder* who refused to comply with the law was likely to be sent away to prison.

After some time Shea reappeared and asked Odette to follow him. Lowe was seated at a desk in the next room, stiff-backed, reading from a thick file. Shea placed a chair on the other side of Lowe's desk and asked Odette to sit down before returning to his own desk on the other side of the room.

Lowe continued reading from the file and didn't look up. It was Odette's file, containing information on her, including an amateurish family tree created by an early squatter and photographs of her taken by government officials who visited the mission to measure, weigh and test for *intelligence.* The file also contained a copy of a letter written by Odette's father, Ruben, demanding he not be separated from his child on the mission; a plea that was ignored. Odette was only saved from a life of institutionalisation when Ruben was given a job at the mine and accommodation at Quarrytown. The file also included Odette's school reports, her employment record as a domestic servant, and a strident letter written by a member of the mining board. After Odette complained about the deaths of her father and husband in the quarry accident, she was described as *an overly headstrong native woman who appears to have forgotten her place in society.*

She glanced across to a blackboard on the wall behind Bill's desk. She was unnerved to see a column on the left side of the blackboard documenting the names of each *known Aboriginal child of any admixture of blood* within the jurisdiction. The second column listed the age and birth date of each child. The third column listed a parent. The final column, beneath the title *caste*, listed descriptions such as *half-caste*, *quarter-caste* and *octoroon.* Odette ran an eye down the board and counted sixteen names. Towards the bottom of the list was the name of her granddaughter, *Cecily Brown.* Alongside it were the words, *near white – caste unknown.* She closed her eyes and willed herself to contain her growing anger.

Eventually, Lowe closed the file, placed a notepad on the desk and picked up a fountain pen, carefully checking both the nib and ink.

'What can I do for you?' he finally asked.

'Well,' Odette said, clearing her throat, 'I'm here to apply for a permit. I need to go on a trip for a week or so. I'll be travelling.'

A muscle in Lowe's left cheek twitched slightly. 'Travelling?'

'Yes. I have a relative, a cousin of mine. She's in the city and I've had word that she's unwell. Very unwell. I need to visit her. It's an emergency.'

Odette looked over to Bill Shea, who was eavesdropping on the exchange. Shea looked away.

'In order to travel to Gatlin, Mrs Brown, you do not need either my permission or a permit, as long as you have no desire to reside there on a permanent basis.'

'It wouldn't be to Gatlin. My cousin lives in the state capital,' Odette explained. 'It's where I need to go.'

Lowe smiled slightly, seemingly amused. 'The capital? And what about the girl? Your granddaughter, Cecily?' he asked. 'Whose care will your granddaughter be in while you're *travelling*, as you call it?'

It was the moment Odette had prepared for.

'She will need to come with me. It's important for her to pay her respects to her auntie. I also want her to attend the cathedral in the capital. We are a religious family, Sergeant Lowe. I would be grateful if you would allow this to happen. I believe it would be important for Cecily.'

Lowe brought his hands together. 'I'm sorry, Mrs Brown, but that will not be possible. Not at all.'

'I beg your pardon?' Odette asked, although she'd clearly heard what he'd said.

'The girl is only thirteen years of age. I've been reading her file. Cecily is classified as an Aborigine.' He raised a finger and pointed to the blackboard, as a teacher might instruct a wayward student. 'By definition, of both the government and the Aborigines Welfare Board, we are responsible for Cecily's ongoing welfare. I'm sure you would be aware, Mrs Brown, that the state government is the legal guardian of the child until she reaches the age of eighteen.' Lowe straightened his back. 'As the representative of the state, and as there is no longer a Justice of the Peace serving this district, all Aboriginal children come under my direct care. I am their guardian. It would be negligent of me to allow the child to travel outside the district.' He leaned across the desk. 'I've been meaning to talk to you about the ongoing welfare of the child. In fact, I will be speaking with all remaining coloured people under my control.' Lowe glanced across at Bill Shea. 'The whole business of native welfare has been neglected in this district for many years. I will not allow it to continue. Your people need certainty, just as we do, as officers of the Crown. None of this is helped, of course, by those troublemakers arguing for citizenship on behalf of your people.'

'What about my travel?' Odette asked, ignoring the policeman's speech. 'My visit to see my cousin?'

'I cannot allow that to occur either,' he answered.

Odette looked closely at Lowe, searching for any sense of understanding. There was none.

'But my cousin is likely to pass away soon,' she persisted.

'That is not my concern. I will not provide you with a travel permit. We must leave it there, Mrs Brown. I have other matters to attend to.'

Odette stood to leave.

'Wait, Mrs Brown,' Lowe ordered. 'There is another issue I need to speak to you about. Your visit here will save me a trip to Quarrytown. Please sit back down.'

Odette watched as Lowe reached for a second folder on his desk.

'You also have a daughter?' he asked casually, disarming Odette. 'This is the station's copy of her Welfare file. Lila Brown, born 29 March 1932. Can you tell me where your daughter is currently residing, Mrs Brown?' Lowe drummed the fingers of one hand on the desk as he waited for Odette to respond.

No answer was forthcoming. Odette had been caught off-guard and didn't know what to say.

'Mrs Brown, can you explain the whereabouts of your daughter?' Lowe demanded.

'My daughter passed away,' Odette finally said, as calmly as possible.

'She's dead?' Lowe looked surprised. He rifled through the file. 'There's no death certificate attached to her file. That cannot be so.'

Odette's mind was racing ahead. 'She died a short time after Cecily was born. She had trouble with her health because of the birth. She went into the Gatlin hospital but she never came out.'

'Did you know about this?' Lowe snapped at Bill Shea.

Odette looked across at Bill, fearful of his response. 'Not specifically,' he answered, nervously.

Odette grimaced, her heart sinking with each laboured beat. Bill was well aware that Lila had run away, and had never bothered enquiring about what happened to her. Admitting to the lapse now would also implicate him.

'But,' Shea added, standing up, literally thinking on his feet, 'any death in Gatlin would be handled by our boys there. They'd have looked after it, the death certificate and any direct contact with the Welfare Board. That would be within their jurisdiction.'

Lowe was clearly annoyed. 'Regardless, we should have a copy of any death certificate in this file. I need you to ring the hospital. They will have their own records.'

'Okay. I'll call on Monday morning.'

'Now. Do it now!' Lowe shouted.

'There's no point in calling them now,' Shea explained. 'The hospital administration doesn't operate on weekends.'

Lowe threw his pen on the desk. He closed Lila's file, picked up a second file and read through it, ignoring Odette. She noticed traces of saliva gathering at the corners of his mouth. She sat and waited for his permission to leave the office. When it wasn't forthcoming, she stood up and quietly left the room, bursting through the main door and into the street, gasping for air like a drowning woman.

Sissy was sitting on the front steps of the police station.

'Sissy!' Odette said. 'What are you doing out here in the dark?'

Sissy got to her feet and scowled at her grandmother. 'What were you doing in there with the police?'

'What was I doing? There's no need for you to question me. Let's get home.' Odette reached for her hand but Sissy backed away.

'You said you were going to see Auntie Millie, but you never. I followed you from home and you came straight here. You lied, Nan.'

'Don't be silly. Of course I didn't lie.'

'You did, Nan. You went in there. I bet you told them to take me away.'

Sissy's accusation shocked Odette. 'Do you really believe that, girl?' she asked.

Sissy refused to answer her grandmother. She stood on the edge of the footpath looking into the gutter.

'Sis, I need to know if you really believe that your nan would turn you out? I'm not wild with you, but I need to know if these people have put so much fear in your heart that you would think that. Please, tell your nan so I can fix it for you. So you can know that would never be true.'

Sissy threw herself at her grandmother, almost knocking both of them to the ground. Odette patted the back of Sissy's head as the child sobbed.

'I reckon you've tired yourself out today, Sis. If I was younger and fitter I'd carry you home from here. But I'm a bit broken down, so you'll need to walk. Or maybe you can carry me,' she laughed.

Sissy wiped her face on Odette's coat. 'I'm sorry, Nan, but I'm frightened about what is happening to us. That boy ...'

'Save your apologies for when you do something really bad, like ride all over the countryside at night on your own. And you leave the worry to your nan. I'll sort this out.'

Later that night Odette sat at the kitchen table, reassured by the rain beating on the roof. It was a sound that had always calmed her. She'd hardly expected hospitality from Sergeant Lowe, but in desperation she'd deluded herself that he might grant her some pity and award her the travel permit. Although having faith in white people could be a futile exercise, Odette had never quite given up on them, a belief she'd inherited from her father, who liked to express the view that there was some good in all people. If there was good in men such as Lowe and Joe Kane, it was deeply buried, Odette thought. She understood that Lowe would never allow her to travel; he was a man incapable of understanding what was in the heart of an Aboriginal woman.

She walked into the bedroom and looked down at Sissy, asleep with an open book resting on her chest. Odette closed the book and sat it on the cupboard next to the bed. She kissed her granddaughter on both cheeks. While Sissy's irrational outburst had hurt Odette, there was something in Sissy's anger that also comforted her. The girl was growing up and she'd need to be strong, even wilful, if she was to survive. Particularly if Odette was not there to guide her. She brushed a wisp of hair from Sissy's forehead. Having recognised her granddaughter in the face of the young Kane boy, she couldn't get the image out of her mind.

Odette made herself a pot of tea and sat at the table late into the night, drained even of the energy to relight the fire in the stove. She agonised over the knowledge that Lila had carried a secret she could not share, even with her own mother. She felt a deep sense of hurt, for herself, Lila and Sissy. She was almost asleep at the table when an unexpected knock at the front door startled her. She immediately thought of Aaron Kane and armed herself with the steel poker she used for stoking the fire.

'It's late here. Who is it?'

A pause was followed by the toe of a boot scraping against the front doorstep. 'It's Bill Shea, Odette.'

Bill? Odette opened the door, the poker gripped in her hand. 'It's a bit late isn't it, Bill? What do you want, coming round here?'

'Please, Odette. Can I come inside? It's best that I'm not seen out here.'

Odette wasn't about to show Shea an ounce of respect. 'You're right, Bill. You wouldn't want to be seen on the doorstep of an Aboriginal house, not this late. But there's hardly a person left around here to see you anyhow. You been drinking tonight?'

Bill looked a little pathetic. 'No. You saw me at the station yourself. I'm sober.'

'Come in then. But keep the noise down. I have Sissy asleep in bed.'

Bill took his cap off and stood awkwardly in the kitchen. He reached into his jacket, took out a piece of paper and placed it on the table.

'What's this?' Odette asked. 'A summons?'

'It's nothing like that. This is your travel permit,' he answered. 'Stamped and signed.'

Odette was surprised. 'How about that? He signed it after all. What changed his mind?'

'Lowe doesn't know about this. And he can't find out.'

Odette picked up the piece of paper and read from it. It stated that she was legally permitted to travel *within the boundaries of the State,* for up to seven days *due to ill-health of a family member.* The permission had been officially stamped and signed by the *local Guardian of Aborigines, Officer William Shea.*

Odette sat down at the table, the piece of paper shaking in her hand. 'You forged this, Bill?'

'I forged nothing. I've signed this legally. I'm still a registered guardian for the district until the end of the month, when I finish up.'

'It says *seven days.* What will happen if I'm not back here in a week?'

Bill shrugged his shoulders. 'Why wouldn't you be back?'

'I'm just asking. What would the other policeman do? Will he come after me?'

'I don't know. He won't be happy, I know that much. He has a thing about your people. Thinks he owns you. I don't know why you just didn't take off and get back here without telling him. He might have got wind, but you'd have been home before the Welfare Board acted.'

'I'll tell you why, Bill. I'll tell you to my own shame. Most of my life I haven't been able to do anything without your lot having control over me. Myself and all the Aboriginal people around here. We're so used to being told what to do, where we can and can't go, all we know is to beg.'

Odette read the details of her travel permit a second time, pondering over what would have motivated Bill to come to her aid. 'Why are you doing this for me *now*?' she asked.

'You've been through enough, Odette. More than enough.'

Odette shook her head slightly. 'That's it?'

'That's it.'

'You've finally understood, Bill? That me and the other women here have suffered enough?' She could hardly look at the man who'd once been her childhood friend. 'So, you reckon you know how much I've gone through?'

'No. I couldn't, Odette,' he said. 'But I'm sorry about what's happened to you.'

She studied the aged grain in the wood of the tabletop. 'You say you're sorry. What about this Kane boy then?'

'What about him?'

'You came across Aaron threatening Sissy. He broke her bike and tried to drag her into a truck. I believe that is the crime of abduction, Bill? What have you done about that, seeing as you reckon I've gone through enough? You have Aaron down at the lock-up ready to charge him, I suppose?'

'I don't have anything to charge him with. When I caught up with him on the road, he told me he was trying to help young Sissy and the child wasn't prepared to say anything different.'

Odette thought Bill's comment so ridiculous she wanted to laugh out loud.

'You're right. A *child.* Sissy is a thirteen-year-old girl, an Aboriginal girl too frightened to say a word. You knew what the Kane boy was up to. And he's still up to. Following Sissy home from school, almost running her down. If nothing is done that boy will follow in his father's footsteps, just like all the other white men round here.' She waved a finger in the policeman's face. 'And mostly, Bill, they got away with it because you turned a blind eye for all those years. You didn't want to know. Don't tell me you know how I feel, and don't you dare say sorry.' She lowered her voice so she wouldn't wake up Sissy. 'Men like Joe Kane, his boy and your boss, the only difference between them and you, Bill, are the different ways you abuse us. You're all the same.'

Shea was taken aback by Odette's outburst. He was stricken by the truth of the words she'd spoken.

Odette held the travel permit in her hand. 'What do you suppose I do with this?'

'Well, it's what you asked for, permission to travel. No one will trouble you as long as you show them that piece of paper.'

'And Sissy? What about her?'

'She can't go anywhere. You should know better than to ask. It's like Lowe explained, your granddaughter is a State ward. You go and visit your sick cousin and leave Sissy with Millie Khan. Or another Aboriginal family.'

Odette was surprised Shea had swallowed the story of the gravely ill relative. She almost felt pity for him.

'You know, Bill, when you were a kid,' Odette said, 'and you spent all your time with us, on the track and playing down along the riverbed, I sometimes thought that you must be a blackfella.'

'I did myself, sometimes,' he said, with a touch of embarrassment.

'After your mum kicked me out of the front yard for playing with you,' Odette continued, 'and barred you from hanging around with us, you were frightened of us, Bill. I can understand that. It wasn't your fault. You were only a child yourself. But the rest of it, everything that's gone on since, I don't understand any of that. What happened to you?'

'I don't know,' he shrugged.

Odette stood up. 'I do. The drink is what saved you from thinking too much, Bill.' She walked to the door and opened it. 'I need you to leave now. Thank you for the travel permit. I'll be using it. I'll be leaving this house and taking my Sissy with me. If you really want to help me, Bill, you can do me one last favour.'

'And what's that?'

'Keep your mouth quiet, at least until we're well away.'

Bill put his cap back on. 'Odette, let me warn you, for your own good as well as your grandchild. You can't be taking her across the State. Not on a bus, a train, or on foot. That permit will get you some freedom, but not her. You're living under the Act, and she's under the Act as well. That girl is not permitted to travel anywhere. It's as simple as that. You take her out of the district and get caught, you're likely to lose her for good. You know that better than me.'

'And if we stay around here, I'll end up losing her

anyway, to either your boss or one of them devils prowling the countryside. I'm taking her with me. And we won't be coming back.'

'Odette, be sensible. Sissy cannot leave this town.' Shea threw his hands in the air. 'Listen to me, please, Odette. It's not as if your Sissy is a white girl.'

A white girl, Odette thought. She slowly nodded her head. 'A white girl. You're right, Bill.'

Odette stood on the veranda, watching Bill leave. She was stuck on three simple words, *a white girl.* As impossible as it seemed, once the idea revealed itself, Odette knew it was their only hope of escape. She went back inside and retrieved a battered suitcase from under the bed. She took out a pair of black dancing shoes, scuffed, and a white lace dress. The shoes, second-hand, had been too big for Sissy when she wore them to the school play the year before. Sissy had played the part of the White Witch, which had amused Odette and Millie Khan. Odette cleaned the shoes with a lump of damp charcoal, followed by a quick polish with her trusted castor oil. Satisfied, she turned her attention to the dress, which she had made herself out of a pair of lace curtains and satin lining. It was now both too short and too tight for Sissy. Odette spent the next hour unpicking the sides of the dress, taking it out and lowering the hem.

Once the repairs were completed she fetched a bundle of letters from a canister above the stove, tied together with a length of string. There were eight letters in all. Odette opened and read each letter, beginning with the first note

Lila had written her after she'd run off, and ending with the final letter that briefly mentioned the café where Lila was working. She then retrieved the jam tins containing the money she'd saved from the gift cards. As Odette sat at the table counting the money, she did not realise the sun had come up. Sissy opened the bedroom door and walked into the cold kitchen. Odette had no time to hide the pile of notes sitting on the table. Sissy had never seen so much money. She sat down at the table, rested her chin in her hands and stared at the bank notes.

'Hey, Nan. You see all this?'

'I do indeed, Sweet. I just counted it.'

'Who does it belong to?'

'Well, technically me. But seeing as we're related, I guess it belongs to you as well,' she smiled.

'That's a lot of money there, Nan. We must be rich.'

'Well, in the world out there,' Odette said, nodding towards the front door, 'it wouldn't make us rich, not exactly, although it would keep us out of harm. But if you're talking about a black woman with a long dead husband and a grandchild to care for, that's a different story. Yeah, I suppose we're rich.'

'Can I touch it? The money?' Sissy asked.

'Of course you can. Pick it up and sniff it if you want to.'

Sissy rested a hand on the pile, but dared not pick up a note. 'Where'd you get it all from?'

'I saved it, over the time I've been doing the greeting cards.'

'And what are you going to do with it?'

Odette picked up the money and folded it into several tight rolls. She opened a kitchen drawer, found some rubber bands and wrapped one around each roll.

'Well, I'm going to use it to help us. I'm not exactly sure how yet, so don't be at me for an answer.'

CHAPTER TEN

'You've had your head in that book all day,' Odette said, handing Sissy a cup of tea. She'd been curled up quietly on the veranda all morning. 'What's the story about?' she asked.

'It's the story of a boy who lives with his grandpa and a dog in a swamp. The dog comes all the way from Africa. And it doesn't bark. The dog can sing instead. It's called a Basenji.'

'Are you liking it? The story?'

'I am. Except I'm up to the part where the dog disappears in the swamp and the boy can't find it. I think it's going to end sad, Nan.'

Odette kissed Sissy on the forehead. 'Too many stories do end sad. The ones I know, at least. I'm off to the graveyard. I'd like you to walk with me, there's something I want to talk to you about along the way.'

'What is it? Can't we talk here?'

'We could. But I need you to come with me. We'll talk when we get there.'

'Will I see any ghosts?'

'Only if we head into town.'

Odette struggled on the walk to the graveyard. She looked over at Sissy and smiled, disguising her pain as best she could. When they reached the mission, she bypassed the church and walked with Sissy straight over to the graves of her parents. 'Please, sit,' she instructed, 'on the ground with your people.'

Sissy sat on her great-grandmother's grave and traced her name and the date of the woman's death with a fingertip. 'Why is it,' Sissy asked, 'that here, next to the day of her birth the word written down is *Unknown*? Everyone knows their birthday, don't they, Nan?'

'Not back then, they didn't. Your great-grandmother, she wasn't born on the mission. There wasn't any mission when she was born. She was free. Born on her country. Birthdays didn't matter so much before the mission days.'

'That means nobody knows how old she was?'

'Well, maybe not the day or the year, but she was a respected woman. That's all we need to know.'

'How did she die?'

'She died giving birth to me. But she was already ill, my father said. Being put here against her will, on the mission, it wore her down. The mission took her away from us.'

After visiting with her parents Odette walked Sissy past the other graves, explaining the connection she had to family and Odette's childhood friends.

'You need to know all of these people,' she said, 'and you must remember them.'

Sissy looked around at the headstones. 'There's a lot of people here, Nan. How will I remember all of them?'

'Through the stories,' Odette said. 'I'm telling them to you, and it will be your job to remember. It's just like the story in the book you're reading. The story of the dog from Africa. You told me about that today, and already I can remember it. Our stories are not written in any books, which means you'll need to keep telling them to your own family one day.'

Odette sat down next to Sissy on a stone bench outside the church. She'd sat on the seat many times as a child, waiting to be called inside by one of the missionaries who would then quiz her about her knowledge of the Bible.

'There's something that I need to ask you to do,' she said to Sissy, dreading the conversation ahead. 'But first, I need to explain something to you.'

'Yes, Nan.'

'My father brought me up to be an honest person. Always. It didn't matter how much trouble our family suffered at the mission, my father, he told me I had to stay true and honest to all people.' Odette's stubborn attachment to honesty and her habit for directness had occasionally caused her trouble. She paused, thinking carefully about what she had to say next. 'I'm going to tell you a new story, Sissy. It's one that we might have to tell together, one to help each other out. It's a made-up story, but one as important as any I've ever told you.'

Sissy was sharp enough to know where her grandmother was heading. 'I think you want me to tell a lie?'

Odette put an arm around Sissy's shoulders and drew her close. 'Yes, it is a lie. But a lie told for an important reason, a good reason. To protect you. My father, he was strong, and he was proud that he was known right across the country around here as a man of truth. Even when white people didn't want to hear what he had to say and it got him into bother, he told the truth. This story, the one we're going to share, he would understand why we might need to lie. I'm sure he would. Do you understand?'

'I think so, Nan.'

Odette knocked at Henry's gate. The padlocks were missing, as was the heavy chain. Henry didn't answer. Odette pushed the gate open. Not wanting to startle him, she called Henry's name. When nobody answered she made her way through the yard. She could hear the distinct sound of a shovel hitting dirt. She followed the sound and found Henry digging a hole about three feet long by a foot wide. Laying in the dirt, next to the hole, was Rowdy. His coat was matted and his body looked as hard as stone. His swollen tongue hung from the side of his open mouth. Henry briefly looked up at Odette before returning to the grim task. Sissy, who held a fear of dead animals, stood back.

'Henry, I'm so sorry,' Odette sighed, looking down at the poor dog. 'What happened to him?'

Henry ignored her and continued digging the hole until he was satisfied the walls of the grave were straight. He dropped the shovel to the ground, walked over to Rowdy, lowered his head and whispered a prayer, ending with an *Amen*. He lifted the dog in his arms and cradled him to his chest before gently lowering the animal into the hole. He bowed his head.

Not wanting to interfere with Henry's privacy, Odette walked across to where Sissy was standing and waited until he'd filled in the hole and patted the last shovel of soil into place. It was only then that Odette's earlier question appeared to register with him.

'He was thrown a bait,' Henry explained. 'This morning, the wind had turned and I could smell him. Must have been dead for all this time I thought he was missing.' Henry walked to the bonnet of a car wreck and returned with a piece of rotten meat in his hand. 'I found this bait on the roof of one of the tractors. Thrown over the fence, it must've been. There's glass all through it. There must've been another bait he ate, I reckon. That's what killed him. You know who it was, don't you, Odette?'

Remembering what she'd witnessed at the Kane farm, Odette had no doubt who had poisoned Rowdy.

'It was that Kane boy,' Henry said. 'Would be nobody but him. That boy, he'll have to pay for this. They've got bad blood in them, the Kanes.'

'Not all of them,' Odette said, thinking not only of George Kane, but of her granddaughter too. Although she understood Henry's feelings Odette worried that revenge would only bring him more trouble. 'I think you should let this rest,' she advised.

'Sorry Odette, but I can't do that.'

Henry hurled the piece of meat back over the fence. He looked across the yard at Sissy. The sight of the dead dog had distressed her.

'What are you here for?' he asked Odette. 'Have you had more trouble with Sissy's bike?'

'No, the bike is working fine. I came here on other business,' Odette said. 'But it can wait. Now is not the time.'

'The time is fine with me, Odette. Rowdy's gone and he won't be back. Nothing I can do about that. Tell me what you need.'

'Is the utility running, Henry? The car you've been driving.'

'Sure is. I haven't started it since I was over at your place the other day. But it goes really good.'

'Do you think you'd be able to drive Sissy and me to the train station tomorrow morning? We need to be there before the seven-ten train. I'll pay for petrol, of course, and your time. You'll need to be early.'

As was his custom Henry gave the prospect serious thought, checking that his early mornings were otherwise free before answering. 'I can do that for you, Odette. Are you two going on a holiday?'

'I wish we were,' she said. 'Not anything as good as a holiday. It's family business. I need you to keep this to yourself. After we've gone that new policeman, Lowe, he might come round asking after us. You can't tell him that you drove us to the station. That's important to us, Henry. Both to me and Sissy.'

Henry frowned. 'I understand, Odette. I think it's best if you tell me no more. You never know if the police will want to torture me or something. You have your secrets and I have my own.'

Odette took hold of Sissy's hand. She had not taken her eyes off Rowdy's burial site.

'We have to go and get ready. You'll be on time, Henry?'

He tapped an imaginary wrist-watch. 'I won't be late.'

~

Later that night, Odette took the framed photograph of Lila down from the wall and put it in her suitcase. She added the photographs of Delores Reed's daughters. After Sissy had fallen asleep, she also fetched Lila's letters and added them to the case, along with her life savings, which she tucked in the inside pocket.

Early the next morning, she laid out Sissy's clothes and brushed her hair. Once Sissy had put the dress and black dancing shoes on, Odette circled her granddaughter, examining her. She was not fully satisfied with the disguise. 'Don't move. We need to do something more.' She went and rummaged through a drawer in the bedroom and retrieved a small compact of rouge. She dusted it across Sissy's cheeks. 'Not too much. If I overdo the colour, it could be a giveaway.'

'Why are you doing this?' Sissy frowned.

'Just adding a bit of red to your cheeks,' Odette explained. 'The right colour.'

Sissy stamped the heel of her dancing shoe on the wooden floor. 'I don't think I want to do this, Nan. I don't want to be any colour. I just want to be here with you.'

Odette grabbed hold of Sissy and shook her, vigorously enough to startle the child. 'Do you think that this makes me feel happy? I don't want to do this either. We don't have a choice. We went over this yesterday. If we stay here it won't be safe for us.'

'We haven't said goodbye to Auntie Millie,' Sissy said, stalling.

'We don't have time to do that,' Odette replied, although time was not the only reason she didn't want to involve Millie in her plan. Odette was convinced that once Lowe was aware that she and Sissy had left town, he'd interrogate Millie and the other Aboriginal women Odette knew. She didn't expect Millie would disclose information to a policeman, but preferred that she not be burdened with her story of escape.

The front gate squealed. 'That will be Henry,' Odette said to Sissy. 'It's time for us to go.'

Odette closed the front door behind her without looking back and followed Henry across the footbridge. He lifted the suitcase into the back of the truck and opened the passenger door with the elegance of a well-trained chauffeur. Sissy hopped in, followed by Odette. It was a tight fit.

Despite Henry not having a licence he drove well enough, although he was painfully slow. Odette became anxious. 'Henry,' she began politely, 'can I ask you something? Can this car go any faster?'

'I reckon it would,' he answered. 'This car has a strong motor.'

With the speed dial stuck on twenty miles an hour, Odette prodded him again. 'Do you think you could try it?'

'Try what?' he asked.

'Try to go a little faster, Henry. The train we're meeting up with, it's the only one for the day. We wouldn't want to miss it and get stuck at the railway station.'

'If you want me to,' Henry replied, 'I'll drive faster. But the roos will be on the move, looking for breakfast. I don't want to bump into one of them.'

'Yes, I need you to do that, Henry. Go a little faster. You watch the road and I'll look out for the kangaroos.'

Henry put his foot down, only slightly, and increased his speed to twenty-five miles an hour. Odette looked out of the window at a line of ghost gums on the side of the road. The car passed the sagging front gate of the Kane farm. She thought of Lila and the horrors Joe Kane must have subjected her to. She felt renewed guilt for not searching harder for her daughter when she first ran away. Odette put her arm over Sissy's shoulders, drew her closer and resolved that this time she would do all she could to locate Lila and reunite her with her own daughter.

The railway station on the outskirts of Gatlin was quiet except for a wind kicking whirlpools of dust into the air. Henry pulled over to the side of the road, jumped out and opened the passenger door. 'We're here.' He grinned. 'I'll get the case for you.'

After setting the suitcase on the footpath, Henry stood back, his arms folded and his hands tucked into his armpits. Odette couldn't help but smile at him. Somehow, Henry Lamb had never grown up. Although he'd been tormented over the years, Henry's innocence also offered him some protection from the stain of the town. 'Thank you, for everything,' she said. 'You take care of yourself, Henry Lamb. Can I give you some advice?'

'You can, Odette.'

'That Kane boy, Aaron. He's not worth your trouble, Henry. You stay away from him.'

'I don't know that I can do that, Odette. I would be happy to if he would stay away from me. I would be happy then.'

Odette had never touched a white man in her life, not voluntarily. She walked over to Henry, put a hand on one cheek, leaned forward and kissed the other. Henry put his hand to his cheek and left it there. Sissy tugged at his shirtsleeve. 'Goodbye, Henry. You can ride the bike anytime you want to.'

'When will you be back, Odette?' he asked.

'I can't be sure.'

The bells on the closing gates signalled that the train was arriving. Odette picked up her case in one hand and took Sissy's hand with the other.

CHAPTER ELEVEN

Odette had not ridden on a train before, let alone purchased a ticket. Gatlin was as far from home as she'd ever been, and she had little idea what lay beyond the town except for what she'd read in newspapers and heard on the radio. She stood in the waiting room and observed the other passengers in line at the ticket window. She took the travel permit from her handbag and approached the window.

'I need two tickets, please,' she said when she reached the front of the queue. 'One adult and a child.'

The young station assistant looked up. 'Are you going to the end of the line?'

Odette presumed the state capital was as far as the train would go. 'Yes. The end of the line.'

'And will the trip be one-way or return, Madam?'

The young man's dimpled face was dotted with acne. Odette couldn't comprehend the question. 'I beg your pardon?'

'Are you coming back?' he asked.

Odette gathered herself. 'Yes, I'm coming back. But I'm not sure when.'

'Okay,' he nodded. 'One-way it is. Would you prefer first class or economy?'

Odette wasn't sure what he meant by economy, but first class sounded foreign. 'Economy, please.'

The boy calculated the fare and Odette handed him the cash and her travel permit. The station assistant handed the permit back to her along with the tickets without reading the document. 'Sorry,' he said, 'this must be yours. Have a comfortable trip.'

Odette had little more than five minutes to get them something to eat. She ordered a Cornish pastie for both herself and Sissy before getting on the train. They walked along the aisle of the carriage searching for their seats. Odette was relieved to find the compartment empty. She placed the suitcase in the baggage rack above their seat, sat down and passed Sissy the steaming brown bag with the pastie inside. The smudges of rouge on Sissy's cheeks momentarily unnerved her. Odette wasn't sure if the journey they were about to embark on was the right choice.

'Thank you, Nan.'

'Don't do that,' Odette urged.

'Do what?' Sissy asked. 'Show my manners?'

'You're not to call me Nan while we're on the train,' Odette whispered. 'You can call me Auntie or even Odette, but not Nan.'

'Sorry,' Sissy said, amused at the thought of calling her grandmother by her first name. She took a bite out of the pastie. 'I know I can't call you Nan, because of our story, but you say I can call you Auntie. Why? That still means that we're related, doesn't it?'

'Well,' Odette explained, 'white families, they like to call the women who look after their children Auntie. When I looked after white kiddies they always called me Auntie.'

'Why?'

'They wanted me to feel like I was part of the family.'

'How could you be part of their family?' Sissy asked. 'You had your own family.'

'Exactly. I've always had my own family. And I was never really part of theirs, shuffled out the back door at the end of the day or asked to sleep over in some rundown shack.'

A white woman, elegantly dressed in a tweed coat and straw hat was standing outside their compartment. She tried opening the sliding door, struggling with her suitcase. Odette nodded towards Sissy. 'Give her some help, Love.'

Sissy jumped down from her seat and opened the door.

'Thank you, Darling,' the woman said, checking the reserved numbers above each seat. She looked at the ticket in her hand and sat down next to Sissy. The suitcase remained on the floor. Odette recognised an opportunity.

'Would you like me to put your case on the rack for you, Missus?'

The woman, who would have been slightly younger than Odette, turned to her and smiled. 'Oh, yes. Thank you. And it's *Miss*,' she smiled.

'Oh, I'm sorry,' Odette said, picking up the woman's bag.

'No need to apologise,' the woman laughed, a little too highly pitched for Odette's liking. 'I'm a single woman.' She straightened the crease in her dress. 'By choice,' she added.

The pain in Odette's side caught her off-guard as she lifted the bag above her shoulders. She struggled and almost dropped the case. The woman did not bother to help. The porter's voice came over a speaker, announcing that the train would not be leaving the station for another fifteen minutes, *due to an unforeseen delay.*

Odette became anxious, worried that the train might never leave. As ridiculous as it was, she imagined Henry Lamb in the police cells at Deane, being beaten by Sergeant Lowe, who would be on his way to the Gatlin train station to arrest her. She willed the train to leave the station. Sissy ate her pastie and watched as the white woman took a compact from her handbag and powdered her already pale face in a round mirror.

Sissy looked up at several framed photographs decorating the carriage walls. *Come and Visit the Countryside* the advertisements read. In each of the pictures there was a scene of the mountains, a coastline and a magical fern gully.

'Auntie,' Sissy said purposefully, after she'd finished eating, 'do you think that we could visit the beach some time?'

'You have never visited the coast?' the woman interrupted before Odette could respond.

'No, I never have,' Sissy answered.

'Well, you are missing out on a wonderful experience. The coast is fresh and clean, and as long as you escape the city beaches, you might never see another soul while walking along the sand. But,' she paused, 'always protect your skin, particularly your face.' She showed Sissy the powder compact. 'I use this and wash with a delicate soap of an evening. The sun never touches me. Hence, I have no wrinkles or blemishes.' She examined Sissy's face. 'You have too much colour already.'

'Colour?' Sissy responded.

'Yes. And at such a young age. Where do you live, young lady?'

'In Gatlin,' Sissy answered, as she and Odette had rehearsed.

'Really? So do I. At least, I did originally. I live in the city now. I've just been visiting family,' she explained. 'I have to detour and see other relatives at the next station. Where in Gatlin are your family located?'

It wasn't a question that Odette had considered, or one that she and Sissy had rehearsed. 'We're not in town,' Odette offered. 'Cecily's family live on a farm outside of town.'

'Which farm would that be?' the woman asked Sissy, without looking at Odette.

'The Kane family,' Odette interrupted, with as much confidence as possible.

'Kane?'

Odette sensed the woman attempting to place the family. Everybody had their position in the district, not just Aboriginal people. The wealthy white people looked down on the poor whites, and almost all white people looked down on Aboriginal people.

'I do not believe I know of them,' the woman said.

'We're closer to Deane than Gatlin,' Odette offered.

'It makes little difference. We know most families in the district,' the woman said. 'My family, we've been in this area from the very *beginning*. We are pioneers. We know everyone.' She raised an eyebrow, waiting on an explanation from Odette.

Sissy decided it was her turn to interrupt. 'Excuse me, have you ever been on a holiday to the mountains?' she asked, pointing at one of the photographs.

The woman's eyes lit up. 'Yes, I have. Several times over the years.'

'I bet it was exciting,' Sissy said.

'Oh, it was so exciting. The air is so fresh and clean in the mountains.'

The whistle blew and the train began moving. The woman took hold of Sissy's hand. She talked continuously for the next hour or so, telling Sissy stories about being sent away to boarding school when she was a child and how lonely she felt at the time. When she could finally get a word in Sissy talked about the books she'd read and her favourite animals on the farm where she lived. She recited the names of her pets, drawing imaginatively on every storybook and novel she'd ever read.

Odette looked out of the train window with one ear trained on a conversation she did not expect to be included in. She was struck by the view outside the train window. The country was familiar and yet alien. The farms, or what was left of them, resembled the neglected properties around Deane. The ancient forests had long gone, their vast roots torn from the earth by machines linked with heavy chains. The dams were dry, and the animals scraping at the ground behind the fence lines were scrawny. Odette didn't see a single person outside the train window.

The conversation between the woman and Sissy eventually fell quiet. The woman had fallen asleep. Sissy got up from her seat and stood by the window. Although she'd played the role of a young white girl well, the charade bothered her.

'Are you feeling alright,' Odette whispered.

'Yes, Nan … Auntie.'

She offered Sissy the paper bag. 'Would you like this second pastie? I can't eat it.'

'No. You keep it for later. You might be hungry then Nanna. I mean, Auntie.'

Odette detected an unease in the girl.

'I don't like doing this,' Sissy whispered.

The woman woke up, startled by the vibration of the carriage crossing a bridge above a river. Saliva had dribbled down her chin while she'd been sleeping and her hat sat crookedly on her head. Sissy thought the woman looked silly and couldn't help but laugh. Odette glared at her to stop. The woman sat up, yawned, wiped her chin and blinked several times. She turned to Odette and yawned again. 'Oh, I do beg your pardon.'

'That's fine, Missus.'

Odette returned to her seat opposite the woman. She could feel the woman's eyes on her, studying her, another habit of many white people.

'Have you always been with the Kane family?' the woman asked.

'Not always. But, I've been with them for some time.'

The woman moved across the carriage and sat next to her, alarming Odette. 'I'm sure you would be interested to know that before I went away to school I was cared for by one of your own people. Although,' she added, 'she came from the desert and she was darker than you. Several shades darker. You have more of a coffee complexion,' the woman observed. She waited for an explanation.

Odette had long ago learned that white people were fascinated with the skin colour of Aboriginal people, and what it might indicate. She'd been similarly interrogated many times over the years. Odette understood that what this woman really wanted to know was how she'd inherited the white blood she carried and who it had come from. Odette didn't know the answer to such questions. All she knew was that the women in her family loved all their children, regardless of the suffering and violence that had created them. She turned to the woman and repeated a fiction she'd told before, the story of the mythical white forebear who'd *saved* her family. Stories of such benevolence comforted white people and would often result in an Aboriginal woman attached to a household being treated with some fondness and even care. Odette ended the tale with the punchline she often quoted. 'The white man who came into our lives, he was a true Christian man.'

The woman sighed audibly. 'You were fortunate. Some of our own men, in the past, were no more civilised than savages.' She looked out of the window as if expecting to see a *savage* that very minute. 'The land out here, it does that to some people. It turns them into savages.' She nodded towards Sissy. 'Are you escorting the girl to the capital?'

'Yes. She will be living with her mother. The family have a home in the city and the mother is living there. She decided to leave the countryside.'

'I don't blame her. I've done the same. Let me suggest that the child remains in the city. It would be for her own good.' The woman leaned closer to Odette. 'You know, I miss my old Auntie Sarah. She came to us with her tribal language only. Barely a word of English. We were able to make a change in her life. My mother sat with her for an hour each afternoon and taught Sarah to read and write.' She raised her eyebrows. 'I had feelings for her, you understand?'

Odette did understand such feelings; those feelings could leave a grown woman being treated no better than a household pet.

'Although she did not like to talk about it at all,' the woman continued, 'we were aware that Sarah had children of her own. They had been brought in from the desert and handed to the Anglicans. Given a proper education. I was fortunate that along with my two older sisters, Auntie Sarah shifted her affection to us. Do you feel the same way?'

'What way?' Odette asked. The woman's shrill voice had given her a headache.

Sissy, counting telegraph poles outside the train window, also wanted the woman to stop talking. She'd never heard her grandmother spoken to in such a way and it annoyed her.

'You and Cecily are obviously very close. I would expect you have affection for her?' the woman said.

'Affection? I love her,' Odette answered.

The comment startled the woman. 'So, you do not have children of your own?' she probed.

'No,' Odette said. 'And you also don't have any children of your own. Why is that?'

The woman was taken aback. She glared at Odette and moved back to her own seat, abruptly ending the conversation.

Sissy moved into the seat beside her grandmother. 'I love you, too, Auntie,' she said, without a hint of performance.

The woman looked from Odette to Sissy. She was troubled. 'I think the child needs to spend more time with her own people,' she said.

Odette had had enough of the white woman. Despite her better judgement she was about to put the woman in her place when her response was cut short by an announcement from the conductor. The train would soon be arriving at the next station. 'All passengers are to leave the train during the period of shunting,' the conductor ordered. The passengers were invited to enjoy a short lunch break.

At the station, the woman stood up and waited for Odette to retrieve her case. Although she felt like slapping the woman, Odette dutifully took the case down from the rack and placed it on the floor. Sissy opened the sliding door. They watched as the woman struggled along the aisle. Odette had been raised to excuse the ignorance of white people, but it was a difficult task. *It will be for your own sake more than theirs*, her father had explained to her many times. *If you can't get them people out of your head, they will hold you down for the rest of your life.*

'Are you hungry?' Odette asked Sissy, once the woman was gone. 'I need a cup of tea.'

'Nan?' Sissy asked.

'It's not Nan,' Odette reminded her. 'I told you, I'm Auntie. You have to remember that.'

'I know it's Auntie. But there is no one here but us. I want to call you Nan when there is nobody else around. I didn't like that woman, and I don't like the way she spoke to you.'

'Don't bother with her. And you do exactly as I told you to do. We both need to get used to this game. You're to call me Auntie.'

Sissy kicked the base of her seat in frustration. '*Auntie*. Do you think that I could have another one of those Cornish pasties? Not the cold one, but a fresh one?'

'You can have two pasties if you want to, as long as you behave.'

'*Auntie*,' Sissy repeated. 'Do you know why they call them Cornish pasties, and not meat pasties?'

'No, I don't,' Odette answered. 'But I bet you do?'

'I do, *Auntie*. I read about it in a book. It's because the pasties come from a place called Cornwall, where miners used to take the pasties underground for their dinner. *Auntie*.'

Odette had thoughts only for the pot of tea she was desperate to enjoy. 'Is that so?'

'Yes, it is. *Auntie*.'

Odette stopped in the middle of the platform and put her case down. 'Okay, Sis. I know you're frustrated and I can see where you're going with this Auntie business. You can give it a rest, as long as there is only the two of us around.'

'Yes, Nan.' Sissy smiled.

CHAPTER TWELVE

The cafeteria was at the end of the main platform. A crowd had gathered around the entrance. Odette saw a policeman standing with two other men, each wearing a dark suit and tie. She and Sissy were forced into a queue behind a group of school students and their teacher. Odette overheard the station master explaining to the teacher that the Immigration Officers were searching for a Polish migrant who'd run away from a local hostel.

'The young fella has got himself into some sort of strife. They're not saying what it is. He absconded before Immigration could get hold of him. They expect he'll try and get away from here by train.'

The Immigration officials watched closely as passengers filed through the cafeteria doors. By the time Odette and Sissy were inside the room it was crowded, with most chairs and tables taken. Odette spotted two spare seats at a table in the far corner where a man sat alone with his back to the room.

Odette shuffled between the aisles and pulled a chair away from the table. The seated man turned around. He was clearly Aboriginal, and about Odette's age. She looked around the room for another place for them to sit. There was none.

'Do you mind if we share this table with you?' she asked.

'I don't mind,' he said, with little enthusiasm, and returned to the newspaper he'd been reading.

Odette sat down and handed Sissy a menu card. 'I'm sure one of them pasties will be on here. But maybe you'd like to try something else. You can choose anything you want.'

Sissy ran a finger down the menu card. 'It says here that they have a toasted cheese sandwich. Could I have one of those?'

Odette, distracted by the Immigration officers moving through the cafeteria, didn't hear Sissy's reply.

'I would like a toasted sandwich,' Sissy repeated. 'Can I have one of those?'

'If you like,' Odette said, keeping one eye on the policeman. He looked about as friendly as Sergeant Lowe. 'You be sure not to move from the table, Sis, and I'll go and order us a sandwich and a cuppa.'

The officers moved systematically between tables, questioning people as they went. Odette stood in line to order, watching closely. Patrons were being asked for identification. One of the Immigration officers had what appeared to be a photograph in his hand and was showing it to people. Odette looked back across the room to where Sissy was seated. The man sitting at the table was talking with her. Once she'd been served, Odette carried the tray of food back to the table. She frowned at Sissy, who was talking animatedly, as if the man was an old family friend and not a complete stranger. Odette sat down, handed Sissy a sandwich and poured each of them a cup of tea.

'Nothing better than a good cuppa,' the man remarked to Odette. He offered his hand, appearing friendlier than he had a few minutes earlier. 'They call me Jack Haines,' he said, his chest rising slightly, as if the name carried some importance. 'I've just been speaking with the lovely young lady here. You've covered some distance today, and you have a way to go, all the way to the capital. Travel like that would wear me out, and I've covered a lot of distance over the years. You've come all the way from Deane, the young girl tells me. It's a lonely place out there.'

Odette was annoyed that Sissy had provided so much personal information to the stranger. 'You know Deane?' she asked cautiously.

'That I do. There aren't many places I don't know. I worked on the shearing for a time. The season would have taken me through nearly every town across the state at one time or another.'

Jack Haines looked harmless enough. Something about his mannerisms reminded Odette of one of her cousins, Marcus. He'd also worked at the mine with her father and husband. Marcus narrowly escaped the accident, but had witnessed the deaths of the other men. Jack Haines, like Marcus, wore a friendly, open face. His voice sounded as if it could break into a show tune at any moment, which Marcus had been prone to do, particularly after a glass or two of beer.

'You spent much time in Deane?' Jack asked.

'I was born over that way,' Odette offered, without being more specific.

'Then you'd be off the old mission out there, I'd reckon. It was the Proddies who ran that place, wasn't it?'

Attempting to withhold personal or family information from another Aboriginal person was never easy. 'That's the one. And you?'

'Oh, I'm a north coast fella, originally. Up near the border. A saltwater boy, I am. Do you mind if I ask your name?'

'Odette Brown.'

'You're a Brown? Okay then.' He nodded his head knowingly. 'You would be related to Jimmy Brown, for sure. I knew that fella well.'

'I'm a Brown by name,' Odette explained. 'My late husband's family.' Odette had a faint memory of Jimmy Brown, from when she was a child. He was taken away before she started school. If Jack Haines expected Odette to get excited hearing the name of a long-lost in-law, he was mistaken. Reuniting with family, if only through memory, could be heartbreaking. As tragic as it was, some of those who'd lost family found it more bearable to forget. 'He could be the same fella,' Odette said casually.

'Not could be. I'd bet he is one and the same. Me and Jimmy Brown were in Kingsley Boys Home together. He used to talk about the mission days at Deane all the time. He had a big mob of family over there.'

'What did this Jimmy look like?' Odette asked.

'Well, he had a big mop of dark hair and he was as thin as a creek snake. That was Jimmy.'

The description was familiar to Odette. All of the Brown men grew up to be thin and wiry.

'Like a snake! That's really skinny,' Sissy said, laughing.

'It is, young lady.' Jack held up one finger. 'Like that, he was.'

'How'd he get to be so skinny?' Sissy asked. 'I bet he didn't eat any food.'

'Eat? Oh, he ate like a horse. Jimmy was as good on the tooth as any fella I've ever come across, even the big boys out on the shearing. I would be willing to wager that boy could have eaten a whole elephant in an afternoon,' Jack said to Sissy, enriching the story. 'One time we stole a dozen bread rolls from the kitchen. We snuck off, just the two of us, and climbed a ladder into the bell tower above the chapel to have our feast. In the time it took me to eat three bread rolls Jimmy had demolished the other nine.' Jack Haines grabbed hold of his ample stomach with both hands. 'As you both can see, I'm a bit of a porker these days, but back then we were built the same. Jack Haines and Jimmy Brown, we were like twins. They'd get us mixed up all the time. Couldn't tell one young blackfella from another.'

Odette couldn't help but ask an obvious question. 'Where'd he'd get to, Jimmy, after the Home?' she asked.

Jack paused. 'I don't know, not for certain.'

It was obvious to Odette that Jack was hiding something. 'Did he get himself into trouble?' she persisted.

Jack's eyes sparkled to life. He slapped his hands together and told Odette and Sissy another story about Jimmy Brown.

'Well, this is what happened to him. Jimmy loved his freedom. We all did, but Jimmy, he could not be held down. It didn't matter to him how many ways they tried keeping him in order, that boy would find a way to escape. He was like that magician fella, Houdini.' Jack chuckled, having transported himself back in time. 'In the Home, we must have lived by a hundred and one rules. Well, your Jimmy,' Jack said to Odette, 'he would have broken every one of them. He was a good kid, but he could never do as he was told. And he was a runner. Took off every chance he got. They'd bring him back and lock him up on his own for a week. Soon as they let him out, he'd be off again, sometimes that very same day. That boy couldn't help himself. His people,' Jack asked Odette, 'I believe they were originally desert mob?'

'Some of them were,' Odette said.

'It figures. I used to get out west to the desert now and then and listened to the old boys tell stories about *freedom days*. My thinking was, if you come from out that way, with a big sky above and the big ground under you, you couldn't survive with a fence around you, let alone in a box with iron bars on the windows.' Jack's tone shifted. 'I mean, a poor camp dog can't survive in a box without going crazy. It has no choice but to give in to its master. Or go on the attack, of course.'

Odette looked up as the policeman moved closer to their table. Their eyes met and Odette quickly looked away.

'So, did Jimmy give up on running away?' Sissy asked.

'Not a chance in a fiery Hell. He woke me up early one morning, said he was taking off and would *never ever* be back. I'd heard it before from him, of course. But that morning, well, he had a fearsome look in his eyes. He had the courage of a dingo, that young boy. He absconded while the rest of us were in the showers and that was the last we saw of him. Jimmy Brown was never heard from again. The lad finally beat them. Got away. I'd bet he's out there now, moving about all over the country. That would be his way.'

Sissy, who'd fixated on the story, applauded. She'd always enjoyed a happy ending.

Jack looked across at Sissy and smiled openly. Odette had listened closely to his story and was grateful to Jack for telling it that way for Sissy's benefit. But the story was partly a lie. Both Odette and Jack knew it without another word passing between them. Jimmy Brown of the Kingsley Boys Home was indeed the same skinny kid off the mission at Deane. And he was a runner. Along with other boys in the Home, including the outwardly amiable Jack Haines, Jimmy was worked into the ground. Each time he ran off he was hauled back to the Home, where the beatings became more severe. In the eyes of the institution, Jimmy had to be broken. In his own mind, he'd decided that he couldn't let that happen. The last time Jimmy Brown ran off he'd tried jumping a ride from a passing goods train. He fell under the train and was killed. His body was returned to the Home for burial in a pair of hessian sacks. After the funeral, the blood-stained sacks were left on display as a warning to any other boy with the idea in his head to escape.

Although Jack Haines continued smiling, the deep pain he'd experienced was obvious to Odette. 'And you?' she asked. 'After the Home? Where did you end up, Jack?'

'Oh, I was lucky. I was sponsored by a fishing business and worked all along the coast from north to south. I love the sea and earned my wage on the boats. Worked with an old boatman, the first decent whitefella I'd ever met. He taught me a lot about working the tides and where to lay the nets. He was a good man. I was about as free as a blackfella could be around that time. When I wasn't working on the boats,

I would head off fishing for myself. Same as we used to do in the old days. Then the boating business went bust, so I tried my hand at shearing with a couple of other boys, a whitefella and a blackfella. We were a team of three. Ten years I was on the shearing. All over I went.'

'And what do you do now?'

'Now I live in the big smoke. The capital. I've just come back for the funeral of an uncle. I'm about to head home.'

'You have family in the city?'

'Sure do. I have a wife, two grown-up daughters and my own grand-kid. They're at home there in the city, holding the fort.' He patted the inside pocket of his suit coat. 'I have a pay packet here. While I was up this way I picked up a bit of work. I'll hand this money over to my wife tonight. She's in charge of the savings at our place.'

Odette had never met an Aboriginal person who had experienced freedom like Jack Haines. Not one who'd lived among white people, at least. It was obvious Jack could tell a good yarn. Odette remained a little suspicious. 'How is it that you get to travel around so much?'

'What do you mean?' He frowned. 'I follow the work.'

'But what about the Act?' She whispered the words – *the Act* – as Aboriginal people generally did. It was a curse, rarely spoken aloud. 'It would hold you back from travelling, wouldn't it?'

Jack scoffed dismissively at Odette. 'The Act doesn't mean nothing to Jack Haines,' he boasted. 'I was finished with the Act years back. It can't touch me. I don't need it. And I'm free of it.'

Odette thought the man a fool. 'You've finished with it?'

Jack raised a hand in the air. 'Hold on, Sis. Showing is better than explaining.' He took a beaten leather wallet from his back pocket and took out a piece of paper, sealed in an envelope. He carefully unfolded the document and placed it on the table.

'There it is,' he said, looking as satisfied with himself as a man possibly could. 'My exemption certificate.'

Odette looked down at the photograph of a slightly younger Jack Haines. 'Exemption?'

Jack threw his hands in the air in mock disgust. Sissy giggled at the display of theatrics. Jack reminded her of a sideshow clown she'd once seen at the Deane showgrounds.

'Gee,' he said, 'you people out here, I think time has passed your mob by. This is a certificate of exemption. It means that I can go anywhere I like, when I like. Even across the border. With some rules, of course,' he offered as a cautionary note.

Odette had indeed heard of the exemption certificate, although she'd never seen one or met a person who actually carried one. As far as Odette knew, nobody from back home had sought an exemption from the Act.

'And what are those rules?' Odette asked.

Jack listed the orders he was subject to, counting on his fingers as he went. 'To start with, to get the certificate I needed to provide testimonials to the Welfare Board from reputable people. White people. I can live where I want and I can have a drink,' he added, winking at the smiling Sissy. 'But I can't give grog to a blackfella. That's rule number one, just about. And ...' Jack hesitated and looked at Sissy.

'And what?' Odette prompted him.

'And ... I can't *fraternise* with Aboriginal people,' he said, lowering his voice. '*Unlawful association*, they call it.' He looked away, unable to hide his sudden shame.

Sissy tapped Odette on the arm. 'I need to go to the toilet.'

'Go on,' Odette said. 'Be sure to be straight back here when you've finished.'

Although Jack appeared strong and proud, Odette couldn't understand how he could allow himself to be shamed in such a way. He sensed her look of disapproval and became annoyed.

'What's with you, woman?' he asked. 'Don't you be looking at me that way. I know what you're thinking. Well, you can get this over and done with and say what's on your mind and I'll be on my way. You reckon I'm some kind of traitor, don't you?'

The policeman, overhearing Jack's raised voice, looked across to their table.

Odette understood the danger of causing a scene. 'I'm sorry,' she said. 'I don't mean to judge. Maybe I don't understand.'

Jack leaned across the table. 'Damn right, you don't. I have a job to do.'

'I'm sure you do,' Odette said.

'Do you know what that job is?' Jack insisted.

The policeman turned his full attention to Jack.

'I really don't need to know,' she whispered, trying to calm him, but Jack was determined to put her in her place.

'I survive the best way I can. That's my job. I was one of six kiddies. I seen three of them taken away, and a sister who ran off before they could get hold of her. They went for all time. I had a big sister left, but the others, I don't know what happened to any of them. I've kept my wife and kids together through everything these bastards have put us through,' he said, looking directly at the policeman, before waving a finger in Odette's face. 'You can try this little trick of your own, disguising your granddaughter, passing her off as a snowflake. Well, let's see how far that one gets you. That's a dangerous game, Sister. And all the pressure, it's on that child more than it's on you.'

'She told you?' Odette hissed. 'I can't believe it.'

Jack waved her protest away. 'She didn't tell me anything. She'd die for you, that kiddie. Five minutes I sat with her, and I can see she has a mighty big heart in her, and that she loves you as much as a child can do. She didn't say a word to me about any of that business, not a word.'

'How do you know then?'

Jack's anger faded from his face quicker than it had arrived. 'Because I see so much strength in that girl, and I see it in you. I might look like a silly old boy in front of these white buggers but I know love when I see it.' He sat back. 'All of us, we have to do anything we can. And none of us needs to be judged. Me or you.'

The Immigration officials and the policeman moved to their table. 'Your name, please?' one of the officials asked Jack.

'John Harold Haines,' he answered.

'Which train have you been on today, John?'

'None as yet, sir. I'm about to catch the train to the capital.'

'You purchased your ticket here?' the second officer asked.

'Yes, I did, sir,' Jack answered, responding in kind to the civil tone of the officer.

The same officer showed Jack the photograph he'd been passing around the cafeteria. 'Have you seen this man about the station area today?'

Odette looked across at the picture of a blond-haired, thin-faced young man.

'No,' Jack answered, barely glancing at the photograph. The official asked him to take a closer look, which he did. 'No, I haven't seen anyone who looks like that. What's he done?' Jack asked.

'That's nothing to concern yourself with, Sir. Thank you for your assistance.'

The uniformed policeman watched Jack closely. After the Immigration officials moved to the next table, he questioned Jack. 'What's your name?' he demanded, with none of the politeness of his associates.

'I just gave it to them fellas,' Jack answered, as nonchalantly as possible.

'Maybe you did,' he said. 'And I'm asking you again.'

Jack repeated his name. He was asked his age and address.

'Do they call you by another name,' the policeman asked, smiling, 'other than John?'

'My friends call me Jack.'

'Jack?' The policeman smiled. 'Or is it, Jacky?' He smirked.

Jack winced. 'No. Jack.'

'Well, *Jack*, you're a long way from home if you're heading back to the city. I presume you have permission to be here?'

'I don't need permission,' Jack said defensively. He picked up the exemption certificate from the table and handed it to the policeman. Odette could see Sissy walking back towards the table from the toilet. The slightest shake of Odette's head was enough of a warning for her to turn and walk in the opposite direction. She sat at a table on the other side of the room, alongside a white family.

The policeman inspected the exemption certificate. 'Well, Jack. It looks like you've been given the keys to the city.' He laughed loudly. On cue, Jack joined in, relaxing, until the policeman suddenly asked, 'Who's this?' He snapped his fingers, without bothering to look at Odette. 'Is this the wife?'

'No, no,' Jack continued laughing, awkwardly. 'I don't know the lady.'

The policeman leaned forward. 'Come on, Jack. I saw you talking with her earlier on. It looked like you were having a lovers' blue. A secret rendezvous at the railway station?' He winked. 'You must be a bit of a romantic, Jack.'

Jack nervously shifted in his seat. 'No, it's not that way at all. We've just been sitting here having a social talk.'

'Really?' The policeman turned to Odette. 'And you would be?'

Odette reached into her handbag and handed him the travel permit.

'You've got a sick relative?' the policeman asked.

'That's right,' Odette said. 'My cousin.'

'They give you free rein just to visit a cousin, when you people have so many of them.' He frowned. 'We're going soft. This citizenship talk. The Commies have you lot behaving uppity.' He looked at the permit a second time. 'Bill Shea,' he sneered. 'Didn't know that barge-arse was still on the job. He's soft as butter, old Bill.' The officer handed the permit back to Odette. 'This document is only good for a week. I don't really care if you want to cat about with old Jacky here, even at your age, but make sure you're back in Deane before your seven days is up. I'll make a point of ringing old Bill myself, to check that you're back where you're supposed to be. In your place.'

The policeman took a notebook and pencil from the front pocket of his tunic and wrote a reminder to himself. He grabbed Sissy's empty chair, placed it alongside Jack Haines and sat next to him. 'These exemption certificates, for them to be valid, Jack, you know you have to stay out of trouble, don't you?'

'Of course, I do,' Jack answered. 'I keep a clean sheet. I've been in no trouble with the police.'

The policeman placed a firm hand on Jack's shoulder. 'You be sure then not to associate with Aborigines, *of any caste*, starting with your lady friend here. If you're caught hanging around the blackfellas, you'll find yourself reclassified and you'll be back with the mob. Do you understand what I'm saying, Jack?'

Jack nodded. 'I do.'

The policeman noticed a half-drunk tea cup and toast crusts on a plate next to Odette. 'Looks like we have a third for lunch. Who's sitting here?'

'Nobody,' Jack answered quickly. 'The dirty dishes were here when I sat down. They're too busy here today for them to clear up.'

The policeman gave Odette a final look before walking away. Jack got to his feet, eager to be on his way. 'We both best get moving or we'll miss the train.'

Odette was shaken by the interrogation, particularly the humiliating manner in which Jack had been treated. 'Yes, you're right.' She stood and picked up her suitcase. 'And I need to fetch Sissy.'

'I'm really sorry about all of this,' Jack said.

'For what?'

'For that copper speaking to you the way he did, showing you, a decent woman, no respect.'

'I was just thinking the same about you, Jack,' she said. 'I'm sorry about how I behaved to you before. I have no right to judge you, no right at all. I can see you're a good man. Whatever you need to do to care for your family, it would be the proper thing. And that policeman, I'd have been surprised if the man treated me any differently than he did. I don't have the time to take blame out on a fella like him.'

'But he was rude to you. How's he without blame?'

'Because they're the ones we deal with every day of our lives. Police. Not the Welfare or the ones who write the rules for the government. Think if you were police, Jack, knowing that one day you'd be told to go into a house and take kiddies away from their family. If you were to treat people with any decency, you couldn't do that job. This fella giving us a hard time, he needs to be angry at us. Maybe even hate us. The only way they get by.' Odette looked across the cafeteria for Sissy. 'I best go,' she nodded to Jack. 'You look after yourself.'

As she stood, Jack gently squeezed her arm and walked away.

Sissy fell in behind her grandmother as she walked past on her way to the toilets. A woman stood at the sink in front of a mirror, applying lipstick. One of the cubicles was locked and the door on a second cubicle was slightly ajar. Odette knocked gently at the door and waited for a response. She heard nothing and pushed the door open. A teenage boy was huddled in the corner. Odette recognised his face from the photograph the Immigration officer had shown Jack. He was petrified. She closed the door and called out to Sissy. 'Come on, let's be going.'

Sissy was curious about the liquid soap dispenser over the sink. She'd never seen one before, and wanted to wash her hands to test it out. Another woman walked into the toilets and opened the door where the runaway was hiding. She screamed with fear and ran from the toilets and into the cafeteria calling for help. The Immigration officers and the policeman ran into the room, found the runaway boy and dragged him out of the cubicle, forcing him to his feet. He was quickly handcuffed and led back through the cafeteria, crying out in a foreign language.

Odette waited with Sissy until the commotion was over before they walked back to the train. In the compartment Sissy rested her head against her grandmother's shoulder. 'That boy back there,' she said, 'the one the men took away. What did he do that was wrong?'

'I don't know, Sweet. Maybe he did nothing wrong. You don't have to do a lot wrong to find yourself in trouble,' she said. 'Not in this country.'

'Nan, I don't want to call you Auntie again. It's not the same. I don't want to do it.'

Odette patted the small of Sissy's back. 'You will have to sometimes but only when it's needed. And I think you're smart enough to know when that has to be without me having to tell you.'

'I will?'

'Yes, you will. You're as smart as they come, Sissy, and you're going to have to trust yourself to know what is best for you.'

'We're in trouble, aren't we, Nan?'

Odette actually laughed, surprising her granddaughter. 'Trouble? Our people have been in one sort of trouble or another from the first day we set eyes on a white person.'

Sissy soon fell asleep and Odette looked out of the window at the changing landscape. The open country was gradually replaced by undulating forest. Odette thought about Jimmy Brown. Jack Haines said he was a born runner. Odette's own family had been the opposite. They'd refused to run, sometimes at great cost to themselves. Odette herself had always felt secure staying put. She believed her strength came from the old people who'd passed on. Without their presence, she was certain she'd have given up her struggle long ago. Now, for the first time in her life, she was experiencing what it felt like to be a long way from home, with hundreds of miles still to go. It was a terrible lonely feeling.

CHAPTER THIRTEEN

The train entered the outskirts of the city. Streets, factories and houses came into view. A tall chimney in the distance spewed dark smoke into the air. Odette and Sissy had seen nothing like the view outside the train window.

'Is this the city, Nan?' Sissy asked.

'I guess so,' Odette answered warily. 'It must be.'

'It looks ugly,' Sissy said.

'It sure does.'

Minutes later the train pulled into the capital's central station. Sissy insisted on carrying the case. As they stepped from the train they were confronted by a wall of moving passengers. Odette had never encountered so many people in the one place. She made the mistake of coming to a halt on the platform and was swept along by the crowd. Sissy reached out for her grandmother. Odette grabbed hold of the suitcase handle and Sissy was carried along with her. Announcements from each of the twelve platforms blended into a singular inaudible garble. Sissy lost her grip and was twice separated from Odette. They were eventually marooned together on a wooden bench next to a booth selling cigarettes, newspapers and sweets. Odette landed on the wooden seat with a thud. Sissy fell beside her, a little stunned.

'This is crazy, Nan.'

'Too right. It's the craziest place I've ever seen.'

Each time Odette considered standing and making a move the crowd gathered momentum. She heard someone calling her name, looked up and was relieved to see the smiling face of Jack Haines, bobbing up and down among countless others. He manoeuvred his way across the platform to the bench.

'It can get pretty wild, this place,' he shouted above the noise. 'But don't you worry, it will slow down soon enough. This lot have just got off work for the day. They call it *the rush hour* here in the city.'

'It's living up to its name,' Odette observed.

'You get used to it,' Jack said. 'I don't mind it anymore.' He leaned forward and spoke into Odette's ear. 'I never asked you, why have you and your young granddaughter come all this way?'

Odette looked across to Sissy. The girl was in a trance, spellbound by the passing crowd. Odette stood up and lowered her voice. 'I'm hoping to find my daughter,' she said. 'Sissy's mother. I haven't seen her in over twelve years and it's urgent that I find her. I'm worried for Sissy. I've been ill of late and I'd like to find her mum so that she can take care of her.'

'Is that the only reason?' Jack asked. 'I saw the way you looked at that copper.'

Odette had little energy to explain the threat that Lowe posed to Sissy. 'That's the main reason I'm here,' she said. 'I need to find my daughter.'

'Do you know where she lives?' Jack asked

'I don't know much at all. I haven't heard a word from her in close to two years when I last had a letter from her. And that didn't tell me much. All I have is the name of a café where she was working at the time.'

'That's it?' Jack frowned.

'All I know is that she was working in this town.'

Jack gestured towards the passing crowd. 'Well, finding her won't be easy. First up, this is not a town, it's a city. A big city at that. They say there's nearly two million people that live here. Do you understand what you're up against?'

'I do now,' Odette answered, her voice straining.

'Does she spend time with other Aboriginal people, your daughter?'

'I know nothing more than what she's written to me. I don't think she wants to be found, to be honest.'

The comment did not surprise Jack. Those who wanted to escape the shackles of the Act, could apply for an exemption certificate like he had. Others passed themselves off as white if they were fair enough, or sometimes Indian if they were coloured, others disappeared completely.

'Your daughter,' he asked, 'is she fair-skinned, like your granddaughter?'

Odette turned to Sissy, who was standing and studying the crowd, wide-eyed. 'No. Lila is more my colour, not quite as dark as me.'

'Okay. You give me her full name and I'll ask around. If

she's got friends inside the community someone will know her and most likely where she is. Where will you be staying while you're here?' he asked.

'I don't really know,' Odette said. She felt silly, not having considered where she and Sissy would be staying. 'I'll need to find a boarding house, I suppose.'

'You two could come home to our place,' Jack offered. 'My wife, Alma, she'd love to have the company. I drive her mad when I'm home. I reckon she'd fall in love with your granddaughter quick smart.'

'I thought you didn't mix with Aboriginal people, because of the exemption rules,' Odette said. She immediately regretted the comment, considering the generosity of Jack's offer. If Jack was offended, it didn't show on his face.

'Well, I don't,' he explained. 'Not when I'm out on the road. The police in them small towns have too much time on their hands. Here in the city, you'd be surprised. It doesn't take much for a blackfellla to become invisible. Most people, they don't know much about us and don't want to know. Except for the ones involved in the citizenship business. And most of them are either Churchies or Union people. As far as the rest go, as long as we keep our heads down and steer clear of trouble, we don't have a lot of problems getting by. It's like we're ghosts.' He chuckled to himself. 'Ghosts from the past.'

'How do you manage that, Jack?' Odette asked. 'Keep yourself out of trouble? I can see you've got some cheek.'

'Years back I set myself strict rules and I stick by them. I only have a beer when I'm in my own home, I pay all my bills up front and on time, and I do the best I can not to answer back. It doesn't always stick, that last rule, but I try my best.'

'There'd be a heavy price to pay for having to check yourself that way, I would think,' Odette lamented.

'There is. For a start, looking down at your feet too often rather than up, like a man should be entitled to do. That's one cost. In the end, it's worth it. I'm not proud of what I've had to do over the years, like having to beg for that exemption paper. I'm not ashamed of myself either. I do what's needed to get by. Simple as that. So, what about my offer? We can put you and the girl up while you search around for your daughter.'

'No, I can't let you do that,' Odette said. 'I'm grateful. I am. But we'll be alright. I know how to look after myself.'

'I have no doubt of that,' Jack said. 'You're a strong woman. A stubborn one too, if you don't mind me saying so. That's a part of what gets you women through, staying stubborn and tough. My wife, Alma, is stronger than any man I've known. Can you at least let me give you something before we go our separate ways?' Jack searched his jacket pockets for a pencil. He picked up an empty cigarette packet from the ground, tore off a stub and wrote his address on the back. He handed the stub to Odette. 'This is where me and my family is at. We're only three railway stations out of the city on one of the suburban lines. Then its two streets away from the station. We're not hard to find. If you change your mind about staying, all you have to do is turn up on the doorstep. We have no lock on the back door and you can sit in the kitchen and make yourself a cup of tea until somebody gets home.'

'Thank you,' Odette said. 'I really am grateful.'

'What's your daughter's name?' Jack asked.

'Lila. Lila Brown.'

'Okay. I'll ask around. Maybe someone has heard of her. If anything comes up how can I get hold of you?'

'I don't know yet.' Odette realised she didn't want to lose contact with Jack Haines. His warmth had impacted on her. 'I'll write you at your address as soon as we have settled, and let you know where we are.'

'Good luck with your search then,' Jack said. He walked away and was quickly lost in the crowd.

Odette put Jack's address in her pocket. She turned to Sissy. 'It's time to go,' she said. But Sissy had already gone.

Odette walked the length of the platform frantically calling Sissy's name. She reached the end of the platform, turned and walked in the opposite direction, without finding her. She searched every platform of the vast station, watching trains pulling into platforms and people pouring in and out of carriages. If Sissy was caught in the crowd, Odette doubted she'd find her. She walked down a ramp to a subway lined with shops: a café, bootmaker, a dry-cleaner and a newsagency. She was too breathless to go on. She sat in a chair next to a weighing machine, dropped her case on the ground and cursed herself for her own stupidity, in not keeping a watchful eye on Sissy. A station porter, riding by on a baggage trolley, noticed her distress and pulled up alongside her. 'Hey, what's up, Love?' he asked, showing genuine concern. 'You look like you need some help.'

Odette looked up at a man with a red bloated face, a white man. He had beads of sweat on his forehead and a worker's cap on his head, cheekily tilted to one side. She did the best she could to compose herself.

'I've lost a girl, in my care. We were sitting down for a rest and I looked around and she was gone. I've searched everywhere and I can't find her.'

He hopped off the trolley and sat next to Odette. 'You tell me how old she is.'

'She's only just turned thirteen.'

'Thirteen. I'm sure she'll be right then.'

'But she's never been to the city before, and she won't know what to do with herself, being alone.'

'Well, when anyone's lost or separated at the station, we tell them to go to the Traveller's Aid Society and wait there to be collected. If she's approached any of our staff for help, that's where she'll be.' He stood up and patted the narrow seat of his trolley. 'You look tired, Love. Hop up next to me and I'll take you up there.'

'You mean on the trolley?'

'I do. Let me take you on a royal tour.'

The baggage trolley chugged along the subway and strained up a steep ramp. Odette was sure people were staring at her as she passed by. The station porter pulled up outside an office and hopped down from the trolley. 'Let me help you down,' he said, taking Odette by the arm. 'You go through that door and make enquiries. I would just about bet my house that she's in there waiting for you. On the off-chance she's not, the ladies in there will help you out.'

'Thank you,' Odette said. 'You've been so helpful.'

The porter looked bemused as he handed Odette her suitcase. 'You shouldn't expect any less, Love.'

Odette walked through the door and saw Sissy sitting at a table with a cup of tea and a biscuit. Sissy smiled when she saw Odette. 'These are chocolate,' she said, holding up the biscuit.

'Where'd you get to?' Odette demanded. 'And why so calm? I've been sick with worry searching for you.'

'I'm sorry, Nan, I really am. You were busy talking to Jack and I needed to go to the toilet. Bad. And I didn't want to bother you. I was going to come straight back to where you were sitting, but when I came out of the toilet I couldn't remember the platform we were on. There were so many people around and so much noise, I got lost. I'm sorry.'

Odette's beating heart eased. 'Well, I hope you are sorry.' She leaned forward. 'Sissy,' she whispered, 'it's best you call me Auntie again.'

'Why?'

Odette looked at two women behind the long wooden counter. 'Because we don't know these people and we need to be careful. I talked to you about this on the train.'

Sissy nervously tugged at her fringe. 'Nan, I'm sorry, but I already told them that I'd lost you. The lady asked who I'd travelled with and I told her my grandmother. I forgot all about the white girl story.'

One of the volunteers walked over to Odette. 'So, you found each other? I'm so pleased.'

'Yes,' Odette said, cautiously.

'Good.' The woman smiled. 'You must have been so worried. Please let me fetch you a cup of tea.'

Sissy placed a hand on Odette's leg. 'You can have a chocolate biscuit as well, Nan. They're free.'

The woman returned with Odette's cup of tea.

'I think I'm the one who should be sorry,' Odette said. 'Your Nan didn't give this adventure enough thought before we took off.'

'You don't have to be sorry, Nan. I was the one who got lost. And you had no choice,' Sissy said.

'How do you mean?'

'When you went to the police station and asked for help, you got none.'

Sissy's comment surprised Odette. 'How do you know that?'

'Because I woke up in the night and heard you talking to Bill Shea. And then yesterday you packed up the clothes and money and took me to the cemetery. To say goodbye.'

'Goodbye?'

'Yeah, Nan. I don't know what we're doing here. But I don't think we're going back to Quarrytown.'

'And when did you work all this out?'

'On the train ride. I did some thinking.'

The volunteer approached Odette. 'I bet that cup of tea has done some good?'

'Yes, thank you,' she said. 'It was just what I needed.'

'Good. Are you returning home to the city or visiting?'

'We're visiting,' Sissy interrupted. 'It's a holiday.'

'How long do you plan to be here?'

'I'm not sure,' Odette said.

'And do you have accommodation?' the woman asked.

'No,' Odette said. 'I'm sorry. We should have planned ahead. We're not experienced travellers.'

'Well, don't worry yourself,' the woman said. 'We can help you out with a hotel. Do you have a preference?'

Odette sighed. 'I would like somewhere that is quiet. Somewhere suitable for children.'

The woman smiled. 'I know just the place.' She walked over to a wooden bookcase and returned with a sheet of paper. 'This hotel is only three blocks from here. You can take the bus or walk. The hotel is small, the rates are reasonable, and best of all it's a temperance establishment. No alcohol. It keeps the riff-raff away.' She handed Odette the sheet of paper. 'There's a map on the back if you need it.'

The pace of the street was frenetic. Odette ordered Sissy to hold on to her hand. 'Don't you dare let go, whatever happens.'

They stood at the intersection outside the station for several minutes while Odette studied the map and looked up at the street signs. 'This way,' she said finally, with uncertainty.

Sissy was fascinated by the sounds of the street, a police siren in the distance, a choir of newspaper boys and the rhythm of marching feet. 'Hey, this is exciting, Nan,' she said.

'You think so?' Odette thought it more frightening than anything else.

Approaching the next intersection, they saw a man standing on the lower rungs of a wooden ladder. A hand-painted sign resting against the ladder announced: *Jesus Saves – at 8 o'clock tonight*. He preached at the top of his voice, competing with the din of the street. A woman standing nearby, wearing what Odette was sure was a wheat sack patterned into an ankle-length skirt, offered her a pamphlet. 'Will you allow Jesus into your life?' she asked. 'He will arrive at our church at eight tonight.'

'Well, I'm glad he's punctual,' Odette quipped. 'But, no

thank you,' she said, with as much politeness as she could summon.

The woman frowned and gritted her teeth. 'If you do not come, you will be punished. Satan will take you.'

Such damnation never frightened Odette. Millie Khan had once asked her if she believed in the devil. Odette had shaken her head. 'No, but even if he was true, this devil fella, how could he be any worse than some white people we know?'

Crossing the street, Sissy arched her neck and looked up at the tall building on the next street corner. As she counted the number of floors she was knocked to the ground by a pedestrian rushing past in the opposite direction.

Odette helped her to her feet. 'Can I make a suggestion? Keep your eyes on what you can see in front of you and not what's in the sky.'

At the next corner Odette turned left, as the map instructed. She searched for the street number, two-twenty-nine, and the name of the hotel, *Temperance Palace.*

'Here it is,' she said to Sissy, pointing at a sign above the entrance.

The hotel didn't resemble the palace Sissy had imagined. The foyer was lined with wood panelling. It was gloomy, with a scent of disinfectant in the air. Odette approached the reception desk and read a small sign: *Please ring the bell – only once!*

'Can I ring it, please?' Sissy asked.

Odette placed her suitcase on the floor. 'Go ahead. But not too loud.'

Sissy tapped the bell, as gently as possible. A young woman with dark hair and olive skin appeared from a doorway behind the reception desk. 'Can I help you?'

Odette had not been in a hotel before and wasn't sure what to ask for. 'I need a bed for myself and the young girl here.'

The receptionist looked over at Sissy. 'Are you and the girl related?'

'I'm sorry?' Odette asked

'Would you prefer two single beds or a double to share?'

Odette had never slept in a double bed, alone or with anyone else. The thought of sleeping in a separate bed from Sissy felt alien to her but she suspected if she asked for a double bed the woman would think it odd behaviour for an Aboriginal 'Auntie' escorting a young white girl.

'We'll have two beds. Yes, two singles.'

'Fine. And how many nights are you expecting to be staying with us?'

Odette looked up at the calendar on the wall behind the reception desk. 'I can't be sure. Two nights, but maybe more.'

'That will be fine. We can book you in for two nights to begin with and take it from there.'

The receptionist handed Odette a card listing the room prices, services and conditions. Odette unbuckled her case and took out several notes. 'Here you are.'

'Oh no,' the woman said, raising a hand. 'You don't need to pay until you're ready to check out. I take it that you want the room?'

'Yes, we will take it. Thank you.'

The receptionist handed Odette the key to the room and pointed out the locations of the dining room, lounge, library and laundry. 'Where have you come from?' she asked.

'Oh, we've travelled a long way.' Odette answered, without offering further details. 'We've been on the train all day.'

'Oh, you must be hungry. I bet you would like a cheese sandwich and a cup of tea,' she said to Sissy.

'Yes please,' Sissy said.

'Wait here for a few minutes and I will arrange food for you and show you the way to your room.'

The receptionist soon returned with a tray of food and asked Odette and Sissy to follow her to their room. Odette trailed behind as they climbed the narrow staircase. She heard the receptionist up ahead, chatting to Sissy as she put a key in a door and unlocked it. 'Here we are,' she announced.

By the time Odette reached the room she was short of breath. The receptionist handed her the key. 'You take care,' she said. She stopped and looked closely at Odette. It appeared that she wanted to say something more, but she excused herself and returned downstairs.

Sissy jumped from one bed to the other and back again. 'Have you seen anything better than this, Nan? Two beds in one room!'

'I've never seen such bad manners from you,' Odette said. 'You'll break something, doing that. Maybe a leg. Or the bed. Hop down and we'll have these sandwiches.'

The décor in the room was similar to the hotel lobby, dark and lined with wood. The beds had been pushed to the walls to create a narrow centre aisle. The room was otherwise bare, except for a Bible sitting on a shelf above one of the beds. Odette sat the tray of food on one bed and she and Sissy sat on the other, eating quietly and drinking tea. When they'd finished, Odette left the tray on a seat outside the room. She took her nightgown and Sissy's pyjamas out of the case. All Odette wanted to do was hop into bed and sleep.

'I need to go to the toilet,' Sissy said.

'It's along the corridor next to the stairs. You go and be straight back. And then I will go after you.'

Once Sissy had gone Odette took the bundle of letters out of the case and untied the string. She opened the final letter her daughter had written her, one of the few with a legible postmark. She read the revealing words: *I'm working at a café, the Arizona. I will send money soon.* When she heard Sissy's footsteps in the hallway, Odette returned the letter to the case and quickly closed the lid.

'Nan, guess what?' Sissy said, standing in the doorway

'Sorry, Love, but I'm too tired to guess anything. You'll have to tell me.'

Sissy held out her hand. 'I can't tell you. Come with me and I'll show you instead. It's a surprise.'

'But I'm tired, too tired for games and you're getting too big to play them.'

'Please, Nan. It'll be worth it.' Sissy guided Odette along the corridor and stopped at a door. 'Close your eyes, Nan.'

Odette did as she was told and blindly shuffled into a room, guided by her granddaughter. Sissy clapped her hands together. 'Open them!'

Odette had never been inside a proper bathroom. Some of the farms she'd worked on claimed to have bathrooms, but they'd been crude affairs, no more than glorified lean-tos at the rear of a farmhouse, constructed from corrugated-iron sheets above a brick floor. The hotel bathroom had white tiles on the floors and walls, chrome taps and a bath as big as the one in the backyard at Quarrytown. The hotel bath was finished in sparkling porcelain.

'Watch this,' Sissy said. She turned on a tap above the bath and pointed to the steam. 'The hot water comes out as soon as the tap is turned on. You don't have to build a fire under this one.' She turned the tap off and on again. 'See, Nan. It keeps on coming.'

Odette was suitably impressed. 'I don't believe a Queen would have a bathtub any better than this one.'

'Well, you're my Queen, Nan. I want you to get in.'

'What do mean, *get in*? Don't be silly. I can't do that.'

'Yes, you can. I'm going to fill it up for you.' She opened a cupboard door. 'And there's fluffy towels in here and tiny bars of soap.'

'I can't do this. Someone might come along.'

'It doesn't matter,' Sissy said. She walked over to the door. 'There's a lock on the door. Nobody can come in. Hop in the bath and I'll get your nightie for you.'

Sissy ignored her grandmother's protests. She put the plug in the bath, turned on the taps and went to fetch Odette's dressing gown. When she returned, Odette was standing in the middle of the room, fully dressed.

'Come on, Nan. You have to take your clothes off.'

'I will after you leave,' Odette said. 'Once you've left I will lock the door.'

After Sissy left Odette stood watching the flow of hot water streaming into the tub. She placed the palm of one of her hands against the white tiled wall. It was completely unmarked; no dust, no mildew, no cracked or broken tiles. She walked around the room, allowing her hand to glide across the cool surfaces. She sat on the edge of the bath and slipped her fingers into the clearest water she'd ever seen. As much as she would have enjoyed soaking her weary body in the bath, Odette could not bring herself to hop in. Such a luxury was more than she could contemplate. She pulled out the plug and stood back. She was struck by how quickly the water gurgled down the drain. She wondered how people could afford such waste. She changed into her nightgown, put her cardigan on over the top, and went back to the room. Sissy was laying on one of the beds.

'That was quick, Nan. Did you have the bath?'

'Of course, I did.'

'Are you sure?' Sissy asked, suspiciously. 'Your hair is dry.'

'It's dry because I didn't wash it. How many times have I told you that you never wash your hair before getting into bed. The cold you catch could kill you. Are we back with your twenty questions?'

'Nope. I was just wondering.' Sissy didn't want to worry her grandmother more than she was already.

'Well, wonder no more. I'm dead tired. You're going to have to chat to yourself if you have anything more to say tonight. I will be fast asleep.' Odette didn't bother turning down the blankets. She lay on top of the bed and fell asleep.

Sissy looked across at her grandmother. She didn't know what Odette was suffering from, but she now realised that her grandmother was sicker than she'd let on. She got down from her own bed, pulled the bedspread and blankets off the top and used them to cover Odette. Sissy turned the light off, stood in the darkness for a moment, and then climbed into bed beside Odette. She wrapped her body around her grandmother's, and was comforted by the old woman's warmth.

CHAPTER FOURTEEN

Odette rolled over, lifted her arm and accidentally slapped Sissy in the face. She opened one eye. 'Sorry, Bub,' she croaked. 'Your Nan can be a clumsy old girl sometimes.'

Sissy giggled and patted Odette on the cheek. 'You always do that.'

'No, I don't.'

'But you do,' Sissy whispered, playfully. She turned onto her stomach. 'What are we doing today?'

Odette rubbed her eyes and coughed. 'Well, I have to go out this morning, and I need you to stay here in the hotel. I have to see a doctor in the city.'

'What sort of doctor?'

'A specialist is what they call them.'

'I want to come with you, Nan.'

'I'd love you to do that, keep me company. But I could be waiting awhile. It's best for you to stay here. I'll feel better knowing you're not sitting around with strangers. Hey, we should get out of bed, both of us. We'll get dressed, have breakfast together and then I'll have to get going. I don't want to be late.'

After breakfast, Odette spoke to the receptionist and arranged a time for Sissy's lunch. Odette searched the pages of the telephone book and found the address of the café that Lila had mentioned in her last letter, the Arizona.

'Are we far from King Street?' Odette asked the receptionist.

'No more than a fifteen-minute walk. Let me write the directions down for you.'

Odette left the hotel with the address of the Arizona café in her handbag. Walking through the city she was awestruck by the crowds in the streets – men in suits, young women in beautiful frocks and older women wearing cleaning aprons. She watched the faces of the young women in particular, speculating that any one of them could be Lila. She was drawn to a woman in a red floral dress with dark hair and coffee skin. As the woman brushed by, Odette had to resist the urge to reach out and touch her. The distraction caused her to walk straight past the café. She turned back and found the café shut. There was a handwritten sign taped to the door: *Open at 11.* Odette had more than an hour to spare.

The State Museum on the corner opposite caught her eye. Odette crossed the street and walked up the steps into the grand foyer of the building. Unknown to her, the museum had been built using the same stone mined by the Aboriginal workers of Quarrytown. The floor of the entrance hall was finished in colourful patterned tiles and the ceiling was decorated in gold leaf. A marble staircase ran either side of a large central statue of Queen Victoria. Odette had never seen such a fine building.

She listened to the echoing footsteps and whispers of a group of schoolgirls walking up the stairs. Following them, she found herself in a cavernous room lined with cabinets full of antique guns and swords, stuffed animals and skeletons, and row after row of colourful but dead butterflies. Odette leaned forward and examined the wings of a spectacular specimen. It was similar to the butterflies she'd sometimes seen in the bush on the outskirts of Deane. She shook her head with dismay. It made no sense that a person would do something as senseless as kill and spear a butterfly and put it in a glass case.

The next room contained a menagerie of stuffed snakes, gorillas and birds. One side of the hall housed a display of dioramas – *Cultures of the World.* In the first scene, Odette stood before a collection of penguins crossing an imaginary ice shelf. Behind them stood a mannequin, a fur-coated hunter, poised to spear a fish. A group of young boys stood in front of the adjoining diorama. One of them imitated the sounds of a monkey and beat his fists against his chest. His friends laughed at him. *More of them poor gorillas,* Odette thought. Approaching the diorama, she discovered the boys were not mimicking a monkey, or any other animal, but an *Ancient Aborigine.*

Odette stared at the figures of a man, woman and two children sitting around a campfire. Each of the wide-eyed figures, painted jet black, were unable to contain their broad smiles. One of the schoolboys turned, looked at Odette and whispered in his friend's ear. Odette turned away too quickly and crashed into another display case. She was confronted by a full human skeleton, the bones held together with copper wire, screws and metal rods. The skeleton was separated from her by a fine sheet of glass. Odette read the label attached to the display case – *Aboriginal Woman of Australia.* She backed away in horror and hurried from the building. When she reached the front steps she was gasping for air and sat down. The sight of the skeleton shocked her. It reminded her of seeing her own skeleton, X-rayed at the hospital in Gatlin. The schoolgirls Odette had followed earlier were also sitting on the steps. They wore pleated woollen skirts, monogrammed blazers, long white socks and polished shoes. Each girl wore her hair long and plaited, or tied in a ponytail with a red ribbon. Odette tried to imagine Sissy sitting among them. Would she fit in with these girls? What would she have to say for herself? *Sissy could do it,* Odette thought, *hold her own.* But the thought vanished just as quickly as it had come. Sissy wasn't one of them and never would be. Odette could pass her granddaughter off as white, out of necessity, but the child could never be one of them.

When Sissy went back to the room after breakfast she opened Odette's suitcase, looking for a book to read. Instead of her book she found the picture frame that held the photograph of her mother. It was empty. She couldn't understand why Odette would have removed the picture. She laid the empty frame on the floor. Even though she knew she shouldn't, Sissy couldn't help but search through the case. She took out Odette's woollen cardigan. A corner of a cigarette packet fell from one of the pockets. Jack Haines' name and address was written on it in pencil. Sissy returned it to the pocket. She took an envelope out of the case, opened it and found two photographs. She stared at the faces of two mysterious young girls. She put the photographs on the floor beside the empty frame. The girls were fair-skinned and their hair was such a rich red it appeared to be on fire. She looked from the older girl to the younger one and back again. They were very much alike, obviously sisters. She continued rummaging through the case and soon found the rolls of money she'd seen Odette counting at the kitchen table. She returned the money to the zip pocket where she'd found it. A bundle of letters, tied together with string, was her next find. Sissy untied the string and lay each of the envelopes on the bed. She read the address on the front of the first letter. *Mrs Odette Brown, c/- Deane Post Office.* She turned the envelope over. There was no return address. She spread the letters on the bed in the order she'd found them. She was desperately curious to read them even though she knew she shouldn't. She snatched the first envelope from the bed, stuck it in the sleeve of her cardigan and left the room.

The receptionist heard Sissy coming down the stairs. 'Are you hungry again, already?' she asked.

Sissy had decided the night before that she liked the receptionist. 'Yes, I am.'

'Well, breakfast has finished and the cook is on a break, but no matter. You find a seat in the dining room and I'll make you something.'

Sissy felt important seated at a table with a proper cloth napkin, unchipped crockery and matching knives and forks.

'I'm not much of a cook myself,' the receptionist said. 'Would you settle for a bowl of tomato soup and a sandwich?'

'Yes, please,' Sissy said.

'Good. I didn't introduce myself last night. I'm Wanda.'

'Thank you, Wanda,' Sissy replied. She dabbed her lips with the clean napkin. 'I'm Sissy.'

As she ate, Sissy thought about the letter tucked into the sleeve of her jumper. It scratched at her skin. When she'd finished her soup and sandwich, Wanda brought a plate of biscuits over to the table.

'Here you are.' Wanda continued to stand at the side of the table while Sissy concentrated on a cream biscuit. 'You've come a long way,' Wanda said.

'Yes, we did. We were hours on the train,' Sissy answered, taking a second bite of the biscuit.

'Where did you begin the trip?'

'From Gatlin. But first we drove from where we live at Deane, with Henry Lamb. He's Na ... Odette's old friend from when they were younger. He drove us to the station.'

'Deane? And that's where you've always lived?'

'It is.'

'And Odette? She's your?'

Wanda's questions began to bother Sissy. She didn't answer, hoping it would be enough of a signal for Wanda to leave her alone. The receptionist tried a different tack. 'Odette, she's a lovely woman, isn't she?'

Sissy thought carefully about her answer. 'Odette is a very nice lady.' She wiped her mouth with a cloth napkin. 'I have to go now, to our room.'

'We must talk again,' Wanda said.

'Yes,' Sissy answered politely. 'When Odette comes back.'

Walking slowly up the stairs, purposely counting each step as she climbed, Sissy regretted taking the bundle of letters from her grandmother's case even though she already knew she was about to read them. She was certain they contained information about her. When she opened the door she looked across to the bed. The letters were waiting for her. She took the envelope from the sleeve of her cardigan, sat down, slowly opened it and took the letter out, carefully unfolding the sheet of writing paper. She read the single, blunt paragraph several times before picking up the second envelope.

Sissy read each of the letters. They had little to say and explained nothing about why her mother had left her, what she was doing with her life, or when she might return home. Worst of all, her mother hadn't talked about her at all. Sissy had only been mentioned twice as *the baby.* She was furious. She'd conjured so many fanciful but loving thoughts about her mother over the years. It wasn't that the letters told her a different story about her mother, but that they told her nothing. She picked up the first letter and tore the envelope down the centre. She tore it again and again into smaller pieces. She ripped the remaining letters apart with increasing anger, eventually leaving a frenzy of confetti across the bed and on the floor.

The tolling of church bells in the distance roused Odette to her feet. She struggled down the museum steps and made her way back across the street to the café. A waitress was sweeping the footpath out the front. Odette waited until the waitress went back inside before following her in. The blinds were drawn across the window. Odette could hear the voice of Hank Williams wailing a familiar chorus. She'd heard the tune many times on the mantle radio in her kitchen at home. The sadness in his voice appealed to Aboriginal people.

'Take a seat,' the waitress called from the open kitchen.

The café floor was covered in black and white chequerboard tiles and the walls were decorated with pictures of Hollywood movie stars. Odette sat at a booth, opened her handbag, took out the photograph of Lila and placed it on the table.

The waitress came over to the booth and pulled a pencil from behind her ear. 'What can I get for you, Love?'

'Do you have any food?' Odette asked.

'Yeah, it's all on the board there,' the waitress answered, nodding in the direction of a blackboard menu above the counter.

Odette couldn't read the menu from such a distance. 'I'll just have a drink, please.'

'Yeah. What? Coffee? A cold drink?'

Odette had drunk coffee only once before in her life. Although she'd enjoyed the smell, the drink had tasted awful.

'Do you have tea?' she asked.

'Tea?' the waitress replied. 'Yeah I can get you a tea. Some milk and sugar with it?'

'Yes, please.'

Odette watched the waitress cross the floor and tried to imagine Lila working in such a place. She realised it was difficult to imagine her daughter at all after twelve years. The waitress returned with a weak white tea, slopping over the sides of a mug. She plonked it on the table. Odette had the photograph of Lila in her hand.

'Excuse me,' she said, just as the waitress was about to walk away.

The waitress clicked her fingers together. 'You don't have to tell me, Love. I forgot the sugar.'

'No. It's not that. It's something else.' Odette showed her

the photograph. 'I'm looking for this girl. I believe that she used to work here, in this café?'

The waitress glanced briefly at the photograph. 'Wouldn't have worked here. The boss doesn't hire the young ones. They're too much trouble.'

'No. This was taken many years ago. If she'd worked here, it would have been around two years back.'

'I was working here then,' the waitress said. 'What's her name?'

'Lila. Lila Brown.'

'Lila? We've had no Lila in here, not in my time, and I've been here for five years or more.'

'Can you take a closer look?' Odette asked. 'Please. It's important.'

The waitress took the photograph from Odette and studied it more closely. 'Hang on. Are you sure this girl's name is Lila?'

'Yes. That's her name,' Odette said. 'Why?'

'Well, she looks a lot like Lorna. She worked here maybe two years ago. Could have been a bit less. She was here for maybe six months and took off out of the blue. This one, in the picture, she's a lot younger. But I think it might be the same girl. Hold on, let's get a second opinion.'

The waitress walked over to the counter and called out, 'Alfie! I need you out here.' She walked back to the booth. 'The boss is on his way out. He studies the form guide about this time every morning. Hasn't picked a winner in a year. We'll ask him.'

The boss, Alfie, was aptly built, like a jockey. He wore a crumpled and stained powder-blue suit.

'What do you want, Sheila,' he grumbled, without so much as a nod to Odette. 'I'm working back there.'

Sheila picked up the photograph. 'Take a look at this picture and tell me who it is.'

'What's this, a joke?' he asked. 'I don't give a fuck who it is. I'm organising my bets. You should know better than to interrupt.'

'Come on,' Sheila laughed. 'It's a game, Alf. See if you can guess who this is and I'll give you a prize.'

Alfie snatched the photograph from Sheila, tearing it along one edge. He squinted at the portrait and nodded his head. 'Yeah, I do know her,' he said. 'It's Lorna.'

'You recognise her?' Odette asked, excited.

'Yeah, I know her. She worked here for a few months and then one day she shot through with a Greek fella. When she started here she told me she was Maltese, but I pegged her for Greek straightaway. Didn't I Sheila? It all made sense when she ran off with him. He came in here every morning for a coffee. Yeah, a wog bloke, he was.'

'What was his name?' Odette asked.

'Don't know. Some of our regulars called him Zorba, but I never asked what his true name was. She was a good worker, Lorna. But jumpy.'

'What do you mean?' Odette asked.

'Well, when she first come in for work and I asked her if she had experience she rattled off at least a dozen pubs and cafés in cities and towns along the coast that she'd worked in. Been to more places than Lucky Starr.'

'And while she was here,' Sheila added, 'she was always talking about taking off for the sun. Up north somewhere.

She could never keep still. Unless you put a kid in front of her, of course.'

'A child?' Odette asked.

'Yeah. A kid or a bub. Both did the trick. Anytime one of the working girls came in here with a kid, Lorna would be straight across to the table wanting to nurse it, slobbering it with kisses and hugs. She was as clucky as a girl can get. She had none of her own and I don't reckon her bloke was keen. If you ask me, he was some sort of gigolo. Or a crim. He always had money on him, but as far as I know, he didn't have a job. You know what them foreign blokes are like. They can talk smoother than silk underwear.'

'Do you know where she went, after she left here?'

'Sort of,' Alfie said. 'She sent us a postcard to show she had no hard feelings over me pinching her on the arse now and then.' He winked. 'She was a good sport, Lorna, with that sort of stuff.'

'Could I see it, please? The postcard?' Odette asked, checking her disgust.

'Are you two related?' he asked. 'You don't look much alike.'

'No,' Odette said. 'I'm just a friend of the family. They live in the country and asked me to ask after her.'

Alfie went into the kitchen, returned with a postcard and handed it to Odette. On the front was a picture of a wide sandy beach and deep blue sea. Odette turned the card over. She recognised Lila's handwriting. The card read, *Enjoying the good life with my man!* Odette dropped the postcard on the table. The waitress was looking at her closely when she finally looked up. She tore up the bill.

'Hey, the cuppa's on the house, Love,' she said to Odette. 'You take care.'

Alfie and Sheila walked back into the kitchen. Standing up to leave, Odette overheard them talking. 'You know that she's an Abo, the old girl there,' he said. 'I can pick 'em, most races of the world.'

'So fucking what, Alf? Can't you see she's upset?'

'Upset? Hey, I was just saying. You don't see many of them around here these days.'

Odette walked several city blocks with little sense of purpose, cursing her own stupidity. She'd convinced herself that she would simply arrive in the city and find her daughter waiting for her in the crowd. Now she could see how foolish she'd been. She'd been tested many times in her life but had always managed to find a solution. Back in Deane she sometimes sat by the river and talked with the old people, seeking guidance. There was nobody in the city for her to talk to and she didn't know what to do next.

When she opened the door to the hotel room the first thing she saw was the photographs of Delores Reed's young daughters on the floor. The remains of Lila's letters were strewn across the carpet. Sissy was asleep on the bed, her face buried in a pillow. Odette picked up a scrap of one of the letters and read the faded words. She slowly retrieved the treasured letters, one piece of paper at a time. When she'd finished cleaning up the mess, Odette stood by the bed. The child did not stir. She sat on the spare bed and sifted the mound of paper between her fingers, recreating the sound of a child running through fallen leaves. She felt no anger towards Sissy and, to her surprise, felt some relief that the letters had been destroyed. She'd held onto them over the years in the hope that one day they might have something more to tell her. They never did.

Odette dropped the scraps of paper into the bin. When she turned, she could see Sissy had woken and had one eye open. She was closely watching her grandmother.

'I read them all, Nan,' she said. 'The letters. She never said one word about me in any of those letters.'

'You're right, Sis. She didn't.'

'She mustn't have wanted me,' Sissy added. 'If she'd loved me, she'd have stayed with us. She went away because of me.'

Odette took Sissy's hands in her own and kissed them. 'Don't you be thinking that. Of course she wanted you.'

'If she wanted me, why would she go and not let us know where she was?'

Odette was stuck for a reply. Discovering the truth about what had happened to Lila would only harm Sissy further. 'She had troubles I've only now come to understand. Your mother did love you.' She cupped Sissy's cheeks in her hands. 'And all I've ever wanted is for you to feel love. For her, me, but most of all for yourself.' Odette held her granddaughter in her arms, rocking her gently.

Sissy's eyes were raw and swollen from crying. 'I'm sorry I looked in your suitcase, Nanna.'

'Shush,' Odette whispered. 'There's nothing for you to be sorry for.'

'Those girls, in the photographs, with all the red hair, who are they?'

'They are two poor girls who lost their mum many years ago. I was given those pictures by a man who knew her. I've thought of throwing them away, but I can't do it. It would be wrong of me.'

'I'll take care of the pictures, if you want me to, Nan.'

'We'll see. You have more than enough to deal with, without looking after a pair of orphans.'

Sissy put a hand on her grandmother's cheek. 'I had lunch and spoke to the lady downstairs. She was asking me questions. More questions than I ask you.'

'That would be a lot of questions. What did she want to know?'

'Where did we travel from?'

'And what did you say?'

'I told her that we came on the train from Gatlin, and that we lived in Deane.'

'Oh,' Odette said. 'And what else did she ask?'

'She wanted to know about you. How you were related to me.'

'And what did you say to that?'

'I pretended that I didn't hear what she said.'

'And that was it? She didn't ask anything more?'

'No. I came back up to the room. Is there something wrong, Nan?'

Odette couldn't understand why the receptionist would be interested in her. 'I'm sure she was just being polite. She seems like a nice young woman. You forget about all of this worry. I want you to go to the bathroom and wash your face and hands. And then your Nan is going to take you out.'

'Take me out? What does that mean?'

'It means, we're going to eat out at a nice café, like people do in the city.'

They washed over a sink in the bathroom together, brushed each other's hair and put on fresh sets of clothes. Odette took a ten-pound note from her roll of money and put it in her handbag. 'Are you ready for a night out?' she asked Sissy.

There was a knock at the door. Wanda was standing in the hallway.

'Can I help you?' Odette asked.

'Oh, I didn't realise you were back,' Wanda said. 'I was just checking to see that everything was okay with your … the young girl.'

Odette stepped into the hall and closed the door behind her. 'There's no problem here. Everything's fine with the girl,' Odette insisted.

'Oh, good. I thought she might be lonely. I decided to pay a visit.' Wanda hesitated, reached forward and took hold of Odette's arm, startling her. 'My name is Wanda Harrison,' she said urgently. 'My people are from down south near the border. Along the river.'

'Your people?'

'Aboriginal people. I was taken from my mother when I was four years old. I was brought up in the Saint Mary's Home.'

Odette had heard terrible stories about the infamous Saint Mary's.

'After we came out of the Home,' Wanda explained, 'the Welfare Board would billet us here at the hotel until we were found places in domestic service. I must have made an impression on the manageress. She asked if she could keep me on. She looked after me, sent me to business college here in the city. I'd been working here five years when I decided to try and find my family,' Wanda continued. 'I took a week's holiday, got on a bus and went back home, searching for family. But the reserve was gone. The houses and streets, everything had been bulldozed.'

Odette could see Wanda was desperate to tell her story. It was the way of many Aboriginal people. They kept their silence and their secrets until they found somebody they could confide in.

'Did you find anyone?' Odette asked.

'One cousin out of a mob of ten. The young ones had taken off before they could be picked up. The oldies, my cousin didn't know where they went to, except for two aunties. I searched after them, to see if they had information on my mother. One of the aunties had died. I found the other one. She used to care for me when I was a baby. She was living in a room at the back of a pub where she scrubbed the toilets for meals. It was awful.'

'And your mother?' Odette asked.

'I have no idea what happened to her. I thought you might be her when you walked in here yesterday.'

'Me? How could that be?'

Wanda sighed and leaned against the hallway banister. 'Because any older Aboriginal woman I set eyes on, I really believe she could be my mother. Never is, of course. I'm so sorry that I was nosey with the girl before. I should have let her be.'

'I'll hear none of that,' Odette said. 'You've done nothing wrong. I'm only sorry that you did not find your mother.'

'You are related to the girl, aren't you?'

'She's my granddaughter. She's all I've got.'

'Can I ask you something else?' Wanda asked.

'Go ahead.'

'Can I have a hug?' she asked, in a tone so hushed Odette could barely hear her.

Odette smiled. 'Yes, Bub. Yes.'

The women embraced. Wanda savoured the scent of Odette's hair, the touch of her skin and the warmth and strength of the older woman's body against her own. She listened for Odette's breathing and the rhythm of the older woman's heartbeat. It was the first time Wanda had felt the touch of an Aboriginal woman since the day she had been taken away from her own mother.

Wanda didn't want to let go. 'Thank you, Auntie,' she finally whispered. 'Thank you.'

Later that night, as Odette lay in bed, she could feel a dull pain under her ribs. She didn't want to disturb Sissy with her restlessness. She got out of bed and went down the hallway to the bathroom. The bright fluorescent light startled her. She covered her eyes and studied her face in the mirror. The drama of recent weeks had taken its toll. Odette chastised herself. 'You are a stupid woman. You're a silly old gin.'

She felt heat rise in her chest. The room began to sway and Odette's legs turned to jelly. She collapsed and knocked the side of her head against the bath. Her deep red blood spread across the stark white floor.

CHAPTER FIFTEEN

Lowe sat at his desk inspecting the point of a perfectly sharpened pencil. On the other side of the room Bill Shea was going through the motions of shuffling a pile of gun licence applications. Shea had only days left on the force before his retirement and was expecting to go quietly. Lowe was so disgusted by Shea's general tardiness, he could hardly look at him. Instead, he stared out of the window to the main street. It was an unseasonably warm afternoon. *A walk will do you good, man*, Lowe decided. He marched across to Shea's desk. 'I need you to go out and interview that imbecilic junkman.'

'Henry Lamb? What's he done?'

'It's not about what *he's* done. He's had trouble with vandals out there and has complained twice this past week about someone firing a shotgun into his fence. He says it's happened half a dozen times now. I don't want him back in here taking up our time. I can't make sense of the man. Go out there and get a statement.'

'A statement from Henry Lamb won't make a lot of sense,' Shea huffed. 'The yard has been shot up, broken into or set fire to over the years. Giving Henry grief is the local sport for young fellas round here.'

'And what have you done about it?' Lowe insisted.

'Sorry?'

'What have you done to put an end to this *sport*, as you refer to it?' Lowe asked. 'We're not in this job to tolerate yahoos driving around the roads with loaded guns. The people of this town must accept the law. And it is our job to enforce it. Get out there now and interview him. I want details – days, times, the names of anyone he may have had trouble with.'

A northerly wind rattled the window frame. Lowe wasn't concerned one way or another about Henry Lamb's fence. He wanted Shea out of his sight.

'Okay,' Shea said. 'I'll head out there tomorrow.'

'No, you won't,' Lowe ordered him. 'I want you there now.'

Shea finally looked up at his boss. 'You mean today?'

'Yes. Right now.'

Shea picked up the set of keys for the old ambulance.

'Leave the van,' Lowe ordered. 'It may be needed. You will have to walk.'

Shea glared at him. Lowe smiled, aware that the officer lacked the courage to defy him. 'Off you go now,' he added. 'Be sure to take your notebook and a pencil with you. And while you're out there, ask this Lamb fellow when he last saw Odette Brown.'

Lowe noticed Shea bristle. 'Why would I ask him that?'

'Because I haven't seen Mrs Brown since she was in here seeking a travel permit. I have also been to the school and spoken to the headmistress. Cecily Brown has been absent. Do you have any idea where they may have gone?'

Shea shrugged his shoulders. 'Maybe to Gatlin.'

'Why would the woman go there?'

'Some of them from back on the mission have family in Gatlin. People moved there after the war to work in the steel mill. Odette could have gone visiting.'

Lowe dismissed the suggestion. 'When that woman came into this office, she did so with the clear intention of travelling further than Gatlin. I cannot accept that her disappearance is a coincidence. I suspect that Mrs Brown has unlawfully left the district with the child.'

'Odette might be uppity from time to time but I couldn't see her doing that,' Shea said, attempting to deflect Lowe's suspicions. 'She's lived here all her life.'

'She has indeed, and it is here that she belongs. Be sure that you question Lamb about her.'

'I don't see what good this will do. Henry's a simple man. This is a waste of time.'

Lowe turned his back on Shea. 'I decide how your time is spent. Now, do as I say and get out there.'

Lowe heard the heel of Shea's boot scraping against the wooden floorboards. He turned around. Shea was closing the top drawer of his desk. 'What are you waiting for?' he demanded.

'Nothing. I was just thinking, why are you bothering with this?'

'Because we must be able to indicate that we have exhausted all means to locate the family,' Lowe answered. 'I intend to report Mrs Brown to the Aborigines Welfare Board. She must be held responsible for her decision to abscond with the child. The insolence she has conveyed towards myself and this office will not go unpunished. Additionally, we, in our role as local guardians, are ultimately responsible for the care of Cecily. We must ensure that we fulfil our duty to her, which includes investigating the cause of her absence.'

'And what is it?' Shea asked. 'Our duty?'

'Perhaps you should familiarise yourself with the Bible? We have a flock to manage and I am determined to have the child, Cecily, in my care, whatever it takes.'

Lowe followed Shea out of the office and stood on the steps of the police station observing the slow movement in the street. Millie Khan came out of the store opposite. Lowe followed her.

'Excuse me,' he said, 'but I need to ask you a question, Mrs Khan.'

She stopped and looked him up and down, unable to disguise her contempt. She pulled the stub of a cigar from behind her ear and studied it for a moment. 'I doubt I could help you with anything at all, Sergeant,' she answered.

'You couldn't possibly know that,' Lowe smarted. 'I'm yet to ask you a question.'

He watched as Millie took a box of matches from her trouser pocket, lit her cigar and filled her lungs with a generous amount of smoke. 'It wouldn't matter a lot what question you asked me,' she explained. 'I don't know anything much about anything, unless it has something to do with horses. White folk have been telling me since I was a child, that being a native there wasn't a lot I could learn. I heard it so many times, I reckon they must be right. I do know a bit about a gelding and the best way to deal with him. What about you, Sergeant? Are you a horse man?'

Millie's attempt to distract Lowe irritated him. He could see she wasn't easily intimidated. 'I believe you are an acquaintance of Odette Brown?'

'She's no acquaintance of mine. Odette Brown is my closest friend.'

'And when did you last see her?'

Millie had last seen Odette the day she'd returned from Joe Kane's farm. She scratched the side of her head. 'Well, I don't think I could be really sure when that would have been. It may have been this week sometime. Or it could be the week before this one. You know how it is with us? My people, we're not so good with dates and times. What's that thing your people have? I reckon there'd be one in your office, on the wall there.'

'I beg your pardon?' Lowe asked, his frustration growing.

'What do you call that thing, with the numbers all over it? The calendar. That's it. If I had my own calendar I could tell you what day I last saw that girl, Odette. I'll have to ask my Yusie to get me one of them calendars for Christmas.'

Lowe couldn't decide if Millie Khan was stupid or crafty, although he assumed she was most likely both. 'You need to be careful, Mrs Khan, with the manner that you carry yourself.'

'How's that?' she asked, dropping the cigar butt to the ground and grinding it under the heel of her riding boot.

'As a native woman who enjoys the support of the State …'

Millie looked defiantly at Lowe. 'I enjoy no support from the State, as you call it, Sergeant. My name is Mrs Millicent

Khan. I am the wife of Mr Yusuf Khan. He's a free man whose father came to this country from the Punjab. My husband purchased the property we live in with hard-working money from the old stockman who took it away from my people and then hired my own father to work for him. Me and Yusie paid good money for a patch of land stolen from my people. Our children and grandchildren, all of them inherited the Khan name. We take nothing from the government, we are free to do as we want.'

Lowe's authority was rarely questioned by anyone, let alone by an Aboriginal woman.

'You may not feel that you owe us, or that you are responsible to us but Odette Brown certainly is. And she will soon be made aware of the fact. The child, Cecily, must be returned to Deane, for her own welfare.'

'Welfare? Oh, you've looked after the welfare of our young girls for a long time now. Most of them are dead, disappeared, or were sent mad by what you did to them in the institutions. That's not welfare, Sergeant. I think your own law would call that murder.' Millie turned her back on Lowe and walked away.

Bill Shea cursed his boss as he walked out to Henry Lamb's yard. Thoughts of his looming retirement were not enough to calm his anger. He unscrewed the cap on the bottle he'd taken from his drawer and stashed in his pocket before leaving the station. He took a long swig, savouring the warm liquid. He wiped his chin and took a second drink before knocking at Henry Lamb's gate. While he was waiting for the junkman to answer, he walked the length of the fence. It was riddled with holes. Shotgun cases littered the track. Henry had opened the gate and was quietly observing him, studying the bottle in his hand.

'How are you, Henry boy?' Bill asked, soothed by the alcohol.

'I suppose I'm good,' Henry answered, defensively.

'Really?' Bill took another drink of rum. He'd almost emptied the bottle in three gulping mouthfuls. 'I don't see how that could be, Henry, with these young fellas using your front fence for target practice. Couldn't miss, I suppose,' he laughed. 'Did you see who did this? My sergeant has sent me out here to investigate.'

'I didn't see them,' Henry said. 'But I did hear them. I know that truck engine. I know the sound of all sorts of engines. One from the other.'

'I bet you do,' Bill said. He took his notebook and pencil from his pocket, examined them as if they were foreign objects and put them back where he'd found them. 'Tell me then, Henry, whose truck are we talking about?'

'The truck engine that I heard belongs to the Kane boy. He's been coming by here with his brother. It's the older one who is all the trouble. I come down to the station and told your sergeant about it, but those boys, they keep coming back.'

Shea offered Henry the dregs of the bottle. 'You want a drink?'

'No. I have never had a drink and don't want one. My father, he was a drinker. I think it made him crazy.'

'I know all about that,' Bill mused. He took a last drop,

emptying the bottle, and hurled it into the scrub. 'Well, Henry,' he said. 'The next time Aaron Kane comes by here, we want you to come into the station and make a statement.'

'I have to go inside now,' Henry said. 'I'm working.'

'Before you go,' Bill said, almost forgetting Lowe's instructions. 'Have you seen Odette lately? She's not up at her place and the boss wants to know where she is.'

The two men looked suspiciously at each other.

'Haven't seen her at all,' Henry answered. 'But then, I haven't been outside this gate, not until you banged on it. I'm working in here.'

Shea huffed. 'Alright then. Alright. What are you working on?'

'I'm just working,' Henry said. 'I have valuables in here that need fixing.'

'Well, you keep on fixing and stay out of harm's way. See you, Henry.'

Shea made his way slowly back along Deane's Line. His mouth was parched and a pain ground away in his head. He approached the old saddlery. Millie Khan was hanging over her front fence, keeping an eye on the policeman staggering along the road.

He stopped at the gate. 'Good afternoon, Millie.'

'Hey, Bill, you don't look so well,' she said. 'You're the second policeman I've seen this afternoon. Must be a crime wave going on.'

'Do you happen to have a drink in there?' Shea asked.

'Oh, no Bill. We don't take alcohol. You should know better than to ask. Yusuf is a Muslim man. He's always been of the belief that the grog is an evil.'

Shea scratched at an insect bite on the side of his neck. It began bleeding. 'He said that? Evil?'

'Oh, he did.'

Bill grinned, stupidly. 'You know, Millie, I can't ever remember your husband speaking a single word.'

'That's his way,' Millie shrugged. 'Yusuf has never been a fella for idle chat. I suppose he's never had a word he wanted to share with you.'

Millie said goodbye and went into the house. Bill wandered on, his only thought was for another drink.

Lowe stood in front of the list on his blackboard, concentrating on only one name, *Cecily Brown*. The telephone rang. He picked up the receiver. 'Deane Police Station.'

'That you, Bill?' the male voice on the other end of the telephone asked.

'No, it's Sergeant Lowe. I'm in charge of this station.'

'Oh. It's Sergeant Carter. I'm with Central Highlands. What's happened to Bill Shea?'

'He's about to retire. This is his final week. If this is a personal call, it may be best if you call Officer Shea after hours, at his home.'

'No. This is police business. I've been working with a couple of Immigration boys, tracking down a young Pole who'd run off from one of the migrant camps. And—'

'And what?' Lowe interrupted, impatiently.

'And I came across a couple of Abos, a bloke and a sheila. She came from over your way. The old girl showed me her travel papers. I had nothing to hold her on, but I wouldn't be surprised if she was doing a runner with this fella. He was travelling on an exemption tag. A bit of a smart-arse.'

'What has this got to do with my station?' Lowe asked.

'I'm getting there, Sarge. We found the migrant kid and were hauling him to the lock-up when I saw the woman again. She had a young girl in tow. Might have been a white kid, I couldn't be sure. The woman was dragging her by the hand. I would have grabbed them on the spot, but the Immigration boys were having trouble with the Pole, who was resisting, talking some wog bullshit. I had to give him a clip with my baton to shut him up.'

'The woman,' Lowe asked, suddenly interested in the conversation. 'Did you get her name?'

'I did. I wrote it down. Her name was Odette Brown.'

Lowe gritted his teeth. 'Do you have any idea where they were heading?'

'The only train leaving the station that afternoon was on its way to the capital. The fella she was with was a John Haines, who goes by the name of Jack. He was catching that train, too.'

'You say she had a travel permit,' Lowe asked. 'That's not possible. She approached me for permission to travel, for both herself and the child, and I refused. You obviously did not see the documentation for yourself,' Lowe said, attempting to chastise the officer.

The comment insulted the policeman on the other end of the line. 'I'm not an idiot. I wouldn't take an Abo's word for anything. She had the permit, alright. It was signed by your offsider, Bill Shea. That's why I'm calling.'

'Are you certain?'

'Like I said, Sarge, I'm no idiot.'

Lowe held the receiver in his hand and stared blankly across the room. In that moment Shea staggered through the door. The stench of alcohol filled the air. Shea bumped against his desk, collapsed into his chair and, ignoring Lowe, started searching through the desk drawers.

'Hello? Are you still there?' Carter asked, on the other end of the line.

'Yes, I'm here,' Lowe answered. 'I appreciate the information. It is vital to a situation that I'm dealing with. I will need to talk to you again, but for now I have something more urgent to attend to.'

Lowe slammed the receiver down. Shea had his head tilted back and his eyes closed. Lowe walked across the room and kicked the leg of his chair. Shea fell to the ground, awkwardly sat up and laughed. 'Hey, you take it easy there, Sergeant. Or I'll have you arrested for assaulting an officer of the Crown.'

'Get up!' Lowe demanded. 'Get up, you drunkard.'

'Take it easy. I'm just throwing myself a little send-off. No harm done. I don't suppose you'd like to help me to my feet?' Shea comically stood to attention. 'What can I do for you, Boss?' He laughed, having found courage in the bottle.

Lowe rested a hand on the officer's shoulder. He wanted to make sure Shea heard his next words. 'Bill, there is something that I need you to know. It's information that I need you to fully understand.'

Shea grinned, rocking slightly on his feet. 'Sure. Whatever you need to say, Boss.'

Lowe glanced at the telephone on his desk. 'I have just spoken to Sergeant Carter from Central Highlands.'

Shea's vague recollection of the name was not helped by his drunkenness. 'Don't know that I know the bloke.'

'You may not know him, but he is certainly aware of you.' Lowe paused for effect. 'He tells me that he has recently come into contact with Odette Brown and her granddaughter, Cecily, travelling by train. When she was confronted by Sergeant Carter, Mrs Brown was able to produce a travel permit, executed at this police station.' Lowe leaned forward and whispered in Shea's ear. 'The permit was signed by you, Bill.'

'By me?' Shea asked, as if he genuinely did not understand what Lowe was talking about. 'I signed it?'

'Yes, you did, Bill. And as a result, you are in serious trouble.'

Shea's eyes began to water. He raised a hand as if there was something important he wanted to say, but could not get the words out.

Lowe slapped him on the cheek. 'Please do not embarrass yourself, Bill,' he said, almost affectionately. 'Let me assure you that there is nothing that you could say at present that would be of any assistance to you. What I need to do is firstly find Odette Brown, and secondly, rescue the child, Cecily, and put her in our protection. You understand that, don't you, Bill?'

Shea nodded his head and began sobbing, without fully knowing why.

'And, of course,' Lowe added, 'you are due to retire very soon, which presents me with another matter of urgency. I will be furnishing a report that will, no doubt, have you charged with negligence. You will not be retiring, Bill. I expect you will be dismissed, dishonourably. Which means,' he said, smiling, 'that you will be receiving no pension. You will leave the force with nothing more than the grubby uniform you are wearing.'

Shea began to wail. It was a sound Lowe was familiar with, like the cry of an abandoned child. His face darkened and he reached out, grabbing Shea by the throat. 'Did you think you could undermine me, you useless drunk?' He shook Shea like a rag doll. The officer collapsed to the floor, rolled on his side and vomited. Lowe towered over him. 'Be out of this station before I return. And clean up your mess before you leave.'

Lowe put his cap on, left the station and walked briskly past the courthouse, his hands clasped behind his back.

Shea kicked over a rubbish bin and chair and swept an arm across Lowe's desktop, scattering files across the floor. He opened the top drawer of his desk, took out a service revolver and clumsily checked that the gun was loaded. He went into the bathroom and opened the door of his metal locker. He rifled through it and retrieved a small flask of rum. He took a swig, rinsed his mouth and spat on the floor. He took a second drink, which he managed to hold down. He left the station and was hit by the glare of the sun. Lowe was nowhere in sight. He walked down the centre of the main street, the revolver in one hand, dodging the occasional passing vehicle and cursing the drivers. People walking along the footpath scattered behind parked cars and into shop doorways. When he reached the end of the street Shea crossed the red dirt track and slid down the bank of the dry riverbed.

'You dog, Lowe!' he screamed into the air. 'You fucking rotten dog!'

Shea took a final drink from the flask and threw the empty bottle to the ground, smashing it. He stumbled and fell, then crawled into the shadow of the bridge that crossed the riverbed. He took off his shoes and socks, followed by his tunic and shirt. He sat bare-chested, shifting the revolver from one hand to the other. It finally settled in his right hand.

'You dog, Lowe,' were the last words Shea uttered.

Yusuf Khan found the policeman's body late the next afternoon. Officer Shea was almost unrecognisable, his bloated face slumped against his bloodied chest. When Yusuf returned home and told Millie of his discovery, Millie seemed unsurprised by the terrible news.

'How long has he been there?' she asked, casually.

'I'm not sure, woman,' Yusuf said. 'He smelled off. A day. Could be more.'

'Had to be yesterday. I saw him stagger by here in the afternoon. Poor old Bill. He should have stuck with us when he was a kid. Growing up itself can be a curse for white people.'

Millie sat down beside her husband. 'I need you to keep this story to yourself, Yusie. This is none of our business. This is white folks' trouble and we don't need to be involved in this. If we go talking to that new copper about this, no good will come of it. We're deaf and dumb on this.'

A further two days passed before Shea's body was found for a second time, by a young boy who'd skipped school and gone down to the riverbed to smoke cigarettes. Shea had no wife or children, and little effort was made to locate his extended family. To ensure the officer's violent death did not impact on his own reputation, Lowe prepared a dossier for the state coroner, outlining a history of drunkenness, years of misdemeanours and his recent dereliction of duty, ensuring that if Bill Shea was to be remembered at all it would be as a failure.

CHAPTER SIXTEEN

Odette woke in a haze with no idea where she was. She opened her eyes, rested her chin on her chest and looked down at a fresh white sheet covering her body. Opposite her was an elderly woman lying in bed, her mouth agape. Odette tried turning her head and felt stiffness in her neck. She looked down at her toes, poking out of the sheet. She closed her left eyelid, adjusted the focus of her right eye, and read the card attached to the end of the bed rail. *LIQUIDS ONLY.* Above it was a name: *Miss Betty Haines.*

A nurse walked past and noticed Odette was awake. 'Hello, Betty. You're back with us. Fantastic. Let's get your obs done.'

Betty?

The nurse took Odette's blood pressure and temperature and wiped Odette's face with a wet cloth.

'Let me get you a glass of water. Your brother will be pleased to hear that you're awake.'

'My brother?' Odette's throat was raw and swollen.

The nurse patted Odette on the forehead. 'It's no surprise you're a little confused. You've had an operation. Several days ago.'

'What operation?'

'It's best for the duty doctor to explain the details to you. He'll be doing his rounds later. What I can say is that you had no capacity in your left lung because of a tumour pushing against it. The doctors were amazed that you had no medical complaints before the collapse. You also have some swelling and stitches in the side of your head. You had a fall. Your brother said that you'd been *as good as gold* until the emergency. You must be strong as an ox, Betty.'

Odette didn't feel strong at all. Nor did she understand why the nurse continued to call her Betty.

The surgeon visited later that morning and explained to Odette that while the operation to remove the tumour had been complicated, it was found to be benign.

'Your brother says that you had no signs of illness or pain before you collapsed in his kitchen. Is that so?'

'Yes,' said Odette evasively.

'That's quite remarkable. Your family live close to the hospital and we have checked all of our records for your medical history, but you've never been a patient here. Did you ever see a doctor about your condition?'

'No,' Odette answered. 'Never''

The doctor shook his head. 'Extraordinary.'

Odette slept through the afternoon. When she woke, Jack Haines was standing at the side of the bed with an Aboriginal woman. 'I'm Alma,' the woman whispered. 'Jack's wife.' Jack had tears in his eyes. Odette assumed something was wrong.

'Sissy?' she asked. 'Where is she?'

'She's fine. Just perfect,' Alma said. 'She's top-shelf, that girl. There's nothing wrong at all. Don't worry about Jack. He's pleased to see you back with us, is all. He told me that he didn't know if you'd come good and I told him he was talking the way men always talk when a woman is ill. They think there's either nothing wrong with us or we're on our deathbed.' She tapped Odette on the wrist. 'I told him you'd have been through tougher times than this, and that you would pick up.'

'But my granddaughter?' Odette asked again, her voice hoarse.

'You can shush up about that one,' Jack said. 'She's safe at home with us and our own granddaughter, Lidia. Your girl will be dancing the hula when we tell her you're finally awake.'

Odette remained confused. 'What happened to me?'

'You had a fall in the hotel,' Jack said. 'The young one there, Wanda, she was in her room along the hall and heard a thump. She found you.'

Odette looked at the card with her new name on it. She raised her eyebrows inquisitively.

'I've never had to think so quick on my feet,' Jack laughed. 'The ambulance brought you here and that girl, Wanda, she took Sissy to her room and kept her safe. Lucky for you, she asked Sissy if you had people in the city. The girl said no, and then she remembered you had that stub with my name and address written on it. Wanda brought Sissy to our house, and me and Alma came straight here. They were doing these tests on you, and they told us we couldn't see you unless we were related. Straightaway, I told them you were my sis. I had to give the nurse a name.'

Odette continued to frown.

'Don't you worry,' Alma said. 'While you're in this bed you're Betty Haines and you live with us. Anyone asks a question, you tell them you're feeling poorly and don't remember any more for now. We'll sort the rest out as soon as we can get you out of here.'

'Where will I be going?' Odette asked.

'You'll be coming home,' Alma said.

Sissy was waiting for Odette outside the Haines' house the morning she was released from the hospital. When the taxi pulled up and Odette got out, she was so happy to see her granddaughter she almost cried. Sissy hesitated for a moment before running to Odette and comforting herself in her grandmother's loving body. 'You're here, Nan! You're really here!'

The Haines family kitchen was warm and smelled of lemons. A girl around the age of six or seven was sitting at the kitchen table drawing on a sheet of butcher's paper with a black crayon. She looked up from her handiwork and smiled at Odette.

'This is Lidia, our own granddaughter,' Alma said. 'Her mum, our daughter, Carol, is on afternoon shift at the tyre factory around the corner. She doesn't get off work until eleven. Say hello to Odette, Lidia.'

The girl chirped 'hello' and went back to her drawing.

One wall of the kitchen was covered with photographs. Under each picture were names, dates and places. On a shelf above the kitchen stove Odette could see decorated spears and a carved wooden bowl, similar to objects she'd seen on the mission. When the mission closed its doors they were put on display at the Deane courthouse.

Alma asked Sissy to take Lidia into the yard to play. The three adults sat around the table. The silence bothered Odette. She was worried that she and Sissy were an imposition on the family. 'I don't want to bring trouble, Jack,' she said. 'I've been thinking about the exemption rules you spoke of at the railway station that day, and how you're not supposed to associate.'

'Don't worry yourself over rules, I'll take care of that. And you're no trouble to us, not at all,' he said. 'I grew up learning how to survive. We have to be careful, for sure. Whether you and the child are around or not, we'd be on our guard. That's the way life is for us.' Jack removed a small black and white photograph from the wall. It was a portrait of an Aboriginal woman sitting on a metal drum in front of a shanty, its walls and roof made from flattened kerosene tins. 'This is my sister, Betty. It was taken about twenty years ago,' Jack said.

Odette studied the picture.

'Betty was two years older than me, and always looked out for me,' Jack said, looking across the table at Alma. 'She was a beautiful woman, wasn't she Love?'

'Oh yes, she was,' Alma agreed. 'A beautiful woman with a beautiful heart.'

'I made a choice about the exemption certificate when the cousin of a mate of mine came down to the plant – we were working in a foundry at the time – and told him that the

Welfare were out at the Bend. That's what we called it, where we lived at the time. It was a shanty town of our own, on the river. This fella said the Welfare had been around looking for my mate's kids, a little boy and girl. Well, he took off. Ran all the way home, grabbed the family and was out of there.'

Odette could hear the strain in Jack's voice. 'You don't need to tell me this.'

'I do,' he said. 'That's when I made my mind up to apply for the exemption. Betty was living on the Bend too. She had no kids of her own, but she was a mighty auntie. I let her know what I was going to do, thinking she'd have a go at me, Betty being such a proud woman.'

Jack looked at Alma and sat quiet for a moment. 'Tell Odette what she said, Love. It sounds better coming from a woman.'

'I remember that day well,' Alma said. 'I was washing Carol in the tub when you told her. Betty smiled and made a joke of it. "Well Jack," she said. "If you want to get on your high horse and act up like you're some sort of white man, I'll need to be around to put your black bum in its place." She got the exemption for herself as well.'

'We'd decided we'd best get on the move,' Jack said, 'and Betty decided to come so she could be around the kids.'

'Where is she now?' Odette asked, dreading Jack's response.

'We worked our way south,' Jack said. 'It was during the war. It was horse and cart back then. Anything with a motor in it had been given over to the government to run the farms or for military work. We worked our way down through the basin, fruit-picking, shearing. Any work we could get, we took. One morning, Betty was sitting in the back of the cart, we were out west, maybe a hundred miles from where you hail from, and she died, right there in front of us. Heart, I reckon.'

'Oh, I'm so sorry,' Odette said.

Jack looked to Alma for support. 'Go on, Jack,' his wife said. 'You can tell her. We know we can trust you,' she explained to Odette.

'There wasn't a lot we could do,' Jack said. 'The cost of a decent funeral was out of the question. We had no money and nothing to trade. The Welfare Board has always offered to bury us blackfellas for free, of course. But a pauper's burial in a shared grave? I wasn't having it. The spot we stopped that night, it was where Alma's people come from originally. Not mine and Betty's people, but Alma's. We talked it over. Everyone had their say, including the kids. I spent the next three hours digging my sister's grave. I made sure it was nice and deep so no trouble would come to her. We covered her up, and then I scattered some rocks and brush about so no one would know the ground had been disturbed. She's out there now, being looked after by Alma's people.' Jack slumped in his chair, his face drained.

'We told no one,' Alma said. 'We didn't know if we'd done something criminal, or if there'd be suspicion about how she passed.' She lifted a tea-towel out of a straw basket in the middle of the table. Underneath was an envelope. She handed it to Odette. Inside was an exemption certificate in the name of Elizabeth May Haines. The photograph had faded badly. Elizabeth had been born the year before Odette. 'You can live here for as long as you like,' Alma said. 'You'll be safe here.'

'I can't live here,' Odette said. 'She's your sister, Jack. It wouldn't be right to take her name.'

'It couldn't be more right,' Jack answered. 'She was never happy about the exemption. She knew she had to do it, but she wasn't happy. Betty would be relieved helping out a sister. She'd want that for you, and for your Sissy.'

'I'm not comfortable with this,' Odette said.

Alma took hold of Odette's hand. 'You don't have to be, not yet. You've been to Hell and back as it is. You have a good rest, take your time and think it over.'

The family sat around the kitchen table that evening. Sissy did not leave Odette's side. After dinner Odette emptied her suitcase and called Alma into the small room off the kitchen where she and Sissy would be sleeping, in the same bed as Lidia. She handed Alma a roll of ten-pound notes.

'I can't take this much money,' Alma said.

'You have to take it,' Odette insisted.

'Why?'

'Because, first up, I saved it knowing that one day I would need to use it to help Sissy. And you and Jack are doing that. And second, I know what generosity is. Your heart is full of it. This money will help you spread it round a little more.'

All night, Odette mulled over Jack's plan, unable to rid herself of a concern that it was wrong to pass herself off as Jack's sister. She felt it would be disrespectful to the memory of Betty's own life, and that it would require Jack and Alma to carry on with a lie that could land them in trouble. More than that, Odette couldn't conceive that she would spend the remaining years of her life pretending to be someone other than herself. She had her country to return to one day, and she would do so in her own name, alive or dead. The next morning, she explained her decision to Jack and Alma and what her alternative plan would be.

'Are you sure about this?' Jack asked.

'I'm sure. I've never been more grateful than what I feel for you two. You saved my granddaughter. But I can't be someone who I'm not, Jack. It would be no good for me or your family.'

'What about Sissy?' Alma asked. 'What's best for her?'

'All I can do is hope this will work out for the pair of us.'

Jack suggested a meeting with a lawyer to get advice.

'What good can a lawyer do for Aboriginal people,' Odette asked. 'It's the law that keeps us in our place. My father taught me that.'

'She's right, Jack,' Alma said. 'The law has never been there to help us.'

'Well, you're both right,' Jack said. 'But you need a lawyer who can explain how their law works, and the best way for you to tackle it.'

'Do you know such a lawyer?' Odette asked.

'I do. And he's a good man,' Jack said. 'He's doing work on the citizenship business. I think he's one of them communist fellas old Bob Menzies wanted to outlaw.'

'A communist?' Odette had heard the word back in Deane over the years, in less than complimentary ways. 'A Red?'

'Yep. A Red. I've found them to be decent people,' Jack said. 'And more to the point, they don't charge for their services. I don't mind what they're called. I'll take a Red ahead of a white man any day of the week. We should go and see him at his office as soon as you're feeling up to it. It'll take a bit of time to get things in order.'

'In the meantime,' Alma insisted, 'this is your home, Odette, as much as it's ours. And I won't have you leaving here until I'm satisfied that you and the girl are safe.'

CHAPTER SEVENTEEN

Lowe stepped from the Gatlin train, arriving in the capital in the black suit and tie he'd exchanged for his police uniform. He checked his watch. It was after five in the afternoon. The Aborigines Welfare Board's office was closed for the day. He'd called ahead to report that Odette Brown had absconded from Deane without permission but the conversation had alarmed Lowe. The young clerk on the other end of the line seemed bemused that the police sergeant had reported the matter at all.

'Has she committed a crime?' the clerk asked.

'You must know she has,' Lowe answered. 'As I have explained, she left my jurisdiction without permission. She is also travelling with the child after having been ordered that she could not do so. She expressly disobeyed me.'

'Sorry,' the clerk apologised, 'but we tend to leave it to the guardians in the regions to sort these problems out for themselves. Give her time. I'm sure she'll come back. Most of them do.'

‘We’re not talking about a runaway horse here,’ Lowe shouted down the line. ‘This is a woman determined to defy my authority.’

‘That may be,’ the clerk replied. ‘If you can provide me with the woman’s details, I’ll ensure that we put a note on her file and we will make enquiries.’

‘Is that all?’

‘It is at the moment. The country’s going through a credit squeeze and we haven’t had any new staff through here in two years.’

Lowe put the telephone down. Since arriving in Deane he’d documented the living arrangements and conditions of every Aboriginal family under his control, and kept a keen eye on each family. Cecily Brown was the only child left on the blackboard unaccounted for. Lowe could not allow the situation to stand. He had the address for Jack Haines, the man whose company Odette was likely to be keeping. If the Welfare Board were not prepared to do their job to the fullest, he would do it on their behalf.

The hasty enquiry into Bill Shea’s death and the arrangements for his funeral had delayed the sergeant’s departure from Deane. He’d wasted precious time tidying up the mess Shea left behind. The boy who’d found the body hadn’t reported it until hours later, when he confessed to his parents that he’d skipped school for the day. When the boy’s father reported the grim discovery Lowe had asked Doctor Singer to accompany him to the riverbed.

‘I have no idea what state the body is in,’ he told the doctor. ‘Perhaps you could assist with an examination?’

‘If it’s of help,’ Doctor Singer said.

By the time they arrived a small crowd had gathered beneath the bridge. Lowe ordered them to retreat further along the riverbank. Although the face of the body was unrecognisable, Lowe had known immediately who it was. He looked down at the service revolver balanced on Shea's gut, then up at the crusted clots of blood on his neck and the hole in the side of his head. The flabby rolls of skin on his arms and legs were covered in insect bites. An army of bull-ants swarmed over Shea's right foot and had burrowed into a wound on the tip of his big toe.

Doctor Singer removed his jacket, rolled up his shirtsleeves and crouched over the body.

Lowe casually turned to Doctor Singer. 'It's my man, Bill Shea.'

Doctor Singer was surprised. 'He was a colleague of yours, Sergeant? Did you know him well?'

'I hardly knew him at all,' Lowe said, circling the body. 'I do not believe I will need a report from you after all, doctor. This is straightforward enough. I'm sorry to take you away from your office.'

'There is no need to apologise. I can examine the body and forward a report if you like.'

'No,' Lowe answered, forcefully. 'It will not be needed.'

The boy who'd found the body was standing on the edge of the crowd with his father. Lowe ordered the boy to accompany him. 'Hurry,' he ordered. 'I need to speak with you.'

'I'll come with him,' the father said.

Lowe ordered him to stand back. 'I need to speak to the boy alone. Please remain here.' He waved to the boy a second time. 'Down here, immediately.'

The boy refused to look at the body. He pinched his nose between a finger and thumb and gagged.

'When you found him here, did you see anybody else around?' Lowe asked.

'Nup, I saw nobody,' he answered.

'What were you doing here?' Lowe asked.

'Nothing,' the boy said.

'Nothing? Don't be stupid or take me for being so. You wouldn't have been down here without a reason. What was it?'

'I was having a smoke,' the boy answered. 'That's all.'

Lowe grabbed the boy by the arm. 'Look at me, son. Did you see anyone down here when you were enjoying your cigarette?'

The boy shook his head. 'I saw nobody.'

'I need you to look at the body,' Lowe ordered.

'But I don't want to look.'

'But you must. This is a crime scene,' Lowe explained. 'You are a witness to that crime. Now, do as I tell you and look at the body.'

'No,' the boy cried.

'Surely, this is not necessary?' Doctor Singer asked. 'The poor child has been traumatised by what he has witnessed here. There is no need for this.'

'Don't tell me how to do my job, Doctor. I asked you here to observe the body and nothing more. I am the law in this town and I need this boy to look at the body.'

Lowe wrapped his large hands around the young boy's shoulders, lifted him from the ground and forced the boy to look directly at the corpse. 'Is it in the same position that you found him? I need to know. You look and then you tell me.'

The boy gagged and Lowe released him. The boy ran back to his father. The policeman took a handkerchief out of a pocket and wiped his hands. He could see that Doctor Singer was looking at him with disapproval. 'Do you have a problem?' he asked.

'I don't think that was at all necessary,' the doctor said.

Lowe folded the handkerchief and returned it to his pocket. He was not about to be chastised by the man. 'I have greater concerns than the boy's delicate state.' He retrieved the revolver from the body and examined the chamber. 'I can't leave the gun here, it's loaded.' He pointed the gun in the doctor's general direction. 'Seeing as you are here, could I ask you a question.'

'What is it?'

'Odette Brown, I believe she is a patient of yours?'

'Yes, she is my patient.'

'Do you see her regularly?'

'I have seen her more than once, but I wouldn't call it regularly.' Doctor Singer answered, annoyed by Lowe's intrusiveness.

'I need to know when you last saw her and what you are treating her for,' the sergeant insisted.

'Why is that?' he asked. 'Is the woman a suspect here? Surely not?'

'Of course she's not a suspect in this incident and I'm certain you know that, Doctor. I'm seeking information on another matter. What can you tell me about Odette Brown's health?'

Doctor Singer didn't hesitate. 'I can't disclose such information. To do so would betray the privacy of my patient, which I am not permitted to do. By law.'

Lowe stepped forward. 'Does such a law apply to citizens and non-citizens equally? The woman is a native under the law. You do know that?'

'Yes, I do. But Sergeant, this is a matter of confidentiality between a doctor and patient. Citizen or non-citizen, this is first and foremost a matter of trust between myself and my patient. I would never seek to betray that trust.'

Lowe looked at the tattooed numbers on Doctor Singer's arm. 'You are new to this country. I believe you are a Jew.'

'Yes, I am Jewish.'

'The native people of this land are agitating for the rights of citizenship. I have actually heard one of their speakers claim that they have suffered as the Jewish people suffered during the war,' Lowe said. 'In my experience, both here and in Europe, it only does such people harm to dwell,' he added.

'Why is that?' Doctor Singer asked. 'You do not believe people suffered, Sergeant Lowe?'

'Only as much as we all suffer through life,' Lowe said, looking directly at the doctor. 'There's nothing particularly noble in casting oneself as a victim. I firmly believe there is courage in silence.'

Lowe booked into a city hotel and ordered dinner in his room. After he'd eaten he walked across a bridge and down to the port. Although he had visited some of the largest centres in Europe, he'd spent little time in the big cities of his own country. He walked along the foreshore. The lights of the city reflected off the water. Lowe felt almost at peace with himself.

He noticed the brief glow of a cigarette in the shadows. He slowed and saw a homeless man resting against a pylon.

'Do you have a shilling there,' the man asked, 'for an old soldier?'

Lowe looked down at the man. 'You're a returned serviceman?' he asked.

'I am. Can you help me out with a deaner?'

'Oh, I have a shilling,' Lowe said. He took a leather wallet from his pocket and took out a pound note. 'I have more than a shilling. I have this,' he smiled.

The homeless man held out a hand.

'But I will not be giving it to you,' Lowe explained. 'Or a shilling. Giving you a penny won't help you.'

'But I need a feed.'

'Then, work for it.' Lowe ignored the curses following him. When he reached a concrete jetty he noticed several cars were parked at a strategic distance from each other. The windows of the cars had misted. He wandered slowly past the first car and heard music playing on the radio. In the next car, he heard muffled voices. At the end of the jetty was a wooden shed. Lowe noticed the silhouette of a couple leaning up against the door, a man pressing into a woman. He stood and watched for several minutes before walking back to the hotel.

Back in the room, Lowe opened his briefcase. He took out Cecily Brown's file. He also had Lila Brown's file with him. He was no longer convinced the young Aboriginal woman was dead. Before getting into bed he opened the curtains, ensuring he would rise with the sun. He lay on top of his bed, without a blanket, and slept.

Early the next morning Lowe walked to the station and boarded a suburban train. Looking out of the window, he watched as the wide thoroughfares of the central city gave way to narrow winding streets and houses jammed against each other. He got off a few stations later and studied the address in his notebook, provided by the officer who had questioned Jack Haines at the railway station. A few minutes later he stood across the street from a nondescript terrace house. Lowe was about to cross the street and knock at the door when it opened. Odette Brown and her granddaughter appeared. They were followed from the house by an Aboriginal man, who spoke briefly to Odette, smiled at the girl and waved at the pair. Lowe followed them along the street, keeping his distance. They arrived at the station just as the train arrived. Lowe could see the child, Cecily, holding her grandmother's hand.

'Where are we going?' Sissy asked Odette as the train pulled into the station.

'Oh, we have to go to an important meeting this morning.'

'Who are we meeting with?'

Odette needed to gather her thoughts. 'I'll tell you once we're on the train. Is that okay?'

'Yes, Nan.' Sissy could feel the morning sun on her face. 'It's a nice day, Nan.'

'It is.'

'Are you feeling better, Nan, since the operation?'

'I'm feeling good, and I'll feel a whole lot better if you just give me a little time to myself so I can sort out my thinking.'

'Okay, Nan,' Sissy said, already eager to hear what Odette was thinking about. As they were about to board the train, Sissy turned her head and looked at the man in the dark suit entering the next carriage. She sat close to Odette, desperate to tell her grandmother that she was sure she'd seen the policeman from Deane. She could see by the look on her face that her grandmother was still doing her *thinking*, and thought it best not to bother her. It wasn't until they arrived at the central station that Sissy tugged at Odette's arm. 'I saw him,' she said.

Odette couldn't hear Sissy above the noise of the crowd. 'Pardon?' she shouted.

'The policeman, I saw him.'

Odette frowned. 'Which policeman?'

'The one from home. The one we're running away from.'

'Don't be silly. You couldn't have seen him, that's just your imagination running wild. We have to get a move on.'

Sissy wouldn't budge. 'I *did* see him, Nan.'

Odette searched the crowd of faces hurrying by. Sissy saw a look of unease cross her grandmother's face. As they made their way out of the station and along the street, Odette stopped occasionally and looked up at the street signs. Each time she did so, Sissy also looked anxiously over her shoulder.

'We're here,' Odette said. 'This is where our meeting is.' Sissy looked up at the Coat of Arms above the building. She read the name on the brass plate out the front. *Aborigines Welfare Board.*

'What is this place, Nan?'

'Like I told you, this is where our meeting is.'

'And who are we meeting?' Sissy asked.

'Well, if we're lucky,' Odette smiled, 'somebody who can help us out of our mess.'

CHAPTER EIGHTEEN

Along with every public building Odette had entered, the foyer of the Aborigines Welfare Board was dominated by the national flag, alongside the Union Jack of the Empire and a portrait of the young Queen Elizabeth. Odette introduced herself to the woman at the front desk and told her she had an appointment. She was asked to take a seat and wait.

'Can you please tell me what we're doing here, Nan?' Sissy persisted.

'Well, it's not all that easy to tell,' Odette admitted. 'I want us to be able to stay here in the city, and to do that I need to have some documents approved.'

Sissy looked at the neatly dressed blonde woman behind the counter. 'White people, they don't need documents, do they, Nan?'

'No, they don't.'

Odette's name was called. 'Sissy, I need you to stay here while I have this meeting. You're not to move from this seat.'

Odette was ushered into a small office by a young man wearing a suit and tie and bookish tortoise-shell eye glasses. The clerk introduced himself as Michael and shook her hand, surprising Odette.

'Please take a seat,' he said. 'I will be assessing your application today, Mrs Brown. I understand you have come to apply for a certificate exempting you from the Aborigines Protection Act?'

'Yes. For myself and my granddaughter, Cecily Brown.' While Odette didn't feel comfortable about yet another white man *assessing* her, on this occasion she had little choice but to comply.

The clerk looked down at the sheet of paper in front of him. Odette glanced at it, but could not make sense of the writing.

'Your granddaughter, Cecily, she is thirteen years of age, I believe?'

'Yes, that's right.'

'Technically,' he said, 'your grandchild cannot be granted an exemption as she is under the age of eighteen. But,' he added, 'if your application is successful, you will be granted guardianship of the child. Therefore, she would also be exempt from the Act, provided that certain criteria are met and maintained, such as her regular attendance at school and general health and welfare.'

It annoyed Odette that her care for Sissy should be questioned at all. She held her tongue, remembering Jack Haines' warning that some people who worked at the Welfare Board had started their careers as reserve managers and were resistant to relinquishing control of Aboriginal people. 'Some of them old-timers are set in their ways and they don't like us being exempted from anything,' Jack had said. 'You need to be thinking about young Sissy the whole time you're in there and not speak out of place.'

Looking across the desk at the face of the youthful clerk, Odette could not imagine he was old enough to know anything about the predicament of her people.

'Do you have the relevant documents we require from you, Mrs Brown?' the clerk asked.

Odette handed him the testimonials. Both documents remained sealed, as required. She had no idea of their contents. The first letter was from the woman who ran the gift shop in Gatlin. The clerk silently read the statement. It outlined the longstanding business arrangement the shop-owner had with *Mrs Brown, a reliable woman of independent means.* Attached to the letter were carbon copies of invoices, indicating a regular income for the previous three years. *I am happy for this business arrangement to continue*, the letter concluded. The second letter, written by Doctor Singer, offered ongoing sponsorship to Odette and attested to her *trustworthy character*, a comment that would have come as a surprise to Odette, seeing as she'd only met the doctor twice. She'd only written to him for support as she knew of no other white person who might vouch for her.

The clerk put the letters to one side without comment. He picked up another document and held it in his hand. 'This is a copy of your granddaughter's birth certificate. It states: *Father Unknown*. Have attempts been made to ascertain who the father of the child is?'

'Well,' she hesitated. 'The father took off before the child was born.'

'Do you know if the father was a native? Or white?'

Odette thought of Joe Kane, and how much she despised him. 'He was a white man is all I know, but not his name or any more.'

The clerk himself hesitated for a moment. Odette was sure she detected a glimpse of something more than efficiency on his face. 'Your daughter—'

'I haven't seen my daughter in over ten years,' she answered. 'I've looked everywhere for her.'

'You would most likely be unaware then, that your daughter, Lila May Brown, successfully applied for an exemption certificate eighteen months ago. In her application, she stated that she had no living relatives or dependants.'

The revelation shocked Odette. 'Eighteen months ago?'

'Yes. At the time, she made no mention of the child, Cecily.'

'What does that mean for us?'

'Well, essentially, your guardianship of the child is strengthened, as there is no other claim on her. Do you have your own birth certificate?' The clerk patted a hefty file sitting on the desk. 'We were not able to locate one in your file.'

'Is that my file?' Odette asked, shocked at its bulk.

'It is.'

'What's in there?' she asked

'I'm sorry, Mrs Brown, but all information regarding your history remains confidential. It's the property of the Aborigines Welfare Board.'

My history, Odette lamented.

'We do have an additional item flagged here,' the clerk said, removing his glasses. 'An issue I need to question you about.'

'A flag? What is that?'

'A matter of concern.' The clerk held his glasses in one hand and used them to animate his conversation. 'The local police sergeant in Deane states that you left the district without permission, immediately after he had instructed you not to. He also states that he explicitly instructed that the child was not to leave the district under any circumstances.'

Odette felt trapped. She didn't know what to say.

'However,' Michael said, picking up the support letter written by Doctor Singer, 'this letter appears to provide an explanation addressing the sergeant's complaint.'

Odette did her best to show no surprise. 'It does?'

When Odette had written to Doctor Singer, she'd been honest in providing her reasons for leaving Deane. *I believe I was left with only one choice, to protect my own flesh and blood.* Before writing to the Welfare Board about Odette's character, Doctor Singer had reflected on the conversation he'd had with Sergeant Lowe the day he discovered Bill Shea's body.

The clerk read aloud to Odette from Doctor Singer's letter:

> *'Mrs Brown's medical situation was urgent and it was vital for her to attend hospital. I saw it as my duty to contact the relevant authorities, but failed to do so. Any negligence, in not notifying Sergeant Lowe, of Mrs Brown's necessary absence was my fault alone. Therefore, I take full responsibility.'*

'I believe the doctor is stating that it was he who had planned to notify the police on your behalf,' the clerk offered. 'Is that so, Mrs Brown?' The clerk smiled.

Odette detected warmth in his face.

'I would presume, Mrs Brown, that as you were quite ill, you would not have been able to contact Sergeant Lowe yourself due to your medical condition. And therefore, the task would have rested with Doctor Singer, as he clearly indicates here?'

'Yes,' she answered tentatively. 'I believe he was going to do that on my behalf.'

The clerk bundled the papers together and closed the file. 'Thank you, Mrs Brown. If you could wait in the front office, I will come and see you as soon as a decision has been made.'

Odette returned to the waiting room. Sissy had behaved herself and not moved from her seat.

'Did you get the document?' she asked Odette.

'Not yet, Sweet. But it shouldn't be too long now.'

When her name was called a second time Odette once again took a seat across from the young clerk. He handed Odette the documents she'd provided, including the testimonials and Sissy's birth certificate. 'You will need to retain these in your possession. They could be of help to you in the future.' He then handed Odette two additional documents. 'Here is the certificate granting you exemption from the Aborigines Act. And this is an additional document granting you provisional guardianship of your granddaughter, Cecily Brown. You will need to attend the Registry of Births, Deaths and Marriages to formalise the second arrangement. It is a straightforward matter that should take no time at all.'

Odette picked up the exemption certificate and read the order that she was not to associate with *any person of Aboriginal extraction*. Her sense of shame was relieved by the content of the second document, informing her that Sissy could legally remain in her care.

'That's it?' was all she could say, somewhat bewildered.

'That's it. Congratulations, Mrs Brown.'

He offered his hand. Although Odette felt that there was nothing at all to be congratulatory about, she continued the pretence, as Jack Haines had coached her.

'Thank you,' she said.

'Please let me show you out,' the clerk offered. As he opened the door Odette was horrified to see Sergeant Lowe sitting on the bench next to Sissy, a hand resting firmly on her thigh. The policeman looked up at Odette, his usual stony expression replaced by a self-satisfied grin. 'Well, here you are, Mrs Brown.'

'Sissy, come to me!' Odette called. 'Come to your nanna.'

Sissy jumped up and ran to Odette's side. Lowe stood and straightened his tie.

'Mrs Brown,' he said. 'It's pleasing to find you here. I was about to enquire after you when I saw young Cecily sitting here alone.'

'She's not alone,' Odette said. 'My granddaughter is with me.' She looked nervously at the clerk.

Lowe brought his hands together. 'Well, I'm sorry, but she will not be with you much longer. You left the district of Deane without my permission. What's more, you have illegally transported a State ward without authorisation. You've broken the law, Mrs Brown. And the officers of the Welfare Board in this very building have been notified.'

'Sissy is no ward, she's my grandchild.'

'In fact, she's both,' Lowe smirked. 'But legally, she remains a child of the State, and I am the local representative of the State. I'm here to arrange for Cecily to be taken into care.'

'Can I have your documentation, please?' the clerk asked Odette.

'You're not taking it from me?' Odette responded, mistaking his intentions.

'Please, Mrs Brown,' he insisted.

'Sorry, I didn't catch your name?' the clerk said to Lowe.

'I have not provided my name. I am the head of the Deane district police. Mrs Brown is a native living under the legislative protection of the Act. She has abused that protection, which I have previously notified this office about.'

'Are you suggesting that Mrs Brown has broken the law?' the clerk asked.

'I am *suggesting* no such thing!' Lowe shouted, angered by the young man's tone. 'Odette Brown has no rights in this matter. The law is clear.'

'But she does have rights. Mrs Brown left your jurisdiction under the authority of Officer Shea, who at the time was an authorised guardian. She has since successfully applied for an exemption certificate for herself, excluding her from the Aborigines Protection Act. She has also been granted legal guardianship of her grandchild. She is free to leave here with her granddaughter today.'

'That cannot be possible!'

'But it is. The matter has been assessed by this office and resolved in Mrs Brown's favour. Unless it can be found that the child is suffering neglect, she cannot be removed from her grandmother's care. At present, there is no case for her to answer under the Act we administer.'

'You administer nothing!' Lowe screamed. 'The police out there, all over this country, we have kept these people in their place. Without us, do you know how many half-caste children there would be roaming around?'

The clerk stood his ground. 'As I have said, Mrs Brown has complied with the Act, and she and her granddaughter are free to go.'

'Neglect?'

'Excuse me?'

'You just said a child can only be removed by the court in a case of neglect?'

'I did,' the clerk answered, 'but there is no evidence of it in this instance. I'm sorry, Sergeant, but I am not prepared to discuss the matter further in the presence of the child.'

'I'll be discussing this with somebody other than an overgrown choir boy,' Lowe said. He glared at Odette and stormed out of the room.

'I'm sorry about this,' Michael apologised. 'You shouldn't have been put through that ordeal. Can I give you some advice, Mrs Brown?'

'White people have been giving me advice all my life,' Odette said. 'You might as well have your say.'

He gave her an odd smile. 'White people?'

'Yes. People like Lowe, the priests, white women who think they're a godsend to me, doing me a good turn. All types of people. What's your advice?'

'I wouldn't return to Deane in a hurry, if I was you,' he said.

'Is that it?' Odette asked. 'Your advice?'

'That's it.'

'Well, I don't want to disappoint you,' Odette said. 'You have been a real help to me and Sissy today, but you don't need to tell me that. I'd be something of an old fool not to know that I won't be going home. Not while that man is around, at least.'

'Good,' he smiled. 'You two take care.'

At the Haines' house that night Odette placed her exemption certificate in an envelope and sealed it. She opened her suitcase and took out the photographs of Lila and Delores Reed's daughters. 'Do you think we could find a home for these girls on the wall?' she asked Alma.

Alma picked up the photographs of the Reed children. 'What beautiful girls. Are they family?'

'No,' Odette said. 'I met their mother many years back and it's important to me that these girls are not forgotten.'

'Well, we'll find a place for them. And your own daughter, Lila, as well.'

Odette relayed her encounter with Lowe and how the young clerk had stood up to him. 'Never would have expected that,' she said. 'There was something about that young fella.'

'Like what?' Alma asked.

'I'm not sure. Silly as it sounds, it was as if we were sharing a secret.'

After they'd eaten and cleaned up, the two women, along with Sissy and Lidia, sat around the table playing a game of cards. Jack rolled himself a cigarette. 'I'm going outside for some fresh air.'

'Save yourself the need and don't have a puff,' Alma laughed.

Jack opened the front door and sat on the veranda, enjoying his cigarette. The moon was full and the street was peaceful. He felt deeply for Odette, knowing what a gut ache it was, having to live with the humiliation of an exemption certificate. He had just finished his cigarette when he noticed a man standing on the footpath on the opposite side of the street, watching him. Although the man resembled an undertaker, in his dark suit, Jack knew instinctively it could only be the policeman, Lowe.

Jack stood up and slowly walked down the steps to his front gate. 'You after something?' he asked.

Lowe stepped onto the footpath. 'Tonight, no, there's nothing I'm after,' he said. 'But tomorrow, or the next day, or next week, I'll be back.'

'There's no need for that,' Jack said. 'You don't have any business with this house.'

'But you're wrong. I do,' Lowe said. 'You have the child, Cecily Brown, staying here. Her welfare is my direct concern.'

'You don't need to be concerned at all about that child,' Jack answered. 'She's being taken good care of by her gran, and by us. Family.'

Lowe put his hands behind his back. 'Don't be stupid, man. You people can't look after yourselves and you know it.'

Jack had put up with similar insults all his life. 'We're getting by the best way we can. We don't need anyone to run our lives.'

'You might think you can get away with this but you're wrong,' Lowe said. 'That woman, she was only able to walk out of that office today because some young fool was determined to undermine me. But as he advised me himself, all I need to show in regard to the child's obvious neglect is *due cause.* I'll be back, Mr Haines, and I can assure you that I will find that cause.'

'This is my house,' Jack fumed, 'and you won't be touching any child that is under my roof.'

The women in the kitchen overheard Jack's raised voice. 'What's going on?' Odette asked.

'Oh, that will be Jack talking to the Italian fella next door,' Alma explained. 'I'll just go and see what they're on about.'

'Listen closely,' Lowe continued. 'You may believe that you have some rights, but you're mistaken. The exemption certificate is called the *dog collar* for good reason. You best check yourself, Mr Haines. I should not have to remind you that you have your own grandchild to consider.'

'You lay a finger on her and—'

'And what?' Lowe smiled. 'If you dare interfere with the operation of the law your exemption certificate will be torn up and you could find yourself in great trouble. Think about that, Mr Haines. You can either support the irresponsible behaviour of Odette Brown, or you can protect your own family. I'll leave the choice to you. For now.'

The policeman walked off.

You'll never stop, you bastard. Jack was enraged. He walked along the side of the house and picked up the tomahawk that he used to chop wood. He was about to open the front gate and follow Lowe down the street when Alma called to him from the veranda.

'Leave it be, Jack.'

'What do you mean? I'm doing nothing but going for a walk.'

'A walk? With an axe in your hand. You put it back and get yourself inside.'

'I can't, Alma' Jack said. 'This one, he's not going to stop, Love. None of us are safe while he's around. I have to do this.'

Alma wrapped her arms around her husband. 'Do you really think that killing a policeman would save us, Jack Haines? You'd end up in gaol, or maybe hanging by your neck. What hope would I have on my own, keeping this family together.' She shook him gently. 'Don't think he's the only one out there, Jack. It will be a long time before change comes for us. You can't kill them all.' Alma gave her husband a passionate, full-lipped kiss. 'You're a good man, now behave like one.'

Jack rested the tomahawk up against the wood stack. 'What will we do, then?'

'What we've always done. Keep our heads down, think smart and get on the move again if the need comes.'

CHAPTER NINETEEN

Months later, Odette was sitting in the local hall, along with Sissy and the Haines family. The room was crowded. The audience were listening to different speakers on stage, talking about Aboriginal citizenship and rights. Odette had never heard Aboriginal people talk so strongly in public, at least not in the company of white people. After each speaker finished, Sissy, seated next to Odette, clapped as loudly as anyone in the hall. Afterwards, Odette bumped into Wanda Harrison, the receptionist from the hotel.

'Oh, that was so inspiring,' Wanda said. 'I think real change is going to come to our people.'

'We can only hope,' Odette answered, as cautiously as ever. She looked across to the other side of the hall and spotted Michael, the young clerk from the Aborigines Welfare Board. He smiled at Odette.

She tapped Wanda on the shoulder. 'That young fella over there, is he white or an Aboriginal boy?'

'I'm not sure. I've never seen him before. What do you think, Auntie?'

'I can't be sure either, but looking at him out of his suit and tie, he could be one of our own people. I can't be certain.'

'Well, if you don't know, Auntie, no white person would know either. I'm sure of that.'

Odette walked out onto the footpath and took Sissy's hand. Jack and Alma joined them. 'That was a big night,' Jack said.

'Yeah. Strong people. White people, too,' Odette observed.

'Yeah. More and more whitefellas come to the meetings these days,' Jack said.

'I don't want to sound ungrateful,' Odette added, 'but do you believe we can trust them, white people?'

As was his way, Jack began answering the question with a story. 'When I was a small boy, maybe six or seven years old, my family, we worked together picking fruit. Back in those days, you had to pay a deposit for an empty crate, then you filled it and waited on the farmer to pay you at the end of the day. One time we were working, in the burning heat, without a feed, not even a water break. We must have filled half a dozen of those crates between us. My dad, he was real proud of us kids for working as hard as we did. When the farmer came along, we all stood to attention, waiting for him to settle with Pa. And he did, at one half of the rate he paid the white pickers.'

'He robbed you?' Odette asked.

'You bet he did. He robbed us.'

'So, what are you saying, Jack, that the white folk at this meeting tonight are out to rob us?'

'No,' he answered, 'I haven't finished the story yet.'

'I thought you'd know by now,' Alma interrupted, 'Jack takes his time getting to the punchline.'

'The next day,' Jack continued, 'after the picking was over, we moved to another farm for work. It was even hotter than the day before. None of us wanted to do the work. Not because we were lazy or anything. We knew Pa had been robbed and we knew it was wrong. My older brother, Johnny, he had an argument with the old man, called him a silly old fool. It changed nothing, of course. We were ordered to get on with it and do the work, and we did. Pa was the boss of the family and his word stuck.' Jack paused and began rolling himself a cigarette.

'And what happened?' Odette asked, a little impatiently.

'We filled them crates and stood by, just as we had the day before, although we young ones slouched a little because we were certain our old man was about to get burnt again and we felt bad for him.' Jack took a long drag on his cigarette. 'Well, the farmer came by, checked the fruit for bruising and then paid my father, in full, a white man's rate, plus a cash bonus and a free box of fruit thrown in.'

Jack smiled at Odette. 'I never forgot that moment. Whatever else I might have thought about them whitefellas, that one time, it stuck with me. Then one day, this was years later when my dad wasn't in such good health, I asked him about that time on the picking. I said to him, "How did you know to trust that farmer fella only one day after we'd been robbed by his neighbour?"

'"I didn't trust him," he said to me.

'"Then why did we spend the whole day in the heat picking if you thought we might be robbed again?" I asked.' Jack took a final drag on the cigarette and ground it under the heel of his boot. 'The old man said what he'd done had nothing to do with trust. "White people aren't ready for trust," he said. "But some days we don't have a choice but to take a chance with them. We were down to nothing at the time and I had to take a chance on that fella. I had no other choice but see my family starve."'

'So, that's what we're doing?' Odette asked. 'Taking a chance with these white people? That's a risk, isn't it Jack?'

'It is,' Jack agreed. 'But for now, it's all we have.'

Odette thought about Sergeant Lowe and when he would next interfere in their lives. Jack seemed to have read her thoughts.

'We've been dealing with the devil for a long time now and he's not going away. They could make me the prime minister of this country and the devil would be there at my shoulder. Yours too, Odette.'

'Hey, no more talk of the devil,' Alma said, nodding her head towards Sissy. 'We've had a good night. Let's enjoy some peace.'

'We have had a good night,' Jack agreed. 'What I'm saying is, we can't put our faith in anyone but our own people. This citizenship is coming. Whatever else happens, it could put more of the law on our side.'

'And until that happens, Jack, what will we do?' Odette asked.

'Hope,' was the only response he was left with. 'It's all we can go with.'

EPILOGUE

Sissy finished packing the car for the road trip. Lidia had volunteered to go along for the ride. While Sissy was grateful for the offer, it was a journey she needed to take alone. Auntie Alma had been baking and packed the provisions for the long drive – sandwiches wrapped in tin foil, a slice of Sissy's favourite apple and pear cake, and a flask of tea. Uncle Jack was sitting in his battered chair on the front veranda, enjoying the morning sun. Lidia helped her sister-cousin lift the last bag into the boot of the car. Sissy gave Alma a hug and said goodbye to Jack.

'Where you off to again?' he asked. Uncle Jack's short-term memory had been increasingly failing him, although he was able to remember the days of his childhood in detail.

'I'm going west, Uncle. I'm taking Nanna home.'

'Oh,' he said, excited by the news he thought he was hearing for the first time. 'What sort of car are you driving?'

'My Torana. I've had it serviced and put new tyres on it.'

'Good,' he said. 'Good cars them Toranas. Are you taking a shotgun with you?'

'No,' Sissy laughed. 'I wouldn't know what to do with a shotgun, Uncle.'

Jack was clearly disappointed and shook his head. 'It's wild country out there. A fella told me one time, I wasn't more than a boy myself, and he said that a man should never head west of the Range without a shottie, both barrels loaded. And a mad crazy dog at his side just in case the gun jammed. You have a mad dog with you?'

'No, Uncle. No mad dog and no gun.'

'Don't you be a fool, Jack,' Alma said. 'It's 1980. The days of the wild west are long gone.'

Jack raised a bony nicotine-stained finger. 'Hey, not out that way. Could still be 1880 for a blackfella out there. Them white boys are prehistoric, that's what they are. Haven't seen a television, I bet.'

'Don't be stupid, Jack,' Alma sighed. 'They've had TV since 1956.'

'Not a colour one, I bet. That would be a shock to them dinosaurs,' he laughed.

'Ignore him, Sissy,' Auntie Alma said. 'When was the last time you were out west, Jack?'

'Can't remember,' he shrugged.

'Well, I can. You've been a city boy for a long time now. And a soft one at that. You haven't moved your bum out of that chair in years.'

Sissy hugged her uncle, kissed Lidia on both cheeks and walked to the car with Auntie Alma, nursing a parcel wrapped in brown paper.

'Are you sure you'll be okay on your own?' Alma asked.

'I know I will, Auntie. Nanna will be with me all the way. It's been five years now and she needs to be back home with her people.'

Sissy opened the passenger door and Alma sat the parcel containing Odette's ashes on the front passenger seat.

'Do you reckon I should buckle her in for you?' Alma laughed.

The women hugged. Sissy felt Alma's tear on her cheek. 'I'll be back safe, Auntie. Don't worry.'

'You take the best care of both of you.' She looked at Jack. 'He really has become half a fool, but not a complete one. You might not be in need of a gun out there. But be careful just the same.'

Sissy pulled out of the driveway and navigated through the suburbs of the city until she reached the open highway. She switched on the radio, turned it up and sang loudly. Around lunchtime, she pulled into a petrol station in a small country town and ate lunch sitting under a tree. By the afternoon, she'd crossed the ranges, and hit the flat expanse of the west.

Arriving in the main street of Deane the first thing Sissy noticed was that the old picture theatre had been bulldozed and replaced by a used car yard. The courthouse and police station were chained and padlocked. When she reached the end of the street and turned onto the gravel road by the old riverbed, her heart skipped a beat. She could see a bent figure on the side of the road up ahead. As she got closer she saw it was a woman wrapped in a shawl, supporting herself with a walking stick. Sissy pulled over and got out of the car.

‘Auntie Millie?’

The woman lifted her head. ‘Say it again, the words you just said.’ Her face was deeply wrinkled. She had whiskers on her chin and a film across her eyes.

‘Auntie Milly Khan!’ Sissy said. ‘It is you!’

Millie broke into a smile. She didn’t have a single tooth in her mouth. ‘And it’s you,’ she said. ‘Sissy Brown. I’ve been waiting for you for a long time.’

Sissy hugged Millie. ‘You recognise me?’ The old woman was so light and frail Sissy almost lifted her off the ground. ‘And what do you mean, you’ve been waiting for me? Out here on the road?’

‘I know I’m old, but not so silly. I knew you’d be coming through here sooner or later, is what I mean.’

‘How could you know that?’

‘There you are, being silly. The old people told me.’

Sissy knew better than to doubt Millie’s word. She’d witnessed many occasions when *the old people* had provided advice to Odette. It was obvious to Sissy that Millie was almost blind. She guided the old woman to her house. The saddlery had almost been swallowed by the old billabong. They sat together on a dusty couch out the front. Millie rested her head against Sissy’s shoulder.

‘Do you live here on your own?’ Sissy asked.

‘More or less. Yusuf, he’s been gone for over five years now. I still had my eyes then. The Muslim people, his people, they came and washed him clean like a newborn bub, put him in a cloth and took him away. They wanted me to go with them, out to the desert, but I told them no. They could have his body there and I’d keep his heart here with me.’

'Have you got everything you need here?'

'More or less. There's a lady who comes from Gatlin a few times a week. She brings food and cleans up. Gives me a wash and all. She's a church lady. One of them Quaker people. Friends, they call themselves. I've never seen her face, but I know she's a white lady. And a good one.'

'I need to tell you something,' Sissy said.

'You don't need to tell me at all.'

'No?'

'The night your grandmother passed I was inside there, in my bed, having the best sleep in a long time. It was the middle of the night and I sprung up like a young girl. I could hear the wind, coming from the east, which is rare out here. I said to her, "Why are you waking me, Odette Brown, when I'm sleeping so well?" I knew then that my best friend was gone. Did she die in pain, your nan?'

'No,' Sissy said. 'She died in peace. We were happy together in the city. She's out there, in the car. Nanna's ashes.'

'What are you going to do with them?'

'What she asked me to do. Take her home to the graveyard so that she can be with the old people. Would you like to come with me, Auntie? We can go in the car and I'll drop you back at home.'

'Oh, I would love that. But before we go, tell me about your own mum. Did Odette find Lila after you both took off?'

'Odette never found her. But I did. Three years ago. I'd always wanted to look for her, but not while Nanna was alive. She'd been through enough. I found out, from this group, *Link Up*, that my mum was living on the other side of the country, in Western Australia. I drove all the way across the desert to see her.'

'And did you find her?'

'I did. She was living in a house in Fremantle, run by the government. She had a room there. She knew I was going to see her, and when I turned up she was lying on her bed smoking a cigarette. She didn't get up the whole time I was there.'

'What did you talk about with your mum?'

'Nothing really. Not anything that made sense. She knew who I was, and remembered Nanna and this place. It wasn't like she was old. She just didn't have much to say. I went back the next day and took her out to lunch. She never said a word while we ate, just stared out the window at the sea. It was only when we stood up to leave that I saw she had tears in her eyes. I asked her what was wrong. And she just said, over and over, "He came back for me, he came back after me." Does that mean anything to you, Auntie Millie?'

Although she suspected what Lila would have been speaking about, Millie thought it best to say nothing. 'Did you ask her?' she replied.

'I did, but she stopped talking as quick as she started. She hardly said another word. I took her back to her place. I offered to arrange for her to come over and visit me, but she wasn't interested.'

'Have you seen her since?'

'No. I called her once but couldn't get a word out of her. Meeting me upset her, I think. I don't want to put her through that again.'

'I can understand that,' Millie said. 'Once your heart has been cut open it doesn't stop bleeding.'

Sissy helped Millie into the car and they drove along Deane's Line, heading to the graveyard. Henry Lamb's yard was gone. Sissy stopped the car. 'What happened to the old junkyard?' she asked Millie, who was cradling Odette's ashes in her arms.

'Oh, he went years back. Not too long after you and your Nanna left. Henry blew himself up.'

'Blew himself up! How?'

'Nobody was ever sure about what happened. Not exactly. Henry took them Kane boys with him. They were over at the yard with their truck at the time. All three of them were killed. Me and Yusuf, we heard it from our place. The rattling of the windows reminded me of all them times they let off explosives at the mine. They said it was an accident, but Yusie, he didn't think so. He said Henry would have been on top of everything that happened.'

'What? That he killed the Kane brothers on purpose?'

'Well, maybe I wouldn't say it so directly. Yusie always believed that Henry was a genius disguised as an idiot. But then, he also insisted his camels could talk. I felt sorry for Henry when I heard the news. He was such a gentle soul. But that Kane boy, the older one, he was like his father. Both of them were no good.'

Sissy was struck by an unexplainable sense of sadness. 'The younger brother, George, he was different from the other one, wasn't he? I remember him a little. He tried to help me once.'

'Well, it didn't help him, not in the end,' Millie said. 'That boy paid for the sins of the family. That's how it is sometimes.'

~

The mission church and cemetery had been well maintained. A plaque was attached to the front door of the church, stating it was a 'heritage site' protected by government legislation. Sissy took Odette's ashes from Millie and led her by the hand along the narrow path to her great-grandparents grave. She removed the urn from the brown paper and unscrewed the lid.

'Nan asked me to spread her ashes here,' Sissy explained.

'Give me some of her?' Millie asked.

She cupped her hands together and Sissy placed a small portion of the ashes into Millie's hands. Millie pressed her hands to her cheeks and rubbed the ashes into her skin. Sissy sprinkled the remaining ashes over the graves. She closed her eyes and saw Odette's face before her own. She reached out and kissed her lips.

After she'd driven Millie home, Sissy helped her into her house and hugged her. She had a final question for Millie before saying goodbye. 'Hey, Auntie, do you remember the policeman who was here when we left town?'

'I do. He was only here a little while, but I remember him. He was a bad one, that old boy.'

'What happened to him?'

'Well, not long after you and your Nan took off, so did he. We never saw him again. The bugger vanished.'

'You mean he never came back to town?'

'That's right.' Millie turned her milky eyes to the mountain range. 'But he's out there.'

'Out there, Auntie? That's almost twenty years ago.'

'Don't matter. He's wandering around some place. I feel him sometimes. Them bad ones, they never leave you be.'

Although Millie's remarks made little sense, Sissy felt a chill pass through her body.

'From here I'm driving all the way to the centre of the country, Auntie Millie. I'm starting a job in a school out there. I'll call in on the way back and see you, before Christmas.'

'You do that. Maybe I'll still be here. Who knows? I could be gone by then.'

Sissy kissed the old woman. 'Don't say that.'

Millie dismissed her with a wave of her hand. 'Now, you go. Don't be fussing with me.'

Sissy drove a little further along the track and noticed the remains of the old footbridge. It had collapsed into the dry, weed-infested riverbed. She stopped the car and walked across to the single street of Quarrytown. Few of the old huts remained standing. Those that were had been strangled beneath the tendrils and hushed blue flowers of the voracious weed that plagued the area. Little was left of the one-bedroom hut Sissy had lived in with her grandmother, although the old wood stove and chimney stood defiantly in the ruins. Sissy could almost smell a rich brew of tea steaming in an iron kettle, conjuring memories of a much happier time.

She was about to return to the car when she noticed a familiar shape. She walked across the yard and stood at the foot of the old bathtub, overflowing with rubbish. She found a rusted metal bar and used it to clear the tub of weeds, soil, bird feathers and chips of stone. She sat on the edge of the bath, removed her boots and then stepped into the tub. She lay down and closed her eyes. Sissy could hear the birds of old, the birds that spoke to her grandmother. She rested the back of her head against the edge of the bath and felt the warm water caress her young skin. She could feel Odette's fingertips massaging the back of her neck.

Odette and Sissy Brown had come home together.

AUTHOR'S NOTE

The White Girl is a fictional work set in a fictional town somewhere in Australia. The story of Odette Brown and her granddaughter, Sissy, is reminiscent of the experiences of many Aboriginal and Torres Strait Islander people throughout the twentieth century; people of remarkable courage. I would not presume to tell the story of any child removed from family and community, or that of the people left behind to deal with loss and the resultant trauma. What I do hope for with this novel, is that the love and bravery conveyed by Odette and Sissy provides some understanding of the tenacity and love within the hearts of those who suffered the theft of their own blood. I dedicate *The White Girl* to both those who found their way home, and tragically, to the many who did not.

ACKNOWLEDGEMENTS

I want to thank my editor, Jacqueline Blanchard, who likes both a tidy sentence and a clean floor. I also want to thank all the team at UQP, people who have been great supporters of my writing for many years.

My kids – Erin, Siobhan, Drew, Grace and Nina – *you are the champions of the world* (to quote Freddie Mercury). To my grandkids, Isabel – *tougher than the rest* – and Archie – *beautiful boy*, I love you with a big heart. Sara, you are, as always, the rock I roll with.

I also want to thank the deadly three – Kim, Paola and Karen. And finally, Kes, we welcome your tenderness around the house, as we remember Ella with the love she left us with.